THEY SOUGHT VENGEANCE

THEY SOUGHT VENGEANCE

ZACHARY GOLDMAN MYSTERIES
BOOK FOURTEEN

P.D. WORKMAN

PD WORKMAN

ISBN: 9781774685150 (KDP Hardcover)
ISBN: 9781774685112 (KDP Paperback)
ISBN: 9781774685143 (Large Print)
ISBN: 9781774685167 (Lulu Paperback)
ISBN: 9781774685129 (Kindle)
ISBN: 9781774685136 (ePub)
ISBN: 9781774685174 (autonarrated audio)

ALSO BY P.D. WORKMAN

FIND MORE BOOKS AT PDWORKMAN.COM

MYSTERY/SUSPENSE:

Zachary Goldman Mysteries

Private Investigator

She Wore Mourning

His Hands Were Quiet

She Was Dying Anyway

He Was Walking Alone

They Thought He was Safe

He Was Not There

Her Work Was Everything

She Told a Lie

He Never Forgot

She Was At Risk

He Drowned in Memory

Their Walls Were Empty

They Came for Him

They Sought Vengeance

She Was Their Target

His Fear Was Real

She Was Out of Reach

He Was Deceived

She Once Vanished

Kenzie Kirsch Medical Thrillers

Unlawful Harvest

Doctored Death

Dosed to Death

Gentle Angel

Rushin' Death

Posed for Death

Death of a Corpse

Endowed with Death

Shattered to Death

Captured in Death

Currying Death (Coming Soon)

Healed to Death (Coming Soon)

Death's Charm (Coming Soon)

A Bleeding Hearts Valley Thriller

An Abrupt Departure (Coming Soon)

High-Tech Crime Solvers Series

Virtually Harmless

Stand Alone Suspense Novels

Looking Over Your Shoulder

Lion Within

Pursued by the Past

In the Tick of Time

Loose the Dogs

AND MORE AT PDWORKMAN.COM

For secret siblings and sibling secrets

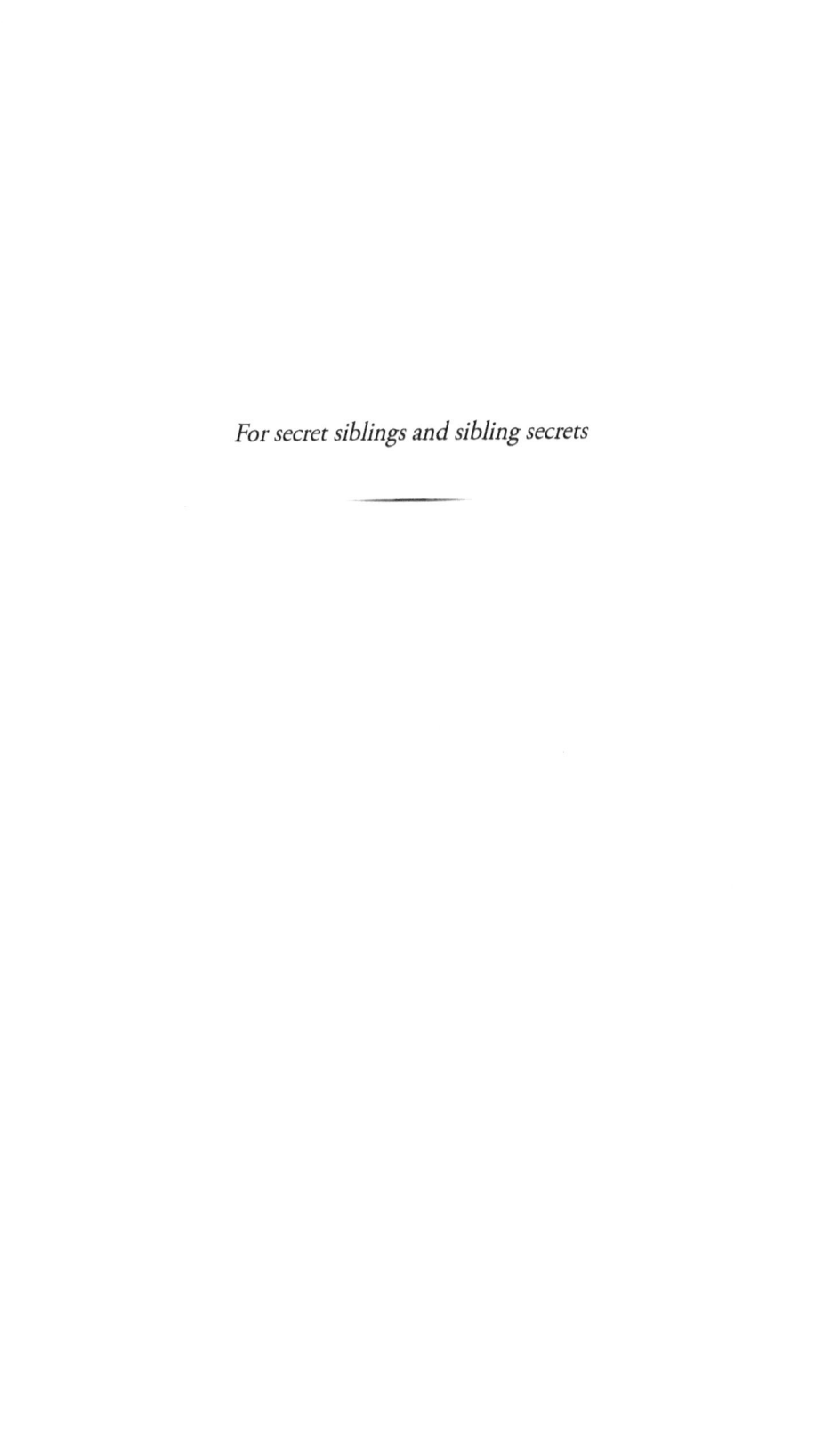

1

The *No Grounds for Alarm* cafe was quiet. The morning rush was over and most of the staff were wiping down counters and chatting idly with each other, taking the time to restock and get ready for the lunch rush. Sun streamed in the front window. A few customers trickled in, ordered their beverages, and either wandered back out of the cafe with blank expressions on their faces or sought out a table and sat down with a computer or other device to work on something important. Or to check out their social media feeds.

Zachary had arrived before the appointed time to check out the location and ensure he wasn't late for the appointment. If there was one way to lose a new client, it was by being late. It didn't matter what the reason was; it could be perfectly legitimate. The client would go somewhere else.

So he sipped his coffee and watched the customers trickle in, speculating which would be Karen Camden. He had a picture in his mind after hearing her voice, but had not run any background on her. He wanted his first impressions to be of her in person, not on social media, in news articles, or wherever else he might find records of her life.

She hadn't had a lot to say on the phone. She hadn't been referred by a friend, but had heard his name in the media on one of his other cases, though she didn't specify which one. A few of them had made the news. Zachary was always a little leery of the potential clients who had seen him in the media. They tended to have unrealistic expectations of what he could or would do. And somehow, those people didn't seem to understand that they would be expected to pay an up-front deposit and that he would be paid for all of his work, whether he came to the resolution they wanted or not. People who approached him because of a business listing or as a referral from another client were much more realistic and likely to pay their bills.

A woman stepped in the door and looked around the coffee shop rather than immediately going to the service counter. She was slim, probably in her mid-twenties to early thirties. Dark brown hair and blue or gray eyes. She had an attractive face but was made up in a very plain style, her hair pulled back in a no-fuss ponytail that made her seem severe. The woman wore a dark green skirt, a white short-sleeved blouse, and black flats.

Zachary smiled and raised his hand slightly. She walked over to his table.

"Mr. Goldman?"

"Zachary." He stood up and offered his hand, which she shook firmly. She had long tapered fingers and dry, warm hands. Her perfume was a combination of light florals with a hint of citrus. "Nice to meet you, Miss Camden."

"That's missus. But you can call me Karen."

She wore no wedding ring. No jewelry except for a gold chain around her neck that disappeared into her blouse and might have a locket, stone, or charm on it. Zachary ran his hand over his own very short black hair, aware that she was also evaluating him. He had shaved for the meeting, but usually had a few days of stubble, which tended to make people look away and discount him. For once, he didn't look too gaunt. The cocktail of medications he was on no longer included drugs that made him nauseated. Kenzie didn't let him forget to eat, and they indulged in a few too many restaurant meals, leading to her working hard to keep from putting the pounds on and Zachary filling out and reaching what his doctor considered a healthy weight for once.

Introductions and initial evaluations out of the way, Zachary suggested, "Why don't you grab a coffee, and then we can get down to it?"

She nodded her agreement and went over to the counter. She glanced at the densely-written blackboard only briefly, and had either been there before and knew the menu, or already knew what she wanted. What she brought back to the table looked like the cafe noir—plain black coffee. Not one of the fancy, calorie-laden varieties that covered the board.

Karen pulled out a chair for herself and sat down. She wrapped both hands around the coffee mug as if she were warming her hands and stared down at the black, shimmering surface. Zachary waited, having a sip of his own cafe noir. It was often difficult for a client to bring their troubles to a stranger. Jumping right in and explaining what they needed was a big step. There might be small talk first. Questions about Zachary's background and references. Fishing to find out his knowledge on various topics or situations while they weighed his words to see whether he was really the right man for the job or if they even wanted to hire anyone. Sometimes it was just too much but, usually, given a period of silence, each would speak up and tell him a bit of their story.

"My father recently passed away," Karen said eventually, not yet looking up from her coffee. "It was unexpected. The police looked into it but said it was a natural death. He had some health conditions." Her shoulders rose and fell. "The coroner said it was heart failure. He had cardiovascular disease. But it wasn't expected," she reiterated. "And… we think that there's more to the story. It was too sudden. There was no warning."

Zachary nodded. "It can be difficult when someone passes away so suddenly."

Karen grimaced. She took a sip of her coffee and put the cup down again. "You think that we're just imagining things because it was unexpected. But there's more to it than that."

"We? Who else is concerned about it?"

"My brothers and I. There are four of us altogether. Three boys and a girl. And the others think that something is wrong too; it isn't just me. We kept going back and forth on it, and we finally decided to… hire someone independent to look into it."

"So the four of you think… what?"

Karen sighed. She looked out the window at the people walking by on the sidewalk. "We think… he was poisoned."

That seemed oddly specific. But maybe something about his death had led them to think that it was poisoning.

"You think he was murdered."

"Yes." She nodded, one jerk of her head. "I guess… yes. That's what we think. Or what we are hoping that you can prove or disprove."

"It might be hard to disprove. There are hundreds of poisons that could have been used. Who do you think killed him? You have a suspect in mind?"

Maybe her mother or a business partner or rival of her father. When people came to Zachary, they had often already built up the story in their minds. And despite the preponderance of murder mysteries on TV and in books, murders were usually obvious and the killer easy to identify. If they thought they knew who the killer was, they were probably right. Maybe the mother, since they had all met together to discuss it and agreed to hire someone.

"Well, one of us, probably," Karen said. A blush started at the base of her throat and chest.

"You or your brothers?" Zachary wasn't sure he had understood her correctly.

"Yes. We're clearly the ones who benefit from his death. None of us were… *close* to him. I know it's probably weird, but we're all… looking at each other, wondering which one of us did it."

"So you decided to hire a private investigator? To investigate *you*?"

"Yes. The four of us." She shrugged. "I mean, we're not going to figure it out by arguing with each other. If one of us did it… then that person should go to prison. We might not have been that close to him… but it's still not right. We can't just divide up the inheritance and give a quarter of it to the killer."

Better that a third of it should go to each of the non-killers.

"Is the estate… significant?"

She nodded, jaw clenched tight. "It's millions."

2

Zachary tried not to react to this declaration. "The estate is worth millions?" he asked, pulling out his notepad and pencil to start jotting the pertinent information down.

"Yes. Even just the house is a couple million. When you figure in all of his accounts, what his company is worth, and the art and furnishings and vacation property… Yeah. It's enough to make all of us very comfortable." She took another sip of the coffee. "It doesn't matter to me whether I get fifteen or twenty million. My motive for finding out if one of the others killed our father is not to get his share. It's just… justice. Because the person who did this shouldn't be allowed to profit from it."

"Right," Zachary agreed. His mind boggled at the very idea of inheriting fifteen or twenty million dollars. Why had they chosen *him* to investigate it? There had to be other private investigators out there who were used to dealing with a bigger fish. Hiring a small one-man—well, two-person—operation instead of one of the big security firms from the city with a whole fleet of investigators seemed like an odd choice. "I am willing to take on the case and have the time for it in my schedule right now. I'll need an up-front retainer." He had his usual rates on a card that he handed out to people but, in light of how large the estate was and their expectations, he might have to increase his rates. "I'll email you the details. And if I need to contract other investigators, I'll let you know first so you can control costs."

"We want you," Karen said firmly, looking Zachary in the face for the first time. "Not anyone else." Maybe they had seen him on the news lately. "We don't want word of this getting out. One person can stay unobtrusive, and we can explain why you're there, but we don't want strangers running around the neighborhood asking questions."

"Well… okay, then. Just be warned that it may take longer to get to the bottom of this with only one person. And my full-time admin, of course. She won't be on site, all of her activities will be remote, and her fees are built into my rates."

Heather, Zachary's older sister, helped him with some of the computer investigations and kept him organized. She would be amused at his calling her a full-time admin, but he didn't want Karen to think she could nix Heather's involvement too.

"But I need to make sure that you understand… I won't necessarily be able to prove that it was murder or who the culprit was. I know that on TV, the private investigator always figures everything out and brings the murderer to justice, but real life doesn't always work out that way. Some cases remain unsolved for years, even decades. You can tell me if you want me to stop investigating at some point. Or I may come to you and tell you that I've exhausted all of my leads. And it might not have happened the way that you imagine."

Karen nodded. "I know it's a long shot. The coroner already said it was natural causes, so that's a big obstacle. But he could be wrong. Sometimes they are."

"I know." Zachary had experienced that before. Getting the medical examiner to reverse his position was difficult, but it could be done. And Kenzie working in the medical examiner's office gave him a bit of an "in." He'd been able to convince Dr. Wiltshire to change his mind and reopen a file before. "I've succeeded in getting to the truth in other cases. It's just a warning… sometimes things are not as they seem. Or we can figure out what happened, but still not be able to prove it and put the culprit behind bars."

"I'll take that risk."

"Okay. Why don't I get the details from you? Your father's and brothers' names. Where or who I should start with. Interviewing you, I assume. And you haven't mentioned your mother…?"

"She died five years ago." Karen's lips compressed into a thin line.

"Oh, I'm sorry. So it's just you and your brothers now? And was anyone living in the same household as your father? Or was he alone?"

"Logan is living there. And household staff. We all come and go as we please; we have our own keys. And we were all home for a family dinner the night he died. Mom had always insisted on having a dinner once every month or so, and we've tried to keep that up, even if it's just the five of us." She sighed and looked away from him. "It's a little suspicious that he would die suddenly right after having dinner with us."

"Right after? While you were there?"

"That night. When everyone had gone home. He died… in his sleep, I guess. In his own bed."

Zachary nodded. He wrote down Karen's name and Logan's, trying to keep his printing tidy enough that he would be able to read it later, but not take so long that she grew impatient with him.

"So there is you, and Logan; tell me something about each of you. And your birth order."

Karen sat back, her posture relaxing. This was more familiar ground. She had talked about herself and her brothers many times before.

"Alex is the oldest, then Eddie, then me, and Logan is the baby."

"Which is why he is the only one still at home."

"He wasn't. He moved out when he went to college. But… things didn't work out. He ended up dropping out and going back home again. If it had been me…" Karen trailed off, thinking about it. "I would have found a job so I could afford my own apartment instead of going back there. I think it was a bad choice."

"What is Logan like?"

"Well, he's the baby of the family, so a little bit spoiled. Actually, maybe a lot spoiled by my mom, but not by Dad. Unless it was because Mom insisted on something. You know, if she told him he had to let Logan do something. But he would only do it grudgingly, under protest. Loud protests, so that everyone knew it was not his idea."

"Was he verbally abusive?"

"I suppose. We never really thought about it that way. Or I didn't, anyway. I just thought of it as Dad being right, because he was always right. If he got after me for something... then I knew that I was in the wrong, because there was no way *he* was. Now that I'm older, I have more perspective, I guess... yes. He was."

"Was there physical abuse as well?"

"No, I don't think so. I mean... he would grab one of the boys and force them to do what he wanted them to. But that's just part of parenting. I don't remember him ever causing any kind of injuries. Not that I knew about. I don't remember any hitting or anything that might have done permanent damage. Just... being rough and forceful."

"Was there any other reason that Logan was spoiled, other than being the youngest in the family?"

"What do you mean?"

"Was he sick a lot? Your mom had a hard time getting pregnant again and knew he would be the last baby? He looked more like her side of the family?"

"Oh." Karen was nodding, thinking about it but already sure of her answer. "Yeah... I guess it was a hard birth, and he was born early. He had learning disabilities. I remember he was in speech therapy before he was five. He was awkward physically, just the kind of kid that gets bullied at school for being different. A dweeb or a baby. So there were a lot of reasons for Mom to want to protect him and make things easier on him."

"Right." Zachary nodded, reflecting on his own learning

disabilities and behavioral problems when he had been in school. His mother had not been the nurturing type and he had not gotten therapy in the earlier years that might have set him on the right course. And when the family had dissolved and he had landed in foster care, group homes, and institutions, there had been no one to spoil or protect him. He'd already been identified as a bad kid, and the foster parents and other adults responsible for his care or education had not gone easy on him.

"I guess I didn't understand that as a kid," Karen said with an embarrassed smile, "I never understood why he got out of responsibilities and was allowed to get away with stuff that I never would have. And why he got all of the attention and help when I was told to work harder."

"Even if she had explained, you probably would have been too young to understand." Zachary hoped this would let her off the hook as far as her guilt toward her brother went. "And they were probably of the school of thought that he should look and act like everyone else as much as possible so you didn't see all of the differences."

"Maybe. I expect more of myself now, but I still catch myself thinking of him as a spoiled brat. That he just needs to quit messing around and work harder, like I was told to."

"What was he going to college for?"

"I don't think he had decided. Just some kind of general upgrading to start with. But he couldn't handle it. I should be more sympathetic about it than I am."

"And then there are... Alex and Eddie," Zachary prompted.

"Right. Alex and Eddie." Karen closed her eyes for a moment, gathering her thoughts. "Alex is the eldest, always the perfect one. The good son who got straight A's and followed all of the rules and did what was expected of him without question. He was the one who got all of the attention and praise from Dad... but I'm starting to wonder if he was treated differently in private. If things were said that none of us the rest of us knew about."

Zachary nodded.

Karen went on, "Eddie was a wild card. He was always a bit of a rebel. Always trying to get away with things." She looked up at Zachary, her blue eyes wide with worry. "I don't see how it could be any of us. I know it must have been, but it just doesn't make any sense. I can't see any of my brothers doing anything to hurt Dad. Even if they were just trying to make him sick and not kill him. I can't wrap my mind around it."

3

Leave that to me," Zachary told her. "Don't worry about it or even think about it. Don't give your brothers any reason to think that you might suspect one of them. If you are right and it was murder, then you need to keep that in mind when you are dealing with them."

"They wouldn't kill me," Karen said with a laugh of disbelief. "Why would they? What would they have to gain?"

"Well… the same as proving that one of you killed him. An extra portion of the estate, divided up among the remaining heirs. Depending on the terms of your father's will, of course, and yours, if you have one."

She colored a little and looked away from Zachary, appearing to watch a young couple a few tables away from them. He wasn't sure whether it was embarrassment that she didn't have a will, or that she did. A lot of young people didn't feel the need for one, and having a will would mean that she was in the minority among her peers.

"I really don't think that I have anything to fear from my brothers. If they killed Dad… well, that's not the same as coming after me for something. For *money*." She shook her head.

"You don't believe that their motive for killing your father was money?"

"Well... I mean, I guess it would be. None of us are exactly crying in our coffee about getting our inheritance early."

"Just... tread lightly. I wouldn't want to put you in harm's way. Let me do the investigating, and stay well out of it yourself."

"I guess since that's what we're paying you for, I can just stay back and let you take care of it."

Zachary nodded his agreement. "So Alex was the perfectionist. What is he like now? What did he become?"

"He's a lawyer. Corporate, not wills and estates. He made that really clear. Big files, companies with a lot of money. Wears expensive suits that he pretends he can afford, even though he isn't getting any of the family money yet and I guess junior lawyers don't make all that much. He's lucky that he doesn't have a huge school debt to worry about. Mom and Dad paid for his education at top-notch schools."

Zachary wrote down that Alex was a lawyer.

"Eddie is an inventor. I guess. I can't show you anything that he's invented. I think it's all really high-tech stuff. Or maybe it just sounds advanced because he's conning everyone into thinking that he's smarter than them and isn't actually speaking gobbledygook. There's a lot of chemistry involved, if I understand correctly, but I don't know how you can invent something with chemicals."

"And Eddie wasn't as close to your father as Alex?"

"No one was as close to Dad as Alex. I think they should have just stopped having kids at one. There wasn't any need for the rest of us and, clearly, Dad didn't care about the rest of us. Only about Alex."

Lots of jealousy going on there. Karen's conclusion might or might not be true, but it was clear that there were years of resentment behind her statement.

"What do you do?"

She breathed heavily and looked outside like she was either waiting for someone or trying to chart the best escape route. "I am... a nurse."

"That's great. I love nurses." Zachary's face got hot after blurting this out. Poor impulse control. It sounded all wrong.

But it made Karen laugh and pulled her out of plotting her escape route to look at him again with fresh eyes. "You love nurses?"

"I don't mean that in any improper way… I think nurses are great. They're the backbone of our medical system. I've had… a number of hospital stays, and I'm always so grateful for the nurses who are so caring and diligent and take care of all of the day-to-day stuff. I don't know what I would have done without them."

Karen looked like she was trying to suppress her smile, but she couldn't hide it. She flushed a little more. "Well, that's very sweet of you. What have you been in the hospital for?"

"Different things…" Zachary didn't want to disclose most of them. "A couple of years ago… I was in a pretty bad car crash. I had a spinal cord injury, but once the swelling went down, I was able to move again. But being absolutely helpless during that time… able to understand everything that was going on but unable to get up and walk around and do all the other things I needed to do to take care of myself… it was really hard. Not just physically, but emotionally. The nurses were so kind and compassionate and helped to take the sting out of doing the things for me that I couldn't do for myself."

She impulsively put her hand over his on the table. "Thank you! It's so nice to hear things like that. Nurses get such a bad rap so much of the time, and I don't know why. The ones that I have worked with have been great. But… full disclosure… being a nurse is not what I wanted out of life."

"Oh." Zachary nodded. "You had other plans?"

"I wanted to be a doctor. Alex was a lawyer, Eddie was a ground-breaking scientist, and I wanted to be a doctor. I didn't see any reason I shouldn't be able to perform just as well as they had."

Zachary nodded, encouraging her to go on.

"Well… Dad paid for Alex and Eddie to go to school. He paid for it all. They both became really good at what they do—I'll give them that—but they wouldn't have had the opportunities they did if they'd had to earn everything on their own or get scholarships to cover it. They worked hard but wouldn't have gotten anywhere without the money."

"But your father wouldn't pay for your education?"

"Oh, he did. But he wouldn't pay for me to be a doctor. He paid for nursing school."

"He didn't even let you try?"

Karen shook her head. "Didn't even let me try. He said that I'd make a really good nurse, and I *am* a really good nurse. But I could have made it as a doctor. I know I could have."

"Wow. I can understand you being upset about that. Was it because… he was sexist? He didn't think that women would make good doctors?"

"No, it's worse than that. He'll see a female doctor. He agrees that some of them are excellent. He just didn't think that *I* had the aptitude."

Zachary winced. "Oh, I'm sorry. That's…" He shook his head slowly. "What a slap in the face."

"Yeah, it was. And it still is. I can't let it go. I know I would have made a good doctor, and he took that away from me."

Karen had apparently not considered putting herself through medical school, as she said Alex or Eddie could have done. She had gone through nursing school and had settled for that.

"Are you still practicing?" Zachary asked, deciding to steer away from any discussion of what might have been if she had made other choices.

"Yes, part-time. But I probably won't once I get the inheritance and don't have to work to support myself. I have two sons. So I have them to take care of, as well as trying to help earn enough for the family to be comfortable. My husband, Dawson, doesn't quite make enough for us to be able to do the things that we want to. We could survive without my income, but not much more than that. I like to be able to do… family vacations, enroll the boys in classes that will help them to get ahead in life, or take just because they are fun. But I couldn't do it on my own, and neither can Dawson."

"Things will change when you get your inheritance."

Karen nodded, watching Zachary scratch a few words into his notepad. She probably knew exactly what suspicions he was making note of. She had, after all, admitted that she was a suspect, equal to her brothers in this one thing.

"Do you have phone numbers for each of your brothers? And is there a time that I could come see the house? Where your father lived when… it happened."

"Well, yes, but… what do you think you're going to discover there? The police didn't see anything suspicious or out of place in his room, so they only took a cursory look around the house. But people have been through there. We all have access to the house. So if one of us poisoned him… we wouldn't leave the evidence there. We would have cleaned it up by now."

"I would still like to get a feel for the house and its layout. What opportunities people had. Or… there are other possibilities as well."

"That he wasn't killed, you mean?" Karen asked. "That it was just natural causes?"

"Well, that remains a possibility. But also… that it was an accident, suicide, or perpetrated by someone outside the household. Someone not in the family. In which case, they wouldn't have had access after your father died to remove any evidence."

"Oh. I suppose. But there are maids and other household staff. Everything will have been cleaned up and put away by now."

"That's fine. I'll look at it in whatever shape it is in. You never know what ideas it might trigger."

Karen nodded. She didn't seem to be opposed to his going to see the house. She only wanted to know what point there was in looking at a scene that had potentially already been contaminated by a dozen or more people.

A question that part of Zachary's brain agreed with. What point was there in going to the scene of the crime?

4

Zachary had been busy uploading his handwritten notes to the cloud and typing out the various questions and avenues of investigation he needed to pursue when Kenzie got home from work, and he hadn't paid her much attention. He'd said hello and asked her about her day, but he couldn't remember her answer, which probably meant that he'd been too focused on his work and hadn't paid any attention to what she had said.

He was trying to be more organized in his work habits, with Heather making suggestions and keeping him on track the best she could. Both of her kids had ADHD, so she had a lot of experience helping them stay on top of their schoolwork and studies. He set up a project for the new case and added his initial tasks into it. Then he remembered that he still had to send Karen a revised rate sheet so she could pay him the initial deposit. He shouldn't be doing any other work before he received that money, or he could get burned. How many times had he taken a client at his word that payment was on its way and gotten deeply into the investigation, only to find out that it had never been sent? Pulling out of a case once he'd gotten into it was almost impossible. Once focused on uncovering the truth, it was painful to withdraw, even if he knew he wasn't being paid.

He added the retainer to the project's task list and gave it the highest priority, then closed his laptop lid, forcing himself to disengage from the case and turn his attention to Kenzie. He sat on the couch for a moment, watching her as she moved around the kitchen preparing their dinner. Her spiraling dark hair bounced when she walked. Her red lipstick was unsmudged and her expression was pleasant even when focused on something else. She noticed Zachary watching her.

"Hey, welcome back."

Zachary was about to say that he hadn't been out, then realized that she was referring to his mental state. His face warmed and he rolled his eyes about his own state of distraction. "Sorry about that. I picked up a new case."

"I figured you must have. You haven't been that hyperfocused since Luke's case."

"Yeah." Despite TV's depiction of private investigators always working on exciting, life-and-death, vitally important cases, Zachary's bread and butter was more routine tasks like skip tracing, insurance fraud investigation, background searches for corporations hiring new high-level staff, and other tedious computer work. Heather enjoyed helping with that, so they split the more prosaic stuff between them.

He really should call Joss, his oldest sister, to check in and see how they were doing. When Luke had been released from jail, Zachary had hoped that things would go back to normal, that Luke would have learned his lesson and decided to stay close to home and follow Joss's rules, and there would be no more concerns about his returning to his addictions or to his former life working with a human trafficking ring.

But Luke was not the type of person who was happy staying at home and living a boring, law-abiding life. Joss had warned Zachary from the beginning that it would be difficult for Luke to let go of the life he had led previously, and she had been right. Luke craved excitement, people around him, the lights and music of clubs, and the praise of his bosses in the trafficking ring as much as or more than he did the drugs and alcohol he was addicted to.

So far, as far as Zachary knew, Luke hadn't gotten back into drugs or the business, but he was back in the party scene, getting away with whatever he could behind Joss's back. She knew more than Luke realized about his activities. But she wouldn't kick him out for disobeying her rules, since the only place for him to go would be back to the traffickers he knew.

"How is Aster?" Kenzie asked, recalling Zachary to their conversation. She had clearly been able to see where his mind had gone at her mention of Luke.

"She's doing okay." Zachary forced a smile to show that he was pleased with Aster's progress. It was her confession that had gotten Luke out of jail, and they had all been worried about how the police would treat her, but things had gone well. "Joss got her into a trauma recovery program that seems like a good fit. She's out of the house, so at least she and Luke aren't encouraging each other to break the rules now."

"And how many other trafficking victims is Joss harboring?" Kenzie smiled. Her feelings toward Joss were warmer now that she had found out that acidic, bitter Joss was mothering girls she had managed to get out of the prostitution business, sheltering them until she could get them into safe homes or programs that would help get them back onto a safer path.

"I don't know," Zachary admitted. He got up from the couch and walked into the kitchen to join her. "Probably half a dozen, at least." Zachary had been happy to find out that the police were so familiar with his sister, "the old lady," not because she was breaking the law, but because she was such a vocal advocate for those victims.

Zachary and Kenzie moved around each other in the kitchen as Kenzie continued to work on the meal and Zachary set the table and got out a pitcher of water and anything else they might need from the fridge. They didn't talk much while doing it, and it was a good transition from being focused on his computer work and everything that was going on inside his brain to focusing outward on Kenzie.

As Kenzie started to set the serving dishes on the table, Zachary sat down. He stared at the casserole that she had set on the table, trying to decide if he would like it. Kenzie pulled a foil-covered loaf out of the oven and Zachary couldn't help grinning. No matter what else she served, she knew that he would gobble up the garlic bread. His mouth started to water as she opened the foil wrapper, releasing fragrant steam.

Kenzie sliced the loaf and put it on a plate well within Zachary's reach. "Now don't just eat the bread! You need the vitamins in the other foods too."

"Mmm-hm," Zachary agreed, the first bite of garlic bread already in his mouth.

Kenzie sat down, smiling in amusement at his greed. "So, tell me about this new case you're taking on. It's obviously something that's caught your attention."

Zachary nodded. It was a minute before he could speak. "I have to figure out what my rates are going to be. They're quite wealthy."

It wasn't that he wanted to take advantage of their position as much as the fact that it would let him give some of the lower-income clients a bit of a break. He couldn't drop his rates too low for them if he wanted to put garlic bread on the table but, when people really couldn't afford his regular rates, it was nice if there was a bit of reserve in the company accounts so that he could still help them out.

Of course, the lion's share of the household expenses was paid by Kenzie, since it was her house and she was also the one who usually did the shopping. But maybe one day, they would buy a house together, and he would have the money in the bank to help pay for it. He'd never been able to afford anything other than cheap apartments in the past. When he had married Bridget, she had not put up with that for long, insisting that she would pay for a suitable home out of her family money.

"That would be nice," Kenzie agreed. She was always encouraging him to charge enough for his services, not to sell himself short with cut-rate fees. "What kind of case is it?"

"One that might have come through your office. A Mr. John Godfrey?"

Kenzie considered this, then nodded. "Yeah. I remember him. The family disagrees with our findings?"

"They think that it was murder. That he might have been poisoned."

Kenzie ate a couple of bites of the casserole. "Hmm. Well, nice if you can get a little extra money out of it. But I wouldn't expect it to go anywhere."

"Medical examiner findings can be wrong. Especially if it was poisoning, and the medical examiner didn't have all the information he needed to find it."

"That can happen," Kenzie allowed. "The police investigation didn't turn up anything significant. He died in his own bed. No signs of violence. Nothing obvious about the body that would suggest poisoning. Why do they think he was poisoned?"

"I need to dig down deeper to find that out. Right now, I think just because it's the only thing they can think of that wouldn't have left a mark on the body."

"There are still options other than poisoning. But that does narrow it down," she admitted. "No gunshot or stabbing. No blunt force trauma. No needle marks or ligature."

"Exactly." Zachary nodded. "And suffocation would leave petechiae, right?"

"Sometimes. Maybe seventy to eighty percent of cases. But not always. And they can be caused by other things. In Godfrey's case, there were no petechiae that I remember. No signs of violence."

"Did you find evidence that he had a heart attack in his sleep? Or a stroke? I don't know what else it could have been, but…"

"They don't leave much evidence on the body. If we have a patient history, then we can speculate. Mr. Godfrey did have a history of heart disease. He was on several medications for his heart and blood pressure."

"Do you know which ones?" Zachary reached for his notepad and realized he'd left it beside his computer.

"You'll need to fill out a request form," Kenzie informed him with a smile. "See if you can get the medical examiner's office to release that information to you."

"I hear it helps if you know someone there."

She shook her head. "Nope. No special treatment. You'll have to beg like all of the other poor slobs."

"The family can request a copy of the Medical Examiner's report. And they might even still have his medication in the medicine cabinet."

"Probably. So you won't need to come to the medical examiner's office?" She batted her eyelashes at him.

Zachary's fork slipped and squeaked loudly across the plate, making the moment comedic. He laughed. "Well, maybe I could come visit for lunch one day this week," he suggested, aware that he was blushing.

Kenzie nodded. "That's a good idea. Pull me away from my desk one day." Like Zachary, she tended to get wrapped up in her work and, while she always reminded him that he had to stop to eat lunch, she usually ended up raiding the sandwich vending machine down the hall from her desk, and frequently told him how terrible it was. Still, he could never convince her to take a bag lunch with her.

"Let's do it," he agreed. "One day when we both need a break."

He had a feeling that he would need to enforce breaks from the Godfrey case if he were going to solve it. Walking away and getting a fresh perspective often yielded positive results.

5

Zachary called up Mario Bowman, a friend on the police force, to make inquiries about the Godfrey case.

"Zach, my man," Mario greeted enthusiastically. "It's been too long! We need to get together one night for pizza and a game."

That had been the promise when Zachary had moved out of Mario's apartment and into his own. Mario had given him a place to crash after Zachary's apartment had been set on fire, and it had stretched from "a few days" to a few months as Zachary had been required to replace all of his ID before he could access his bank account and file an insurance claim before he was able to start looking for a new place. They had gotten along well together, and Zachary had said that they would get together again after he left, but that time was always in the future.

"Yeah. We should. We're always saying we're going to, but why not pick a day? Actually set it up."

"That would be great," Mario agreed, sounding surprised at the suggestion. Maybe he had expected Zachary to brush it off again, as he usually did, with a vague promise to get back to him *someday*. "When are you free?"

"Why not… Friday night? I think I can manage that, and it's enough time that I can let Kenzie know and maybe she'll want to get together with some of her friends."

"She would be welcome to come along." There was doubt in Mario's voice. Whether he thought Kenzie wouldn't want to do something separately, or he only wanted it to be a "guys' night," Zachary wasn't sure.

"No. She likes you, but not that much," Zachary teased.

Mario laughed. "Okay, then. Friday. Awesome."

"And the pizza is my treat." Zachary raised his voice and talked over any objection Mario might raise. "I have to find some way to pay you back for everything you did for me."

Mario chuckled and didn't argue it further. "So, what are you calling me about, Zach? I'm sure you didn't call just to set up a pizza night."

"I was looking for some information, and seeing as you are the fount of all wisdom…"

"Flattery will get you everywhere."

"I am looking for the detective who was in charge of the John Godfrey case."

"Uh-oh, does that mean you're going to be making waves around here again? Let me look…" There was the rattle of computer keys as Mario navigated the internal system. "That would be the fetching Detective El Garcia."

"Garcia?" Zachary scratched the name down, though he was sure he was probably spelling it wrong. "Okay, great. Does she have a direct line?"

Mario recited it to him. "I'll put you through."

"Uh…" Zachary wasn't sure what to say. The other part of the information that Mario usually provided was how Zachary could best get the information he needed. A nice bottle of wine or hockey tickets could go a long way to ensuring that the law enforcement officers he talked to felt well-disposed toward him and would give him any answers they could. "What's she like?"

"She's a tough cop, but fair," Mario said. "I know that's what you hear about all cops, because no one wants to tell you that he's a wuss or she couldn't care less about what's just and right. But Garcia really is. I've seen her in action and she's not afraid to do what needs to be done. Smart and organized. Good interrogator; people want to talk to her and please her. Gorgeous woman—very intimidating when she puts on her tough face. But she's a sucker for kids or old abuelas. Those hard-luck cases get her every time."

Zachary nodded, pleased to have the warning and the insight. He would be prepared for her intimidating front and know how to handle her approach to the investigation. "Got it. You can put me through."

Mario chuckled, and Zachary heard the phone start ringing again. He wondered whether it would go through to voicemail. Not that it mattered; he could just leave her a message. He wasn't expecting her to help him.

"Garcia." The sudden voice in his ear made him jump.

"Oh. Hi, Detective Garcia, my name is Zachary Goldman, and I'm a private investigator—"

"I don't deal with private investigators."

"No, I realize that. I'm just calling you to let you know that the Godfrey family has asked me to consult on their father's death."

"Consult? In what way?"

"To investigate privately to see if there is any indication that it was not a natural death. If it was poison or some other method of homicide."

"The ME has already ruled."

"We'll be requesting a copy of the ME's findings, see if there's anything that we can provide more enlightenment on. I don't expect to be able to come up with anything that would make the Medical Examiner change his opinion, but… well, we need to cover all of the bases."

"You're not going to find anything."

"That's fine. I'm being retained to look. If there's nothing to find, there's nothing to find."

"You just saw a big fat sitting duck and figured you had to have a piece, huh?"

"No. They approached me. I've already told them it's a long shot. But if they want me to look at it, I'll look at it."

"So what do you want from me?" her tone was bullish.

"I don't want anything from you, Detective. It's a courtesy call. I'm just letting you know that I'm working on the case, so if you hear my name or hear that someone is asking questions, you'll know what's going on. If you'd like to tell me anything about the case, I'd be happy to hear it, but that's not why I'm calling. I just don't want to step on anyone's toes or be mistaken for a suspect."

"The police don't share information with private investigators, no matter how polite they are." The last bit was spoken with a sigh and a more relaxed tone.

"No. Though it doesn't sound like there would be much to share anyway. You just did a cursory scene review? Didn't find anything unusual or suspicious?"

"I did more than just look at the site."

Zachary made an encouraging noise and didn't say anything.

"We talked to the family. They didn't raise any concerns. They were surprised, but there wasn't any talk about it being a poisoning. There was no sign of violence. The ME said that it was natural causes. The victim had heart problems. He was on medication."

"That's what I heard."

"What makes the family think that it was homicide now? Why didn't they bring this up before?"

"I suspect… they were too shocked initially and didn't want to raise any suspicions. But they have been talking to each other… and they each think that one of the others did it."

"They think that it was someone in the family?" Garcia's voice grew somewhat shriller. "They think that one of them did it, and they hired you to find out?"

"Yes. They know that they all had motives to kill him. Money, mostly, from what I can gather, but maybe also some emotional abuse as well. So they are all looking at each other suspiciously."

"Well, I hope you have a bulletproof vest, amigo, because I wouldn't want to be stepping between two members of the family accusing each other of murder, if I was you."

"They didn't shoot him," Zachary pointed out, "but maybe I shouldn't accept any drinks from them."

Garcia laughed. "You might want to consider that," she agreed. "As long as you're not getting in my way or demanding private information I can't give you, you can 'investigate' to your heart's content. Just stay out of my way."

6

The Godfrey mansion looked like something out of a fairy tale or Victorian novel. The big house stood in the middle of a lush emerald green lawn, several inches deep and perfectly maintained, and a wide variety of bushes and trees surrounded the house with various rich shades of green and the fragrant smell of ripening fruit. A spotless white porch wrapped around the building. There were several smaller outbuildings. Garage, shed, servant's quarters, perhaps. Maybe a guest house or two.

Zachary got out of his car and just stood there for a moment, taking it all in. He was a photographer at heart, and he immediately reached for the camera around his neck and began snapping pictures of it without even thinking about it. The beautiful house with windows glinting in the sun, the mature peach and plum trees, colorful flowers planted in borders, and not a single brown or withered leaf or deadhead that Zachary could see. A gentle breeze stirred the grass and birdsong filled the air.

He shot a short video, panning over the scene and catching a few birds in flight.

"Excuse me! Just who do you think you are?" A man had come

out from the side of the house where he had not been visible to Zachary and was striding toward him. "What are you doing here?"

Zachary dropped the camera, letting it bounce against his chest. "I'm sorry. Zachary Goldman. Private Investigator with Goldman Investigations." He held out his hand to shake, exuding as much confidence in his position as he could. "And you are…"

He thought that the young man might be one of the gardeners. He was dressed in a white polo shirt and khakis, which Zachary imagined might be an appropriate uniform for a gardener on the Godfrey estate. He was a young man, not particularly attractive. He had a long, oval face and black-framed glasses. His nose was a bit too long, and he didn't appear to have shaved the last few days.

"Logan Godfrey," the young man snapped. "You're the private investigator that Karen hired? I thought you would be more…" Logan looked Zachary over, evaluating him as Zachary had just done. "I don't know. Bigger. In better shape. More like the private eyes you see on TV." He made a show of looking Zachary all over. "I can't even see where you have your gun hidden."

"I don't have a gun. In real life, private investigators are… pretty boring. We're not all those hard-drinking, hair-trigger, womanizing private dicks you see on TV."

Logan grinned and shook his head. "Too bad. I was hoping for some adventure. Well," he made a motion toward the front door. "Come in, I guess. Unless you want to look around some more outside."

"Is there anything else I should see out here? Anything I should be aware of?"

Logan shrugged and shook his head. "How would I know? I just live here."

He went to the door and opened it for Zachary, gesturing again for him to enter. "Go on, no need to block the doorway."

Zachary stepped into the mansion and looked around slowly. He had been in fancy houses before. Bridget had dragged him off to countless dinner parties and other occasions at the homes of her friends. And the house that Gordon had provided her with probably cost more than Zachary would make in his lifetime. So he was somewhat prepared for what he would see in the Godfrey mansion.

The doorway led into a great room rather than a reception hall. It had a high ceiling and lots of stone and woodwork. Rich-looking paintings, sculptures, and pottery. The thick carpets were probably imported from somewhere and cost a fortune themselves.

"This is…" Logan gestured to everything in the room in one motion, then threw up his hands in surrender, "We don't use it. Come into the library, I guess. Unless… did you want to see Dad's room first? Since that's…"

"The order doesn't matter, I don't think," Zachary told him. "Which would you rather do first?"

"Get it out of the way. Looking at his bedroom. I haven't been in there since it happened. I can still… feel him there."

Zachary was uncertain whether Logan was implying his father's spirit still lingered in the room where he had passed away or if he was simply overwhelmed with powerful recollections from his dad's belongings still being there, the aroma of his cologne, and other things that brought back memories of him. He thought it best not to inquire further.

"Let's do that, then," he agreed.

Logan took Zachary up the flight of stairs with the dark wooden balustrade, his movements fast and confident, having grown up in the house. Zachary, however, was out of his element, awkward navigating stairs since his spinal cord injury. He hadn't had a lot of practice going up and down steps, as Kenzie's bungalow didn't require it. Despite Kenzie's reassurances that he looked just fine going up and down stairs, to Zachary it still felt uncomfortable and glitchy.

Logan looked back impatiently when he reached the top of the stairs and Zachary wasn't immediately behind him. He waited, one hand on the rail, and didn't say anything to rush him. But being watched just made Zachary feel that much slower and more awkward. He reached the top stair, using one hand on the handrail to help pull himself up the last step.

"Just down here." Logan once more took the lead.

The carpeting was thick and soft under Zachary's feet, cushioning every step. No creaking floorboards. It would have been difficult to hear anyone sneaking around the house who wished to remain undetected. The master bedroom was at the end of the hallway. Logan opened the door silently. There was a slight change in the air temperature and pressure. It felt like a room that had been empty and cold for more than just a couple of weeks.

The bed was large. A king or maybe even bigger. Longer, to accommodate a tall man without his feet dangling off the end. The ceiling was vaulted and painted with gold embellishments. A stone fireplace and built-in bookcases dominated one wall. The shelves held old volumes bound in leather, maybe classics or even first editions.

Zachary gave a low whistle. "Very nice."

Logan looked around as if he'd never seen it before. "I guess. It was nicer when my mother was alive. Softer." His eyes traveled slowly over the details of the room. "Everything is… hard edges now. None of her things are here."

"I'm sorry to hear about her passing. Karen mentioned she died about five years ago?"

"Yeah. I was still in high school. The rest had all moved on and started their careers. I was a late addition to the family. Unplanned, you can bet on that. Why would my Dad want to have any more kids after the perfect Alex? But I guess Mom wanted a girl, too, so they kept going until they got Karen. Then they didn't need anymore. I was an accident."

"It must have been hard to lose your mother so young."

Zachary had been ten when his mother had walked out of his life. Not dead, nothing as well-defined as that. She just didn't want anything more to do with him. And for years, decades, he had fantasized about her coming back. Changing her mind or saying he was old enough now that she could be a part of his life again. But, of course, that had never happened.

"Yeah, it was hard," Logan agreed. "I think it would be easier now. I don't think it hit the others as hard as it hit me. I felt like… my life was ending too. There was no way I could go on and do all the things she wanted me to. It took years for me to get back on track. And look at me now," Logan offered bitterly, holding his arms out and looking down at himself. "Look at me now."

He looked so lost. Zachary understood why he had dropped out of college. Between his learning disabilities and the loss of his mother's support, it must have felt impossible.

"What did your mother die of?"

Logan sighed and looked away. "Cancer. It was a long battle, but eventually, it won." He paused, lost in thought for a few moments before continuing. "The worst part was that I didn't say goodbye. She was in the hospital for months, and I never visited her once. I was too scared." He blinked rapidly and looked away, his eyes welling up with tears he quickly wiped away.

Zachary reached out to put a comforting hand on Logan's shoulder, but he shook it off.

"I should have been there with her," he said softly. "I should have been there at the end instead of staying away like a coward. I regret that every day of my life. I wish someone had forced me to go, but Mom wouldn't let them. She was always trying to protect me."

Zachary nodded sympathetically, his heart aching for the young man in front of him. He knew what it was like to be alone and helpless in the face of life's tragedies. "I'm sorry, Logan." He swallowed the burning lump in his throat. "I really am."

Logan nodded and took in a deep breath before letting it out slowly. He pulled himself up straighter and squared his shoulders, steeling himself against the memories. "Thank you," he said quietly before letting out another deep breath and looking around the room again. "So, what now?"

7

Zachary took a glance around. "Well, I'll need to take a few minutes to look around this room." There were several doors; one presumably led to a closet and one to an ensuite bathroom. "And at the bathroom…?"

Logan nodded and indicated one of the doors. "Yeah, that one. The double doors are the closet."

"Did you see your father… afterward? Who found him?"

"Yeah, I saw him before the police came. It was Mrs. Kennedy, the cook, who discovered him. He usually takes breakfast in the dining room, but he didn't come down. So she went up to see if he wanted tea or something brought to his room. Sometimes he was… indisposed, especially if he had been drinking all night. She knocked. No answer. She opened the door and went in, but she couldn't wake him and it was pretty obvious that he was dead. She didn't scream and drop the tea tray and go into hysterics like in the movies. She came and got me quietly. Told me that he'd passed, and did I want to call for an ambulance or did I want her to?"

Zachary nodded, impressed by the cook's calm and reasoned reaction. Logan was right about TV maids always shrieking and dropping the crockery when they discovered the lord of the manor dead in his bed. But maybe that was only when it was a bloody murder. A man who simply passed in his sleep wouldn't be as shocking.

"So you called an ambulance?"

"I went in to see him. Not because I didn't believe her, of course. I just wanted to see him myself, make sure he really was dead and nothing could be done for him. I wouldn't want anyone accusing me of not doing CPR or whatever it took to revive him."

"Can you describe what you saw?"

"Everything looked perfectly normal. He was in bed, lying on his side. Mrs. Kennedy had pulled back the blanket and sheet, so I could see that he was still, that he was not breathing. He looked... I don't know. Different. Empty. Like he was just a body instead of a man. Someone I didn't even know. I went over to him, checked for a pulse, couldn't feel anything. But his body was kind of hard, waxy. And cool to the touch. So I knew no one could do anything for him."

"And there were no injuries, obviously," Zachary said. "The medical examiner would have noted any violence in his report. There weren't any signs of a struggle in here? The only thing that had been disturbed was the blankets being pulled back?"

"Yeah. Everything looked just how it should. Nothing knocked over or torn up. I called for an ambulance like Mrs. Kennedy suggested, and they came and said that yes, he was dead, and they said they had to call the police in because it was an unattended death. We had that policewoman and other people in and out of here for a few hours." Logan made a gesture to wave all of that off as unimportant. "And they took him away. Once the medical examiner's office was done, they said we could call our funeral director and he would look after everything else."

As everyone had agreed up to that point, it all sounded routine. Nothing stood out as unusual or showing any negligence by the professionals involved. Just a man who appeared to have died in his sleep.

"Did they ask you about medical conditions?"

"Oh. Yeah. They did. I didn't know much; he kept that kind of thing to himself. I knew he had heart disease and high blood pressure, and was a bit overweight. He'd been on pills for years, but it never seemed like it was getting any worse and he never said that his doctor was worried about anything. Show me a businessman his age who *doesn't* have heart disease and high blood pressure." Logan rolled his eyes.

"Right. Did they ask for his doctor's contact information?"

"They looked at the medicine cabinet and could see all of what he was taking and who it was prescribed by. I don't know if they followed up with the doctor or not. I guess they probably did, but I didn't hear back that they had concerns about anything."

Zachary nodded. He made a few notes in his notebook of facts that he wanted to remember or things to investigate further so that he wouldn't lose track of any stray thoughts. He looked around the room.

"Was there anything on his side table?" If there had been, everything had now been cleared away and straightened up. The bed was made, even though it was no longer in use. Probably with freshly-laundered sheets. There wouldn't be much by way of evidence there.

"Uh… I don't know. I didn't pay any attention. Probably his glasses." Logan tapped his own frames to indicate that he was talking about eyeglasses rather than drinking glasses. "He didn't read before bed. Maybe a cigar and a drink. I didn't notice."

"He regularly smoked and drank before bed?"

"Yeah. He knew he shouldn't, but he said what was the point in stopping now? He already had heart and blood pressure problems. That wasn't going to change if he stopped smoking and drinking. And he didn't want to, so why should he?" Logan shrugged. "It isn't like any of us wanted him to live forever. If he wanted to smoke and drink himself to death, then more power to him."

Zachary felt a pang of discomfort at Logan's callous remark. Zachary knew he shouldn't be surprised by it; Karen and Logan had not hidden the fact that there was a rift between John and his children. That was why Zachary was there, after all. To figure out whether one of John's children had killed him. But Logan's bluntness wasn't going to help matters. If he talked like that to other people and word got back to the police, they wouldn't be as understanding or discreet as Zachary.

"Did the police take his glass or ashtray with them?"

Logan shook his head slowly. "No, they didn't take anything, as far as I know. After everyone left, the staff cleaned up like usual." He looked around the room as if seeing it for the first time. "I guess… I'm pretty sure he had the usual stuff on the side table. It has all been put away now." He walked over to the highboy dresser and opened and closed a few drawers, his expression meditative. "There is a watch missing. I don't know if anything else is or not. I don't want to suggest that someone on the staff might have taken it, but…"

"A watch?"

"Dad had this gold watch that he sometimes wore for special occasions. Not his everyday watch. And… I don't know where it has gone. He wouldn't have worn it to bed, so it isn't like it went to the medical examiner's office or funeral home. The staff…" He trailed off. "Most of them have either been here for years or have been carefully vetted by the agency we hire through. There have never been any thefts before. Nothing of significant value."

Zachary frowned. "But something of less value?"

"I mean… if someone took home the leftovers from a party, or sheets or towels went inexplicably missing… it wasn't worth starting an investigation. Domestics do that kind of thing. Feel entitled to some… perks."

"There has been more than one occasion?"

"I don't know. Over the years, yes. Mom said that was to be expected, and there wasn't any point in trying to stop the petty pilfering."

"When did you notice the watch was missing?"

"It wasn't me. It was Karen. She went looking for it for some reason and kicked up a fuss when she couldn't find it. It will probably turn up at the shop to be cleaned or something like that."

"Is Karen looking for it? Has the disappearance been reported to the police?"

"You'd have to ask Karen. She's taking care of it." Logan gave a snort. “She thought I’d taken it. I told her to go ahead and look in my room or wherever she liked. She wasn’t going to find it.”

“I’ll ask her about it. She didn’t mention it when she hired me to investigate the case.”

“I guess she thought it was just a family affair. That she would be able to turn it up in my possessions.”

Zachary walked slowly around the room, trying to take everything in. He took a photo of the bed and side table in case he needed to refer to it later. Over the fireplace hung a portrait of a man and woman. The man was older, balding, his remaining hair shaven short rather than combed over to try to hide the recession. He wore unattractive glasses with black frames and a dark suit with a white shirt and tie. He was not smiling in the picture, but looked quite stern. His brow was ridged with horizontal wrinkles that Zachary would have expected the painter to omit.

Beside him, several inches shorter, was a woman. Steel gray hair in a bob, wrinkles showing in her neck but not her face, on the thin side and wearing a black dress.

“Your parents?” Zachary asked, just to confirm that it wasn’t a picture of Logan’s grandparents.

“Yeah. Mom and Dad.” Logan gazed at the picture. “I guess that makes me an orphan now.” He gave a short laugh. “Not like I’m going to end up in the street.”

8

Zachary took a picture of the painting, avoiding looking at Logan. He wondered what financial situation Logan was in at the moment. He was expecting to inherit millions, but had not yet. Karen had not said that he was working. Since Logan had recently dropped out of college, Zachary assumed he was not. Had he been getting an allowance from his father? And if he had, would that allowance continue to be paid until the estate was distributed?

Who would get the house? Logan was in a good position. Since he had moved back into the mansion, his siblings would not be able to kick him out without proper legal notice from the executor of the estate, whether that was one of the siblings or a high-powered lawyer somewhere. Logan had certain rights with it being his residence.

Even if he wasn't receiving an allowance from the estate, he was still living in the family home, with access to all valuables, like the gold watch that had disappeared. There were plenty of paintings, statues, books, jewelry, and other movable assets that could disappear and provide Logan with whatever walking-around money he needed before the estate was distributed.

"I'll just check out the bathroom," Zachary informed Logan, gesturing toward the closed doors.

He opened the closet doors first, and looked over the fine clothing arrayed in rows beneath sparkling crystal lights that turned on automatically. He schooled himself not to show surprise. Of course John would have a huge walk-in closet the size of a normal bedroom, with all manner of clothes that had been specially tailored for him, rows of shoes polished to a mirror finish, and ties, cummerbunds, and pocket squares of every color for every occasion.

Zachary walked around the interior, looking in a few shoeboxes and closed drawers to see what else was stored in the closet. There were no boxes of photographs or personal mementos as far as he could see. Those would be stored or displayed somewhere else. There was no need for everything to be crammed into a closet like in the small homes Zachary had lived in.

Logan watched him from the bedroom, curious but unconcerned with what he might find there. Zachary exited and closed the doors. He opened the door to the bathroom, braced for what he would find there. With the opulence of the walk-in closet, he expected the bathroom to be equally grand. As with the closet, the lights automatically turned on, glinting off black marble countertops and shining fixtures. It was not the cramped water closet of an apartment or modest house. There was plenty of room to walk around, or maybe to hold a ball. The bathtub—separate from the shower, which was divided into its own enclosure—was the size of the hot tub at the public swimming pool. Also a mirrored black, it featured seating for at least eight, with numerous jets.

Zachary turned his attention to the medicine cabinet framed in gold. It slid on a track with a whisper, and the inside was not a jumbled mess. Everything was sparkling clean and displayed in precise order. Shaving things in one part of the cabinet, toothbrush and oral care on another row, all of John's prescription and over-the-counter meds arranged with labels facing out, equally spaced apart.

"Just what are you expecting to find?" Logan asked, standing in the doorway.

"I'm not expecting anything. I'm seeing what I find. Being biased toward finding one thing or another can make you blind to what's right in front of your face."

"You think?"

Zachary nodded. "Yes. It can. I don't want to miss anything." He leaned in to read the labels on the prescription bottles. He didn't know what many of them were for, but Kenzie could probably help him out with that and point him toward any that caused potentially dangerous interactions when taken with alcohol or in too high of a dose.

He took several pictures of the bottles for later reference. As Logan had said, the prescribing doctor's name was on each label, and all seemed to have been prescribed by the same physician, a D. Bernard. Zachary would follow up with him later, but didn't expect to be able to get much information about Godfrey. Physicians had to protect the privacy of their patients, and pointing out that the man was dead probably wouldn't get Zachary far. He assumed that the physicians of the wealthy were probably even more close-mouthed than the doctors he had dealt with in the past.

"Logan?" a woman's voice floated in from a short distance away. Logan straightened his posture and smiled.

"Amy? In here." He turned and walked to the door of the master bedroom to look down the hall. "In Dad's room."

"What are you doing in there?"

Zachary could tell that the woman's voice was closer, but she was outside the room and he still couldn't see her.

Logan murmured an answer to her, but Zachary couldn't make out what it was. He closed the cabinet and took another look around the bathroom to see if he had missed anything important. The surfaces were clean and there were few places to hide anything. He wasn't going to look in the toilet tank or toilet paper roller with Logan there. He would be offended to have Zachary treating John Godfrey as if he were a common addict or small-time criminal.

He shut the door to the bathroom, wondering whether it

would shut off the lights by itself, and approached the door where Logan stood talking to the new arrival.

It was obvious from the way the two of them leaned in toward each other and spoke that they were intimately acquainted with one another, which was surprising considering the incongruity in their looks. Logan, though the son of a millionaire, was not the handsome playboy Zachary often saw on TV or grocery store tabloids. He was not what Zachary would have considered attractive to women.

Amy, on the other hand, was a young woman with shining blond hair, sparkling blue eyes, and a well-endowed figure. And she knew how to dress. She was, Zachary assumed, every bit Logan's contemporary in terms of position and wealth.

They made an odd couple. But he'd always thought the same of Bridget when he had been with her. What made her pick an ugly duckling like Zachary? Or, not an ugly duckling, because the ugly duckling at least grew into a beautiful swan, which Zachary would never do. Bridget had, he now knew, thought that she could change him, could mold him into what she thought he should be. That had involved changes to his hair, face, and clothing, as well as her efforts to refine his manners and teach him how to behave around her wealthy and influential friends. But those things were all superficial and, even if she had been able to form him into a picture of the man she wanted, she could not change his brain and fix all the things that the therapists and doctors had failed to address in his lifetime.

At least Logan and Amy were apparently on par socially. Looks didn't matter as much in men. Logan had his learning disabilities to contend with, as Zachary had. But Zachary had learned how to compensate for most of them. He'd found a profession that had worked for him, and maybe Logan would too. Or maybe he wouldn't need to, now that he was inheriting a portion of his father's fortune.

Zachary looked at Logan questioningly. Logan didn't introduce his girlfriend. Amy hung on to Logan's arm and looked up at him. "Logan, honey, who's this?" Her eyes flicked over

Zachary, dismissing him as anyone of importance. "The gardener?"

Zachary considered his clothing, a cross between casual and professional. The gardener? He wasn't wearing jeans or a hat. His fingernails were clean. What made her pick *gardener*?

"Uh, no," Logan said. "This is Zachary Goldman. He's… uh… a private investigator."

"Oooh, how interesting. What is he investigating?" She looked at Zachary with open curiosity, still not addressing him directly, which Zachary supposed was because she saw him as a servant rather than an equal.

"Well…" Logan motioned toward the interior of the room. "Dad. You know. Dying."

9

Amy's eyes got big. "Really? Like... *investigating* investigating it? Whether it was... I thought that you said the coroner said it was natural causes. You already had the funeral."

"They said it was natural causes," Logan agreed. "But the others think... that maybe someone helped him along a little."

"Killed him?" Amy asked in a hushed voice.

"Maybe. I don't know. I think that he was already sick. It was bound to happen sooner or later. It wasn't like he was a young man, and since Mom has been gone and he hasn't had anyone looking after his health..."

"Who thinks someone killed him? Your brothers?"

"Mostly Eddie and Karen, I think. We all said that... we'd been wondering about it. But I think mostly... maybe they think Alex did it, because he was tired of waiting for his inheritance."

"Wow," Amy breathed, "I've never been involved in a murder investigation before. That's crazy."

"It's a weird feeling," Logan admitted. "But I don't think Mr. Goldman has found anything that has pointed toward murder, have you?" He turned his focus to Zachary to ask the question.

"Zachary, please. Well... no. I haven't found anything yet to indicate foul play. But I've also just barely begun my investigation. I wouldn't expect to find anything that fast. Not after the police have already looked into it. Unless they were completely negligent, they would have already checked out most of these avenues. It will take time and effort to find anything they missed."

The woman nodded slowly in agreement. Zachary knew she was picturing all the private investigator movies she had ever seen or murder mysteries she had read and trying to picture Zachary as the suave, hard-boiled, quick-shooting PI.

"It isn't like that," he told her. "It's a lot of routine inquiries and sorting out tedious details. There are no femme fatales or shootings or car chases." He smiled.

There had been at least one shooting and car chase, but he wasn't going to indulge her fantasies. Investigating was just as he'd said, a lot of routine questions and looking around.

Until something popped.

Until some perpetrator decided that he was getting too close to the truth and needed to be taken out of the picture.

But that wasn't going to happen again. Most detective work was boring and mundane.

"So…" He looked at Logan. "We haven't talked about security or what went on the night before your father died. Maybe we could sit down somewhere private and discuss that?"

Logan looked down at Amy, smiling. "Where should we go, the back deck?"

She nodded. "Yes, that would be perfect."

Zachary opened his mouth to object that by "private," he had meant to exclude Amy and to keep it to just him and Logan. But he decided that Logan might just ask him to leave. Logan was still happy to talk to him as long as Amy was there. And maybe he would be open and helpful with Zachary in order to involve Amy in the excitement of the investigation. It was worth a shot. If it didn't work out, he could always come back another day and catch Logan when he was alone.

He nodded and followed Logan and Amy as they went arm in

arm down the stairs and led Zachary through a couple more opulently decorated rooms to get to the back porch.

It was, of course, nothing like any back porch that Zachary had ever seen. The portion that wrapped around the front of the house had been fairly standard. A white fence around a narrow space outfitted with a few chairs and small tables with which to enjoy the fresh air. The back deck was on multiple levels that led down into a garden. He couldn't tell from the house, but it looked as though the hedges at the back of the garden might actually be a labyrinth. The various levels of the deck were garnished with bright flowers and greenery, lounges, a wet bar, a huge stainless steel outdoor grill, and various other amenities. Amy took the lead and took them over to a small grouping of chairs around a glass table, shaded from the summer sun by a large tree.

The smells of ripe peaches and plums wafted over them. Zachary's stomach growled. Zachary, who rarely ever ate anytime but the appointed mealtimes. He was glad no one else appeared to hear it. Logan went immediately to the wet bar. Zachary hoped that he was only planning to have one social drink. Dealing with an inebriated client was not something he enjoyed.

"What can I get you, Zachary?" Logan asked cheerfully. He obviously already knew his and Amy's usual drinks, as he started dropping ice into glasses and opening up various bottles.

"Nothing for me," Zachary said, then decided that might seem ungracious. He needed to keep Logan in a good mood, not make him feel like Zachary didn't appreciate his hospitality. "Just a water or a Coke."

"Those are kiddie drinks. Come on, what do you like?"

"I can't drink because of a medication I'm on," Zachary told him, which was only partially true.

"Aw, they always say that. But I can tell you from experience that most of those drugs you can go ahead and drink a glass or two of alcohol with anyway. They just don't want you overdoing it."

"Sorry. I appreciate it, but I have to stick to the protocol." That made it sound a little more serious. Maybe something that Logan would pay attention to. Meds were one thing. A *protocol* was a whole different level.

Logan shrugged with one shoulder, and Zachary watched him take a bottle of coke out of the refrigerator and pour it into a glass over a stack of ice cubes. He topped the glass with a twist of lime. Nice touch.

"Some people tend bar to help with money when they're going to school," Zachary said.

"Nope, not me. I just like to drink in bars. My bartending is purely recreational."

Logan handed Amy and Zachary their drinks and sat down. He took a swallow of his drink but did not, Zachary was happy to see, instantly drain his glass. He sat with it resting on his knee and looked expectantly at Zachary.

Zachary gave a quick nod to indicate that he understood. "Tell me about any security measures you have in place here. I didn't see any security gate or guards on the property."

"No, we don't do that. No one in this area does. Except maybe the McNabs, but they're nuts! It's like living out in the country here, where people don't even lock their doors. But we do—lock our doors, I mean—we just don't go overboard. No need for a private security force."

"You haven't ever had to deal with any intruders or trespassers? Any threats to the family?"

"No. There's stuff that goes on. People's houses get broken into every now and then. But if you've got a good burglar alarm, you don't need to go hog-wild with the security."

"And you have a good burglar alarm?"

"Sure. State of the art. Or maybe it was state of the art twenty years ago," Logan corrected himself with a chuckle. "It's pretty basic. Open door and breaking glass alarms. Smoke and fire. A hardwired line to the police."

"But you don't keep it armed during the day?"

Logan had not had to disarm an alarm when he had let Zachary into the house. And Amy had walked in without an escort. Unless she had already been inside when Zachary got there and just hadn't been looking for Logan until later.

"No one is going to burgle the place during the day. No, we lock up at night, set the alarm, and sleep like babies until the morning."

"Who knows the passcode? And is it changed regularly?"

"The household staff, the family." Logan tipped his glass to indicate Amy, "A few close family members. And... it doesn't get changed very often. It's too complicated. Changing it, and letting everyone know it has changed and what the new code is."

"But you *do* change it now and then. When someone gets fired. If there are threats."

Logan looked up at the sky. "I think... the last time might have been when I was eight."

Zachary had been expecting a less-than-optimal time frame, but that was a bit much. The passcode hadn't been changed in over a decade? What was the point in even arming it?

"So anyone in the family, who has worked here, or has been a close friend in the past fifteen years can get into the house."

"You need a key, too," Logan pointed out.

"And the same number of people probably have a key? Maybe even more? Have the locks been changed in the past fifteen years?"

"I don't know when they've ever been changed. But we haven't ever had any break-ins."

"And your locks are all pretty basic spring locks and deadbolts. Nothing secure."

"They look secure to me. As long as they look secure to a thief, that's all that matters."

"But they don't. They look like a kindergartner could pick them."

Amy giggled. She sipped her multilayered drink through a straw. "He's really giving you the business, Logan! You'd better beef up the security around here!"

"I guess so," Logan admitted. "I'll tell Alex."

"He doesn't live here, though, right?" Zachary asked.

"No. We all still have rooms here, but he doesn't stay here.

Unless he's drunk or something. But he's sort of the boss with Dad gone. All of the patriarchal responsibilities of the family falling on his head." He snickered. "I wish he *would* fall on his head!"

So security measures were a bust. Pretty much anyone could have walked into the wide-open mansion whenever they pleased.

"And surveillance? Do you at least have a few security cameras?"

"No. Talked about them a lot. But never got around to installing them. Dad didn't approve. Said that a man should be able to have privacy in his own home without anybody filming him. I wouldn't say he's a Luddite, but he had his opinions..."

Zachary nodded. There wasn't much to note down about the conversation, but he scratched out a few phrases about the security anyway. There was no point in beating a dead horse. It was time to move on.

10

"Why don't you tell me about the night before your dad died? From what you and Karen said, I gather that there was a family dinner that night. All of you were here."

Logan nodded. "All of the family," he agreed, glancing at Amy. "Dad and us four. Sometimes spouses come along, the kids, even, but this time it was just the four of us."

Zachary nodded. He had walked past the heavy wooden table in the dining room on the way to the back porch, and he pictured John Godfrey sitting at the end and his four children along the sides. He hadn't yet met all of them, but he had built up a picture of each of the siblings in his head.

"So I assume that you and your dad were here first, since you're the ones who were living in the house."

Logan nodded. "I don't know when Dad got home, I wasn't paying any attention, and it's a big house. But he was growling at Mrs. Kennedy to make sure that everything was ready—as if she hadn't been preparing family dinners for years—and he went down to his study for a drink and to wait for people to arrive. He yelled at me to get myself ready and come down, not to be late for dinner when I was the closest one there."

Zachary raised his brows. "Were you usually late for dinner?"

"Sometimes. I can remember my mom saying the same thing about church. The people who lived the farthest away were always the first ones there, and it was the people who lived just down the street who would be late or hurrying in at the last minute. I guess it was the same thing. I knew I didn't have to drive anywhere, so I didn't get ready until the last minute. And sometimes… I misjudged or got too involved in what I was doing."

"What did you have to do to get ready?"

"Well, I couldn't come to the table looking like this." Logan gestured to his casual outfit. "The old man would have had a coronary." He paused, realizing the inappropriateness of the comment, then shrugged it off. "We had to dress for dinner. Like it was an event. It didn't have to be formal attire, but… at least business professional. Suit and tie. Skirts or dresses for the ladies. Kids too, they couldn't be in jeans or play clothes. None of the kids were there this time. I guess they didn't really enjoy a stuffy dinner with grandpa."

Amy giggled. Logan smiled appreciatively at her response.

"So, were you ready before the others arrived, or did you end up being late?"

"I planned it pretty well. Alex was there already, having a drink in the study with Dad. I joined them. Then I think Karen, and Eddie last." He stared off, thinking for a minute about whether he had the order correct, and then nodded. "Yeah, that's right."

"And everybody started with a drink in the study?"

"Yeah. That was usual."

"Did everyone help themselves to drinks, or was someone pouring?"

"Everybody helped themselves. We all knew what we wanted and where to find it. Karen got Dad another scotch, I think."

Zachary wrote it down in his notebook and jotted down the order Logan had said they had arrived in. That meant that Alex had been alone with John for some unspecified length of time before Logan had walked in. And Karen had given him a drink. Zachary doubted anyone had been watching her very carefully. Why would they? At that point, there was no hint as to what was going to happen.

"Had your father received any threats? Did he have any reason to believe that his life was in danger?"

"No, not that he told me. I mean, I know he got threats sometimes. He laughed them off. Never took any seriously as far as I know."

"Who did he get threats from?"

"I don't know. I was never that interested in his business. I guess… people who thought he hadn't done what he promised, or that he'd turned them down, or snubbed their companies. He wasn't really clear, and I wasn't listening."

"You said he'd been jumpy that night," Amy reminded Logan.

He looked at her, frowning, then back at Zachary.

"Was he jumpy?" Zachary prompted.

"I don't know about jumpy. He was… it was like he was thinking about something else, and then he'd lose track of the conversation and be snapping at people for nothing. Not *that* different from normal, but he did seem a little… anxious, maybe. His head was somewhere else, and he was pacing and looking out the window and jumping on our backs about stuff."

"You too?"

"All of us. He got like that. Acted like he was disgusted with everything we did. No one could live up to his standards, not even Alex."

"You saw Alex as his favorite?"

"He *was* the favorite," Logan told him firmly. He reached over for Amy's hand and squeezed it. Maybe reassuring himself that someone cared about him. His mother was gone and his father had preferred the firstborn to everyone else, but at least Logan had Amy. She looked back at him with a warm smile. Zachary watched her eyes, looking for any sign of masking or deception. He wasn't sure of her.

"What was he getting on your case about? Do you remember?

And did you have any sense about what he might be worried or agitated about?"

"Agitated. That's a good word for it," Logan approved. "I have trouble coming up with the right word sometimes." He blew out his breath, considering. "I remember… he didn't like the way I was dressed. Tie wasn't done up to his liking, and he hated the color—which I knew when I put it on. Mostly he harps about me quitting college. It just wasn't the thing for me though, you know?" Logan appealed to Zachary. "It isn't for everyone. I need… something more hands-on. I'd love to be a carpenter or a welder or something like that. But… that's not what men of our family's social standing *do*."

"He expected you to go to college and… do what?"

Logan snorted. "Something worthwhile. Something he could brag about to his friends. Or colleagues or whatever, because he didn't have any close personal friends. He had the high-powered lawyer, and inventor-scientist, or whatever Eddie sees himself as. He didn't think Karen could make it as a doctor, but he let her be a nurse. Karen was supposed to marry some muckety-muck. He didn't think she needed any education."

"He had a… traditional view of women's positions in society?"

"He was a total chauvinist pig, yes. Like he was still stuck in the fifties. I don't think everyone in our social stratum feels that way. It's like—how can anyone still think that way about women? But those old farts are still out there, trying to push outdated ideas."

Zachary nodded. Despite all of Bridget's intelligence, strength of character, and refinement, there had still been men who had disregarded her and refused to consider that a woman could come up with a worthwhile thought.

Amy patted Logan's knee. "It's a good thing you don't see things that way."

"I learned from my mom rather than my dad. She was a progressive woman. Don't ask me how she and my dad ever hooked up."

"They were probably married before he had any idea about her views on women's place in society," Amy advised. "It doesn't sound like it was something he would have asked her."

Logan chuckled. "No. Definitely not. Shot himself in the foot by not thinking it was worth asking her."

11

Zachary steered the conversation back to the evening before John's death. "So tell me more about that night. Before dinner, in the study, he was acting agitated, lashing out at people, criticizing them. Looking out the window, which might indicate that he thought there was an outside threat. Or he was expecting someone else to come by that night. You wouldn't know if he was expecting anyone else, would you?"

"Not that I know of. He didn't say there was anyone and wouldn't normally see anyone else on a family dinner night. He usually just went from the dinner to his room for a smoke and a nightcap. Maybe read until he went to sleep. And not a lot of people came to the house other than family. A few close friends. But it was his sanctuary. He conducted his affairs at the office and didn't even like taking business calls after he got home."

Zachary nodded and made a couple of notes.

"Did anything happen between meeting in the study for drinks and the dinner? Anything that was said, anything at all out of place?"

"I don't think so. It was all pretty much like every other family dinner. You know how people fall into the same arguments over and over again and never move on?"

"Yeah. I've seen that."

"I've been to family dinner once or twice," Amy said with some importance. "And I'll tell you, it's not exactly the civilized affair they would have you think. There's a lot of… knives in the back."

Zachary looked at Logan. "Just from your father? Or your siblings as well?"

"It's sort of a free-for-all. Mom always tried to get us on the same side. Mediate between us, help us see each other's viewpoints or why we didn't believe the same thing. Dad doesn't exactly egg us on, but he tries to force his own opinion or agenda on everyone. And then we all act like cowards, throwing each other under the bus."

"Do you get along with each other when you're away from him?"

"A lot better, yeah. I mean, I'm still not best friends with any of my siblings. There's so much of an age gap. We didn't really grow up together and I don't spend time with any of them one on one. Taking holidays together, or even just exchanging calls or texts."

"Were there any new arguments or topics of discussion during the dinner?" Zachary inquired.

"I don't know. To be honest, I kind of shut them all off. Focused on the food—Mrs. Kennedy is a really good cook—and zoned out unless someone was talking to me in particular. I'm not interested in their jobs or politics, or even in their kids."

"You didn't notice whether your dad seemed to be attacking one person more than another or more than usual?"

"Seemed like Alex was in a bad mood. Maybe poking at him more than usual. But… I don't know. Dad was just in a state. Growling at anything anyone said."

"Maybe he was coming down with a bug. Didn't feel very well."

"Maybe. Maybe that's what killed him. Like the Spanish flu. Only no one knew it."

Zachary hadn't considered a virus before but, after what had happened with a rogue virus Kenzie had discovered, maybe he should have.

"What did you eat for dinner?"

"Grilled trout," Logan gazed heavenward and licked his lips. "Heirloom tomatoes, asparagus. Locally sourced. And peach pie with our own peaches." He kissed his fingertips. "Delicious."

"I wish I'd been there," Amy told him.

"You know Mrs. Kennedy's cooking. She outdoes herself every time."

"Mmm," Amy agreed.

"Was she the only one involved in the preparation of the food? Did she have help?"

Logan shrugged. "I have no idea. She usually worked alone, but there were other staff around if she needed help with something."

"And any of the other staff would have had access to the kitchen?"

"Only if she wanted them in there. If she didn't want someone underfoot in the kitchen, that was her domain. And that included Dad or the grandkids. Nobody else would have dared to be there."

"Same with the siblings? No one would have gone in there for ice or a snack or to give her a wine to pair with the trout?"

"No. I can't see anyone doing that. I'm the youngest one and, as far as the others are concerned, I am a spoiled brat, but she wouldn't even let *me* in there."

"And once the food came out, was it dished up at the table? Were there communal bowls, things being passed around?"

"No, no," Logan shook his head. "Everything was already plated when it was brought out. Just like at a restaurant."

"Bread bowl, anything like that?"

"No, nothing."

"Did anyone have a special order? Someone who didn't like fish? Did your dad have anything special? Unique to him?"

"Nothing." Logan shrugged and sipped his drink, ice cubes tinkling. "You see? I don't believe anyone could have poisoned him. It's a great theory, but I don't think it has legs. How would he have been poisoned?"

"Were you all drinking the same thing in the study?"

"No. But Alex and Dad were both drinking scotch. From the same bottle."

"And Karen was the only one who poured him a drink."

"Right." Logan grinned. "So, does that make her the poisoner? They say it's a woman's weapon, don't they?" He looked sideways at Amy, and she cuffed him lightly on the shoulder in reproof.

"I don't know if that's actually true," Zachary said. He'd never bothered to look up any statistics on the matter. "But that's what they say."

Of course, a woman could use another weapon, or a man could use poison, so calling it a woman's weapon would just give him an investigative bias, which might blind him to other possibilities.

"Must have been Karen," Logan said, grinning. "Case closed."

"Someone could have poisoned his nightcap. Did someone pour it for him, or did he get it himself? You said that he usually retired to his own room after dinner."

"He could only put up with us for so long. By after-dinner coffee, he'd had enough. He was looking tired. Maybe he *was* coming down with something."

"So did he pour himself another drink in the study, or…?"

"One of the staff would have made sure that there was a full decanter in his bedroom. They knew his habits and that if the decanter wasn't full enough, someone would lose their job, if not their head."

"Who would have done that?"

Logan shrugged. "I don't know. One of the staff. You'd have to ask them about it."

"And the decanter was filled from…"

"A fresh bottle, presumably. There would not have been enough left in the study."

"And his glass and decanter were used every night for his nightcap?"

"Yes."

Anyone with access to the glass or decanter might have placed a deadly poison in the bottom, hoping it would go unnoticed. A poison that was clear and would not react with the scotch, and just a few drops would be enough to kill.

"Where were those kept?"

"In his room. Taken to the kitchen and washed each morning, I assume, and then returned before bed."

Zachary wrote down a few questions to investigate.

"Does anything stand out for you about the evening?" He was careful not to give particular suggestions or directions for Logan to think about, hoping not to influence his answer. He wanted Logan to think of whatever might be tucked away in his subconscious, without any external influence.

"Does anything stand out? No. I guess just what we've already discussed. That Dad was in kind of an agitated or grouchy mood. Usually, he tried to at least put on a mask of civility. But that night..." Logan swore and called his father a couple of names that made Amy press her lips together reprovingly and shake her head.

12

Shopping and meal preparation had always been Kenzie's domain, but she had expressed lately that she wanted Zachary to be more involved in both activities rather than putting it all on her. She had a busy, stressful job, and Zachary should have known better than to saddle her with all of the domestic responsibilities. He was as bad as John Godfrey, expecting Kenzie to play the part of the dutiful wife even when she worked just as hard or harder than he did during the day.

He had offered to do the shopping by himself, but Kenzie had insisted that they do it together, at least a few times, so that he knew her preferences and didn't pick up the wrong thing.

Zachary knew she didn't really trust him to do the shopping and was loath to let it go, even though she had been the one to say it was a burden. And she was right that he was often distracted from less important or less interesting tasks due to his ADHD. There had been too many times when he had only put plates on the table and forgotten about cups, knives, forks, and whatever else was needed. He couldn't deny that. But if he had a checklist, he was pretty good at staying on task. He would get everything on the list and not go home with it only half-completed. And she didn't need to show him what to get; all she had to do was to write down the brand or the size, and he would get what she wanted. He wasn't completely inept.

So they were shopping together the first few times so he could learn, and it was not the equivalent of date night. They might be together and there for a singular purpose, but it was not a fun, intimate activity.

"Do you see this?" Kenzie asked, holding up a couple of bunches of bananas for Zachary. "I don't want you to get the ones that are completely yellow. They'll go bad too fast. Neither of us likes overripe bananas and, if you get the ones that are all yellow, we'll have to eat them within a couple of days."

Zachary nodded. "Green bananas. Check."

"No, not all green, either. If you get these in-between ones," she thrust the bunch toward him, "then we only have to wait a day or so for them to ripen enough to eat. We don't want to wait all week for them to ripen, either."

"Okay."

"I usually get a few that are yellow with just a bit of green, and a few that are more green than yellow so they can ripen through the week."

Zachary nodded. Kenzie pulled three bananas off of two different bunches and put them in the cart. Zachary could remember one of his foster mothers shouting at him for pulling bananas off of the bunch in the store. He had thought that he was being helpful separating them so that when the kids wanted to eat, they just had to pick up one banana instead of pulling it off of the bunch, especially if it was ripe and more likely to tear than come off cleanly.

But his foster mother had had other opinions. From then on, Zachary had known better than to pull bunches of bananas apart at the store. The bunches were *inviolate*. He watched Kenzie blithely ignore this life rule and set the two partial bunches of bananas into the cart.

"Do you need to put them in a bag?" he asked, looking at them.

"No. A bag makes them ripen too fast, or even to get sweaty and go bad without ripening properly."

"Oh."

Kenzie pushed the cart on, talking rapidly about mushrooms in their varieties and packaging options. If she was expecting him to be able to remember everything, she told him…

They were less than halfway through the shopping trip, and he knew he should have been taking notes. There was no way he was going to remember everything. And then she would be upset with him when he brought home the wrong thing.

It was a good thing she had said they would go together a few times. He would take notes the next time. It would mean she would have to tell him some things twice, but he didn't want to act like he was incompetent and she had to do the shopping. He could handle it. He'd been shopping for himself since he had left foster care, hadn't he? He just had to adjust the process to suit someone else's preferences.

Zachary's elbow knocked against a display as they left the produce section and turned into the next aisle. Kenzie whirled around, her face white and eyes wild, hands coming up to protect herself. Zachary froze. She stayed in that defensive position for only an instant, then dropped her hands and tried to look casual. "You startled me."

"Sorry."

She took a deep breath and looked like she was going to lecture him about being more careful and not startling her. But then she closed her mouth and kept walking, acting as if nothing had happened. Zachary kept a little farther behind her and paid attention to his elbows.

Though Dr. B had recommended that Kenzie start therapy on her own to deal with the trauma of her kidnapping, she was still undecided on a doctor or therapist. Zachary understood not wanting to be in therapy. He had fought it most of his life. Not wanting to appear broken. He didn't want anyone to see his weaknesses, much less to talk about them. He had many failings and, despite what Dr. B and the others said, he still felt guilty for his

ADHD, PTSD, and other issues. If he had been stronger and more resilient, he wouldn't be dealing with them. Or he would deal with them in a better way. He didn't like taking medication that changed how he felt and acted and fit into the world around him.

The world was supposed to be getting better for people like him, with more openness about learning disabilities, mental illness, and trauma. But there was still stigma attached to such things, and no one was more aware of that than he was. Of course Kenzie didn't want to admit how much the trauma was affecting her and wanted to deal with it on her own rather than seeking therapy. She might be a medical doctor, but she still had those prejudices built into her too.

"Zachary!"

He hurried to catch up to Kenzie, spurred on by her tone of irritation. "Sorry, I was just..." he trailed off, not sure of an acceptable explanation for lagging behind. He could say that he had been looking at something, but why would he be looking at something that was not on her list? He was supposed to be going by her list.

"Your chicken and stars," Kenzie pointed to the can with the red and white label. "I usually pick up a couple of those. Unless you haven't eaten any lately. And these are the ones that I like..." One of the more gourmet brands, of course, a thick white chicken stew that looked like it had cooked zucchini and tomatoes in it. Who wanted zucchini and tomatoes in chicken soup?

"Great. Those look good," Zachary lied, and put a couple of cans of chicken and stars and a large jar of the gourmet soup into the cart.

"If you want some, we should probably get two."

"No, that's okay. I'll stick with the chicken and stars."

She laughed. As they went by the dried noodle soups, she reached out and touched one of the packages as she looked at them. Probably smoothing it out to see how much sodium it contained. The wrapper crinkled, making him grit his teeth. Even in the busy store, the noise was loud enough to make his skin crawl.

"Do you like—" Kenzie started, and then stopped when her eyes reached his face. "What is it?"

"Nothing."

"You look… upset. Is something wrong?" Kenzie looked behind her, and then at the other end of the aisle, eyes searching for anyone who might be a danger. Who might be planning to attack, or maybe to follow her out of the store, pull a bag over her head, and throw her into the back of a stripped van. "What?"

Zachary shook his head, attempting to maintain a neutral and casual expression. "Everything is fine, Kenz."

"Don't 'everything is fine' me. Something is going on. Did you see something?" She again checked both ends of the aisle.

"No. It was just the noise."

She looked blank. "What noise?"

Zachary pointed to the package of noodles. "The soup package. It crinkled."

She looked at him like he was crazy. Which probably wasn't far from the truth, when he thought objectively about the little things that had been bothering him the last few months, and the defenses he had built up against them, despite trying to act perfectly normal.

"I told you it was nothing," he repeated. "I didn't see anything that should worry you."

"You made that face because the wrapper crinkled."

"Yes."

She smoothed it with her thumb and Zachary turned away before she could see his expression change again.

"What else is in this aisle? Did you need any spices?" he asked her.

"No."

They walked down the aisle, each avoiding looking at the other. A fine pair they made, unintentionally triggering each other. Kenzie had always been the strong, sane one in the relationship and it was difficult to get used to the fact that things he said and did caused her anxiety too.

They were halfway through the store. Zachary looked at the aisle number and list of food categories overhead and sighed. Hopefully, they would not be ready to kill each other by the end of the errand.

13

Zachary waited in the well-appointed offices of Bramwell, Sinclair & Morgan, waiting for Alex. The receptionist's desk was topped with pink marble that complemented the thick carpeting and antique white walls and had been polished to a high shine. The chairs like the one Zachary sat in were thickly upholstered and comfortable, unlike the guest chairs he'd sat in in many doctors', dentists', or lawyers' waiting rooms that forced him to sit up straight or slide out.

The receptionist had a calm, melodious voice and answered calls every few seconds, efficiently dealing with inquiries or putting them through to lawyers. She glanced at Zachary a few times while he waited. Whether because he didn't look like the people who were normally waiting in the offices of Bramwell, Sinclair & Morgan, or because she expected Alex to have come out to get him already, he wasn't sure.

Eventually, a young woman came out and looked around the lobby, empty of anyone but Zachary and the receptionist, and tentatively asked, "Mr. Goldman?"

"That's me," he agreed, taking a moment to struggle from the deep chair and stand. He wasn't sure whether he should offer to shake her hand and ended up giving her a little wave instead. “Zachary.”

“Come right this way, sir; I’m sorry to keep you waiting.”

Zachary followed her into the hallowed halls of the law firm, past several secretaries’ desks overflowing with paper to a small office where a man sat behind a scuffed desk. He was tall and slim, sat up ramrod straight, and smoothed his expensive suit when his assistant escorted Zachary in. Like both Karen and Logan, he had dark brown hair. But he was considerably more handsome, by society’s standards, than Logan.

“Mr. Goldman,” he greeted gravely.

Zachary raised his brows. He sat down in the guest chair, which wasn’t nearly as comfortable as the one in the lobby had been. “It’s Zachary,” he advised.

“Zachary. And you can call me Alex.”

Zachary got the feeling that he was reluctant to be on a first-name basis with a lowly private investigator, but Zachary had forced his hand.

“So… I’m not sure how we begin,” Alex said, out of his element with the interview.

“I’ve talked a little bit to Karen, enough to get the basics of the case and why you were interested in hiring me, and I’ve been to the house to see John’s room and to talk to Logan. I’d like to talk to you about your relationship with your father and then go through the events of the evening before he died. You had a family dinner that night.”

“Yes, that’s right. Of course. My relationship with my father… well, we get along—got along—with each other well enough. We’re both businessmen. Professionals. And over the years, we’ve developed a relationship based on that. Mutual respect.”

“Did you spend time with each other? Go hunting together, out for a business lunch, that kind of thing?”

“Well, no. Our meetings were generally limited to the family home. When one of us wanted to see the other, we would set up a time…”

“Did you go to see him often?”

Alex's jaw clenched. He apparently didn't appreciate Zachary's attempts to nail down exactly what kind of relationship they'd had rather than just taking him at his word.

"I'm sure you know my father and I were both very busy men. I would have liked to have gotten together with him more often, but that just wasn't always possible."

Zachary nodded. "It's hard to keep up with people when there is so much else going on. It's a busy world, and I don't imagine that being a corporate lawyer is a nine-to-five job."

"No," Alex agreed, mollified by Zachary's words. "You're right about that. There have been nights when I have been here until midnight or one in the morning. Days when I've barely gone home to change and then been back here to get back to work again. A junior lawyer like me... we have to keep our billable hours up and get in the cases that will help us to eventually make partner. Dad always expected me to be the youngest lawyer ever to make partner at Bramwell, Sinclair & Morgan."

"Wow. Good for you. Congratulations."

"I haven't made partner yet," Alex growled. He indicated his surroundings. The small office, scuffed furniture and walls, piles of thick files everywhere. "I wouldn't be here if I had."

"Oh, I'm sorry. I misunderstood. You certainly look like you could be a partner. And you *do* have a window."

"Yes," Alex admitted, looking out the window. There wasn't much of a view; opaque blinds were pulled down to cover most of it. "Not everyone gets a view."

"That's right. They must see something in you. Drive. Potential."

"I'm a hard worker and I was always at the top of my class in school. It's different being out in the real world, practicing, working with real clients and real cases. You're not graded the same way anymore. Giving the right answer doesn't always get you anywhere."

"Your father must have been very proud of you. You've accomplished so much."

"Like I said, he expected me to make partner very young," Alex said flatly, speaking through clenched teeth. It was unclear whether this was intended to demonstrate his father's unreasonable expectations or how proud he was of what Alex had already accomplished. It could cut either way.

So Zachary just nodded vaguely.

"It's a good thing you were able to get off the night of the family dinner so that you could see him. You must spend a lot of evenings here."

"I had to make family dinner, come hell or high water. I always made sure that I would be able to get it off."

"What would happen if you didn't?"

"He'd cut me off."

"But you're the oldest. He was so proud of your accomplishments. He wouldn't really have done that, would he?"

"I had no intention of testing how far the old coot would go. I've seen how he treated Karen and Logan—keeping them down. Constantly telling them they could not achieve what they wanted. Do you think he wouldn't do the same to me if I crossed him? Cut off the money, the endorsements, access to his connections?" He shook his head grimly. "I wouldn't do anything to risk that."

"Wow. Tough relationship. I'd heard that he favored you; I didn't think he would do anything to hamper your success."

"I'm sure the others have told you all about how they think I'm the chosen one and never get any of the crap they have to put up with. But that's just not true. They might get more for not living up to his expectations, but I worked hard to get where I am. That favoritism is *earned*, no matter what anyone might think."

"After what I've heard about your father so far, I'm sure it was no walk in the park," Zachary agreed.

"That's right."

Alex stared at him, his gaze direct and challenging, as if daring him to make an accusation.

"I admire your dedication and determination," Zachary told him.

14

"What do you remember about the last night with your father? The evening, your dinner, anything that might have stuck out to you."

Alex considered. He stared off into space. "I don't remember anything out of the ordinary, to be honest. It was like any other family dinner—plenty of verbal sparring, discussions at the dinner table, and good food from Mrs. Kennedy. But in the end, nothing special happened. We just all went back home. It was a shock the next morning to hear that Dad had passed in the night."

"And you think there might have been foul play?"

"I can't help wondering. It was so sudden. And with the others… I mean, none of them have been on good terms with him. As you said, he was a tough guy to maintain a relationship with, and they hadn't had an easy time of it."

"And you think one of them just couldn't take it anymore? Decided to remove him because of something he had said or done?"

"Or to get their inheritance early. I hate to say it, but money is a big thing in our family, and Dad controlled the purse strings. If you needed money and it was something he didn't think was worthwhile, then too bad. You didn't get it. With Logan dropping out of school and Karen's problems, money certainly could have been a motivating factor."

"Karen's problems?"

Alex gazed at him. "Oh, she didn't discuss that with you?"

"I know she wanted to become a doctor, but he wouldn't cover the fees. Didn't think that she could or should be a doctor."

"Well, that's one part of it, sure. But that was years ago. If she was going to kill him over school fees, she would have done something about it then. And Mom was alive then, too. Karen should have appealed to her about it. Mom could still talk Dad into something if she felt really passionately about it."

"But instead, she accepted the offer of nursing school. A compromise."

Alex nodded. "It was probably a relief for her, in a way. I don't think she would have fared very well in medical school." He went on to explain, "Dad was probably right about that. She doesn't have the temperament for it and her grades weren't the best in school, just 'good enough.' Dad would have only accepted the best from her, so he offered to pay for nursing school instead. Less pressure, less emphasis on grades and bookwork."

"And… her current problems were unrelated to that?"

"The woman is a train wreck. Her marriage is on the rocks. She's a nurse, yes, but with the economy and trying to look after her kids during the day, it's all night shifts. When she can get them. So she's struggling to make ends meet. And one of the kids has *problems*, if you know what I mean. I don't know what's wrong with him. She says he is being evaluated, but I don't know what for. He's always into everything, pays no attention to adults, screams and acts out. It's hard enough keeping a normal kid quiet and entertained during a meal. But a long, drawn-out affair like we have, with discussions of politics and world affairs, and a kid she couldn't control… it was a disaster whenever her family joined us. And who knows what kind of trouble he's having at school. The Bentwood Academy wouldn't put up with kids acting out; I'll tell you that."

"Is that where they're enrolled?"

"I don't ask her about her personal business. But that's where they're *supposed* to be. I can't see them keeping wacky Wally there."

Zachary wondered what disability poor Wally suffered from and whether Karen had been able to get him into a program that worked for him. They at least had the means to find a private school or therapist to work with him. Something that many children in the lower strata of society never found. But only if Karen had the money to get him into such a program, and Alex had just said that money was a complicating factor in "her problems."

"Didn't she have the money she needed to get him help?"

"She doesn't make a lot of money working night shifts as a nurse. And that husband of hers, Dawson… I think he's pretty hopeless. Don't know why she married him in the first place. She should have found someone… more adequate. Someone who could provide for her."

Zachary considered a reply like "The heart wants what it wants," but was pretty sure that Alex would disagree. But Zachary couldn't align himself with the opinion that if Karen wanted to have her son taken care of properly, she should have married someone who was in a better position to do so.

"If she's in the midst of having him diagnosed, then maybe she'll be able to find a way to help him by the time she gets her portion of the inheritance," Zachary suggested.

Alex's brows drew down as he considered that. He steepled his hands in front of his face, studying Zachary closely. "Do you think she killed our father for that? To have the money to help Wally?"

"I don't think anything at this point; I'm just listening to what you and the others say. If she was in financial trouble and couldn't afford to educate or treat her son for his disability, wouldn't your father have helped her? Did the four of you have any kind of allowance or trust to draw on? Were there grants or advances given under extraordinary circumstances?"

"We were expected to make our own way. And that's what most of us have done. I don't think Karen ever asked Dad to help her out. She was pretty independent. And if she did… I don't think he gave her anything. There was no trust. We weren't brought up that way. We were expected to work from the start. No one thought they were being raised to a life of leisure."

"You were all given money for your education, though. You didn't have to incur student debts."

"Yes, that's right. I guess you might call that an exception."

"But that wouldn't have extended to the grandchildren? For their education?"

"We're expected to look after our own families. Why should Dad look after Karen's kids?"

"Because Karen didn't have that kind of money, but she would once she inherited. And if he'd paid for her to study to become a doctor, she would have had the money."

Alex shrugged. "Maybe you could have talked Dad into it. You make some good points. But when you grow up trained to listen to his dictates, you don't really think of trying to argue your case."

Zachary nodded. He'd had plenty of experience with homes where questioning or challenging anything the parent said was absolutely forbidden.

15

Returning to the evening before your father died, you said that you don't remember anything out of the ordinary?"

"No."

"But Logan or Karen might have had issues with their father because of money. Because they wanted their inheritances early. It would allow Karen to provide for her sons and she would have been able to leave her husband if she didn't want to stay with him. And with Logan, I guess he would be able to..."

Alex shook his head. "I have no idea what Logan wants to do with his life. Maybe nothing. Maybe he just wants to live off of his inheritance. It's enough that he could live modestly off the interest and never touch the principal. He could find a small house and..."

"He wouldn't be able to stay there?"

"Well, no."

"Who gets the house under the will?"

Alex shifted his position, crossing an ankle over his knee. "Well, that would be me, as the eldest."

"Do you get it outright? Or in a trust? Do you have to live there? Would you be allowed to sell it?"

Alex looked irritated at the series of questions. He shook his head and grimaced. "I haven't had a chance to examine all of the provisions of the will. We have an estate lawyer looking after the probate. He'll get back to me with a list of what goes to whom and if it is outright or in a trust, and the terms of the trust. It was quite a lengthy will and, frankly, I don't have the patience to deal with it. I have my own legal practice to look after."

Zachary nodded slowly. He wrote down his thoughts and questions. He was sure Alex was lying on one point. Alex knew exactly what the provisions of the will were and just didn't want to discuss them with Zachary. From what he had said about Logan not being allowed to live at the house, Zachary assumed that Alex had full control of what happened to the house, except perhaps for the ability to sell it. If the will had set out the terms of who was allowed to live in the house and who was not, then it surely would have allowed Logan to stay. John had permitted Logan to return to living at the house after dropping out of college. Kicking Logan out was part of Alex's plan.

"What was your father's mood that night?"

"The night he died?" Alex stalled by asking the obvious. "Well… I don't know. He seemed about the same as usual." His brow furrowed. "What did the others say? I know he had been worried about…"

Zachary waited, then prompted him when it was obvious that Alex was not going to finish the sentence. "You knew he was worried about what?"

Alex shook his head as he thought about it. "Something to do with work. I don't think it was anything to do with the family, but he'd been funny lately. More… vigilant? Aware of little things going on around him."

"Jumpy? Looking out the window for something?"

Alex's brows quirked up. "Well, yes. Did someone else say something about it?"

"Logan noticed. Thought that he was agitated. More critical or easily irritated than normal. Looking out the window like he was expecting someone else to come."

"Yes." Alex nodded his agreement. "Only, we never had anyone at the house. He wouldn't have invited anyone else over on family dinner night, and once everyone was there, he was still watching. There wasn't anyone to watch for unless one of the spouses had said that they were coming, but Mrs. Kennedy hadn't prepared any more plates; there were no other places set at the table like there would have been if someone else were coming."

"Did anything else stand out for you?"

"No. Nothing else."

"Did your father say anything to you when you were alone together that might have indicated what he was worried about?"

"We weren't alone together."

"You were the first to arrive."

"Well, yes, I was."

"You joined your father in the study before anyone else was there."

"Well, Logan was already there. I wasn't really the first."

"But Logan didn't come down to the study until after you."

Alex shook his head. "Yes, I suppose we were alone in the study for a minute or two before Logan joined us. But…" he shrugged. "We didn't discuss anything of any importance. He didn't tell me what was worrying him or if he thought that one of my siblings was plotting to kill him." He finished on a sharp, sarcastic note.

Zachary nodded. "It was just a routine discussion? A usual topic?"

"I don't even remember what we talked about. Just the inane 'How is work?' and 'Things have been so busy lately.' Nothing of any importance."

"Just small talk."

"Yes, exactly. The kinds of things that two people discuss over drinks while they're waiting for everyone else to join them for dinner. You could have heard the same kind of conversation in every house around us for miles, I'm sure."

"Did you ever ask him what was bothering him? That night or a previous night when you noticed that he was concerned about something?"

"No. I might have if it went on. Several days in a row, or more obviously. I don't know. I just figured that if he had something he wanted to tell me that he would and, since he didn't, it was best if I just kept out of it. That's the way he was. 'Mind your own business and we will get along just fine.'"

"During supper, there wasn't anything that happened or any topic of conversation that would not have been usual? Anything that set that night out apart from any other family dinner?"

"No, nothing at all. It was all routine. The same faces, the same conversations, the same food." He paused and licked his lips. "Delicious food. Mrs. Kennedy is a wonderful cook. To call it 'the same' as anything is really an insult."

"And you all had exactly the same thing? There wasn't anything that might have set your father's meal apart from the rest? No slight variation?"

"No."

"And who served him?"

"Mrs. Kennedy and one of the house girls delivered the plates to the table."

"You don't know her name?"

"I don't know. They come and go. I don't see the point in remembering all of their names."

"You don't know which of them gave John his meal?"

Alex closed his eyes briefly to consider. "I would think that it was Mrs. Kennedy. That she would have served him first and then she and the girl would have served everyone else after him. But I couldn't swear to it in court. That's just my impression… how it had probably happened a hundred times before. If there was some minor variation, I don't know. I wasn't watching the servants. I was talking with my family and checking out the food. And eating. I don't know who handed food to whom."

"I understand. Probably Mrs. Kennedy, but not necessarily. I'll verify with them."

"You don't think that he was given some poison in his meal, do you? He didn't die until hours later."

"Poisons don't generally act as quickly as you see on TV. Some of them may, but not the majority. I'm not saying that he *was* given poison at dinner, just that it is still an open possibility. Something to be explored further."

"The cops didn't think that there was any foul play. They didn't see anything suspicious or think it could be poisoning or any other method of murder."

"I know. That's why you and the others hired me."

Alex looked uneasy. His brow furrowed in thought. "You must think us a peculiar family, accusing each other of murder and hiring you to investigate it when one of us could be the culprit. One of us might be hoping you don't uncover the truth."

"It is an unusual circumstance. But whoever did it, if anyone, has to go with the rest of the group. Doing anything otherwise would focus suspicions on them."

Alex nodded.

"How about after dinner?" Zachary resumed his questions. "How long did you stay after dinner was finished?"

"I didn't stay. We had our dessert and coffee, and I headed for home immediately. An entire evening out of my schedule to play the obedient son takes a lot of time away from work. Junior lawyers are expected to reach a certain number of billable hours, which is impossible if you aren't spending every free hour on client work."

"Be careful," Zachary cautioned, remembering a case he had investigated at Drake, Chase, Gould, an investment banking firm, where they practically worked their employees to death. "If you work too much, it can seriously affect your health. In Japan, there's actually a word for working yourself to death."

"It's a rite of passage for doctors and lawyers. If you aren't willing to make the sacrifices and put in the hours… you'll never make it to the top. Some are more casual with their time, trying to find balance and take an easier path. But those people don't make it to partner at a firm like Bramwell, Sinclair & Morgan."

And Alex was determined to be the youngest lawyer ever to make partner at the firm, as his father had expected him to.

"You can't make it to partner if you kill yourself in the process."

"I'm not killing myself," Alex replied, rolling his eyes.

"And you went straight home from the dinner?"

"Yes, of course."

"You didn't stay to have a nightcap with your father or go anywhere on the way home?"

Alex shook his head. "Of course not. I went home to get a few hours of sleep in so I could get back to work bright and early the next morning."

16

Zachary was to meet Eddie in the cafeteria of his workplace, a medical research facility, as far as Zachary could tell. He would have to ask Kenzie if she knew exactly what Neu Holschmeister Pharmaceuticals GmbH did. It was all Greek—or German—to him. And he had to admit that he was a little anxious meeting Eddie at his workplace when Zachary and Kenzie had previously had a bad experience with a German medical research company. He was sure that Neu Holschmeister was on the up-and-up, but he couldn't help looking around for anyone who looked familiar or suspicious.

He had hoped to be able to pick Eddie out when he saw him, but none of the white-jacketed scientists seemed to bear any family resemblance to the other Godfrey children.

As he looked around, one of the scientists approached Zachary and raised his brows. "You wouldn't happen to be Zachary Goldman, would you?"

"Yes, that's me." Zachary held out his hand. "Eddie?"

Eddie shook his hand firmly. "Yup. Why don't we find a table and sit down?"

The two of them selected a wobbly cafeteria table and sat

down. Zachary hadn't had a chance to buy them coffee, but Eddie didn't seem to feel anything was amiss.

He had brown hair like the rest of the Godfrey children, but his was a different shade, already going gray around the temples. He looked older than Alex, even though Alex was the firstborn. Eddie was also tall and slim like Alex, but his face was entirely different. Zachary couldn't see a resemblance to any of his siblings. All four of them looked different enough to have come from four separate families, when Zachary thought of it.

"Thanks for agreeing to meet me. I hope this isn't too intrusive."

Eddie grinned. "No, I appreciate that you could come here instead of insisting that we meet at home or at the family house. I have so much on the go; I practically live here. I love my work, and going home is just… boring. I shower and change and I'm back here as quickly as possible."

"But your father was able to persuade you to join everyone else for family dinner?"

"Yes, well, family dinner is one of those things that you just don't say no to. So I go under protest. I know I should be happy to see my brothers and sister, but I'd rather be working."

"And your dad?"

Eddie raised his brows. "What?"

"Were you happy to see your father? When you went to family dinner?"

"Eh…" Eddie shifted and grimaced. "No, can't say I was that excited to see him. It was always a surprise to see that he was still alive and kicking. The way he treated his body, he should have been dead years ago. He did have his first coronary after Mom died. Just a small one. Sometimes that is enough to persuade someone that it's time to start paying attention to their health and make some changes to their habits, but not for the great John Godfrey. He just figured he could keep doing the same things and be able to live forever."

"He wasn't worried for his health at all?"

"He said he wouldn't be pressured into giving up the things he loved for a few more miserable years on the earth. He'd rather enjoy his comforts while he was here."

Zachary nodded. "Was there anything he *was* worried about?"

"Dad? What did he have to be worried about? He lived a charmed life. He had all the money he wanted, house, a job he enjoyed. He never worried about the things that the rest of us do."

"Logan and Alex both said that he seemed agitated or worried the evening before he died. Looking out the window, acting like he was expecting someone to arrive or something to happen."

"Really?" Eddie blew out his breath, making a noise. "Nothing that I noticed. He seemed just the same as ever. Ornery and bloody-minded. Picking away at everyone else for not conforming to the roles that he had set out for us."

"Which was pretty normal."

"Since you've already talked to Logan and Alex, I'm sure you know that already. He was overbearing and critical. I'm lucky he decided to accept my life goal to be a scientist and didn't veto it like Karen's medical career. I don't know that I would have had enough gumption to follow through and do this on my own. It's a lot harder when you don't have the money or the great Godfrey reputation behind you."

Zachary could confirm that trying to make something of himself without any money or support had been very difficult, the work of several years and, even then, he had failed a number of times, but kept pushing forward until he was eventually able to build an investigative business that was successful enough to support him. And maybe a family too, if he and Kenzie ever took the next step in their relationship and married or had children together.

"But as it was, John accepted your career choice?"

"He wasn't sure at first. He didn't think it was practical. Didn't really catch the vision. But he agreed that any degree helped prove your worth in the business world, and maybe there was something in a science degree that could lead to a better career somewhere else." He chuckled. "We don't pay our scientific researchers what they deserve. Can you imagine if scientists were paid like professional basketball or football players for what they do? You discover a successful cancer treatment, and a new company signs you on for a twenty-million-dollar contract instead of just getting a pat on the back and maybe an award you can put on your shelf?"

Zachary smiled at the thought. He had no idea how much money researchers or scientists made, but he was pretty sure that it wasn't the lucrative field that John Godfrey would have wanted his son to go into. What would it be like to get life-changing money like that? The siblings were about to find out with the millions coming to them following their father's death. They were about to go from being controlled and directed by him and scraping by with what they considered a pittance, to having the money they needed to solve all of their problems. Karen could escape an unhappy marriage and see that her sons got the education or help they needed. Alex would have the house and enough money that he didn't have to worry about making partner. Logan could live modestly on whatever he got from the estate and never worry about going to school or finding a job. And Eddie… what were his goals and how could they be satisfied with a few million dollars?

"Will anything change with your inheritance from your father?"

It was the direct approach rather than being circumspect about it, but he had the feeling that Eddie preferred straight talk. Zachary knew most scientist types were blunt, not concerning themselves with the subtle shades of meaning and worrying about offending people.

Eddie laughed appreciatively. "What will change? Well, I suppose I'll get a new car. One that won't constantly be in the shop. Will I stop working here and retire to a life of leisure? No. Maybe I don't need to worry about grants and funding. I can fund my own experiments and not have to report to anyone how the money is being used."

"You would still choose to be in scientific research, no matter what?"

"Of course. If you go into what you love, you never really have to work. It's all play."

Zachary nodded. There wasn't much in Eddie's answer. It was off the cuff and he hadn't stopped to think about it. Or if he had considered it before, he was pretending he hadn't.

17

Eddie scratched his chin, which was a little stubbly, even though it was still morning. Either he grew whiskers very fast, or he hadn't bothered to shave that morning. Maybe he had been at the lab overnight and hadn't yet had a chance to go home for his shower and change. Or maybe he'd just forgotten about shaving, thinking about some interesting experiment.

"The money will be nice," Eddie admitted slowly. "I do have a few expenses that I had to stretch to make my paycheck cover and Dad wouldn't have anything to do with. I make reasonable pay here, but sometimes things come up that I wasn't expecting that cost quite a bit."

Zachary considered this. "And you're not talking about car repairs."

"No." Eddie leaned back in the chair, stretching out his lanky figure. He sighed. "The first one is the results of… youthful indiscretions."

Zachary raised his brows. "Oh?"

"I have… a couple of children by women who are no longer in my life."

"Except now they are back in your life."

Eddie chuckled. "Yes, exactly. Those chickens came home to roost. So now, due to my stupidity in my younger years, I have child support and back child support to pay. They garnish my wages until the back support is paid. They can't take the whole paycheck, but enough of it that things are certainly not comfortable. I was living a certain lifestyle... a little bohemian, I suppose. Coming and going as I pleased, throwing money away on things that were just for my enjoyment and had no staying power. Not investing in anything or building my wealth." He rolled his eyes. "You can imagine how my father felt about that. And now I don't have that throw-away money anymore, and I haven't built up any equity or investment accounts."

Zachary nodded sympathetically. It was hard to put money away for the future. The present was so much more... immediate and compelling. It was tempting to spend everything he earned, even if, like Eddie said, it was something that wouldn't bring him any benefit in the future.

"So how long is that going to last? The garnishing?"

"Until I get my money from the estate. Then I'll be able to pay it off and go back to the way things were. Except I'll start putting some money into investments. All of those grown-up things I'm supposed to be doing to raise wealth instead of squandering it." Eddie shrugged, looking slightly embarrassed.

But would he? He hadn't established a pattern of making good investments. People who won the lottery often spent all the money and ended up right back where they had started after a year or two. Eddie might plan to be more responsible in the future, but would he really change?

"How did your father feel about these children? Do you see them? Has he met them?"

"He was not favorably impressed; let's just say that. I do try to make time to see them now and then. Be the responsible father. Have some positive influence on their lives. I'm not with either of their mothers anymore, but I need to take responsibility for my choices. Dad met them—the kids—once or twice. I don't think he ever intended to acknowledge them as heirs or leave them anything, but he did at least get to meet them and didn't threaten to disinherit me over the whole thing."

"From what I've heard about him, you dodged a bullet there."

"Yeah." Eddie cocked his head, considering it. "Or maybe not. You know, he makes a lot of threats, and he does withhold money, but he's never gone as far as to disinherit one of us. He took Logan back in after he dropped out. I don't know if he ever would have written one of us out of his will. But I wasn't going to push it and find out."

"He told you he wouldn't give you any money for child support."

"Oh, yes. He made that quite clear. I was the one who had been stupid. I would be the one to pay the piper."

It made sense to Zachary. He would probably have drawn the line in the same place, if he'd been in that situation. Force his child to take the consequences. To learn from his mistakes. Hopefully.

"And you said that was the first unexpected expense. There was… something else?"

"Yeah." He gazed off into space, thinking about it. "I have some… pretty large hospital bills."

"Oh." Zachary had not been expecting that. Eddie looked like a healthy, strong young man. Maybe he had been in a car accident. Or skydiving. Or had stepped in front of a bus. But why would John refuse to cover medical bills? "Yes, those can grow very quickly. It's too bad that our health care is in the state it's in." Zachary was familiar with onerous medical bills. How many times had he spent a couple of weeks in the hospital and then ended up paying the bills for a year or two afterward? It was no wonder that his savings were almost nonexistent, even with some of the big cases he'd been able to break.

"I have this thing… I sometimes… I'm a very creative person. It's part of being a scientist, researcher, and inventor. I'm curious about things, and I pursue things. Go down rabbit trails, I guess. When I get focused on a thing, even if it isn't the project I'm currently working on, I can get stuck on it. To the chagrin of my bosses. And… as well as it being a problem when I'm supposed to be bringing in one project and get stuck on another, I can get so into it that I forget to eat, don't get the sleep I need, stop going home…"

It hit closer to home than Zachary liked. He too had his obsessions and they had derailed his life more than once. And while he hadn't been hospitalized due to not taking care of himself, he could see how it could happen.

"And you end up in the hospital so they can take care of you and get you back on track again."

Eddie grunted his agreement. He looked at Zachary curiously, maybe wondering why he hadn't acted shocked or horrified at the confession. He wasn't used to an empathetic response to his mental health issues.

"Yeah. I'm always resistant to going. I don't want to leave what I'm working on, even if someone tells me that it's having an impact on my health and life balance. I just… don't have time for it."

Zachary smiled. "And you probably can't understand how other people find it so easy to pull themselves away from a project to go home to the wife or work on something else."

Eddie nodded vigorously. "Exactly! What's wrong with people that they don't dedicate themselves to that one thing? Can you imagine how much more scientific progress we would have if people would pursue their ideas to their conclusion? Not to work on ten different things or to worry about the rest of 'life.' Just staying focused on that one problem until it is solved."

While it was an excellent formula for a mental breakdown, Zachary could catch the vision. How scientists could do so much more if they were focused entirely on one thing, to the exclusion of everything else in their lives.

"So, have you found a medication or therapy that might help you with this? To make sure that it doesn't cause you negative health effects?"

Eddie grimaced and shook his head. "I don't *want* to manage it. It's what makes me successful and has helped me make breakthroughs and find things that no one else even thought of before.

If I medicated that drive away… what kind of scientist would I be?"

"I guess you can't know unless you try."

"And I don't want to try. I don't want to be the same as everyone else. I *need* that edge. I'm not that much more brilliant than anyone else, but I'm a hard worker and I chase the rabbits down. I'm not giving it up even as an experiment. What if I never got it back again? What if I end up some broken-down old man in an institution?"

"It's pretty rare for a psychiatric medication to have permanent effects. The problem is usually that it stops working. Or that you stop taking it."

Eddie shook his head. "*You* don't know what it's like," he dismissed.

"Actually… my last psychiatric stay was in December. For about six weeks."

And how long would it take him to pay the bills for that one? Zachary grimaced at the thought.

Eddie was staring at him. "You? What for?"

"Depression. Suicidal."

"And that was your *last* psychiatric commitment. So you've had more."

"Plenty. Going back to when I was ten. Though that one wasn't psychiatric, strictly speaking."

Eddie leaned forward, putting his elbows on the table and staring into Zachary's face. "That's why you didn't react when I said I had to be hospitalized."

"I did react. Just not the way you expected."

"Yeah. Huh. It's pretty rare for me to run into anyone else who's had a similar experience, apart from people I meet in the hospital. People are very close-mouthed about it."

"There's still quite a stigma," Zachary agreed. "We might be more open about mental health now, but serious mental health issues, the ones that put people in the hospital, are still not talked about. People are quick to admit that they have some depression or anxiety, more and more are talking about being neurodivergent in other ways. Late diagnosed autistic or ADHD. But schizophrenia, schizoaffective disorder, bipolar, suicide attempts, people really don't want to talk about them. It scares them too much."

"Like it might be contagious."

Zachary smiled and nodded. He'd seen that withdrawal too many times. People who suddenly realized that he was *not well* and didn't want to be too close to him. A few tight-lipped, insincere remarks, and they moved on before something rubbed off on them.

"Have you tried a support group?" he asked Eddie. "Other people who have experienced something similar to you? Who are battling ongoing issues with OCD or other illnesses?"

"No. I don't have time for that." Eddie laughed. "I have too much work to do."

Of course he did. Zachary smiled at the observation. He knew how hard it was to pull away from an obsession. Whether it was Bridget or a case he was working on, it had sometimes taken a threat to his freedom or life to break him away from his pursuit. And even then…

"So…" Zachary frowned, trying to sort it out, "why wouldn't your father help you to cover your medical bills? It seems like there is a pretty clear need there. And your mental health issues certainly aren't your own fault."

"He wouldn't pay if I wouldn't take meds and be under ongoing treatment."

"Oh… if you weren't taking care of yourself the way he thought you should be, then why should he pay for something that was the result of your own decision?"

"In a nutshell. Like with the children… deal with the consequences of my poor choices myself."

"But mental health issues are not that black and white. Even treated, there is no guarantee that you would not have ended up in the hospital."

"Tell him that. Oh, wait, you can't. He's dead."

Zachary grunted. And that was why Eddie was better off with his father dead. No matter what the other siblings thought of Eddie's choice not to try medication for his issues, he would get his inheritance, pay the back support on his children, pay his medical bills, and put the rest into a fund that would make money and that he could put it toward his children's future education and any future hospitalizations that he had.

Eddie looked at Zachary steadily.

"Now you see it. Why they think I might have been the one to poison Dad."

18

"Do you think that they consider you more likely to have killed him than any of the others?"

"I'm the crazy one. The one with lots of back bills to be paid. The one who can't control himself."

Zachary shrugged uncomfortably, realizing that all of Eddie's words also applied to him. Is that how his siblings saw him? Tyrrell was the alcoholic and Zachary was the crazy one? The sick one?

"The others all have motives for wanting their inheritance or wanting your father out of the way as well."

Eddie shrugged. "Dad wasn't one for winning friends, was he? Influencing people—sure. But he wasn't great at making people like him."

"That… would seem to be the case."

"Dear old Dad. RIP. Well…" Eddie looked at a large watch on his wrist. "I should be getting back to things."

"I'd like to talk a little about the evening before John's death, if we could."

Eddie slumped back into his chair. "I suppose that's why you're here. We might as well get it over with, because I don't want to have to meet again. No offense, but I don't like interruptions to my work."

"I'll get this done as efficiently as I can," Zachary assured him. "You arrived at the house after Alex. And before or after Karen?"

"After. I was the last one to arrive at the house. Everyone was in the study waiting. Karen had already texted me to make sure I was on the way, because they wouldn't start without me. She didn't want anything prolonging the pain..."

"Were you late or was she just eager?"

"I don't honestly know. Isn't that inconsiderate of me? I left the office in good time, I thought. I should have arrived at the house at about the right time. But she was already texting me, so maybe I was a few minutes later than expected. Dad would have expected me to be there at least half an hour before the announced dinner-time, which was seven. If you're not early, you're late, you know. If you're on time, you're late. But I never subscribed to that theory. I figure on time is on time. If you want me there earlier, give me an earlier time."

"But you don't know for sure what time it was when you got there."

"Only approximate. It would have been around six-thirty. Maybe a little before, maybe a little after."

"Okay. About six-thirty. And the others were all there ahead of you."

"I could usually count on Logan to be there after me, but he was there too early, the little jerk." Eddie bared his teeth in a smile to show that he wasn't serious about the epithet.

"Did you have a drink before going in to dinner?"

"Yes, everyone else already had theirs. I said hello to everyone, helped myself to a glass of wine."

"It sounds like most of the men were having scotch."

Eddie shrugged. "So what? I don't care for the stuff myself."

If he didn't drink the same thing as John, it would be easier to target him. Only John wasn't the only one who drank the scotch, so the whole bottle hadn't been poisoned, only John's cup. If it really was a poisoning, which was yet to be determined.

"And you didn't notice any difference in your father's mood than any other night?"

"No. Honestly. But I'm not always the best one for noticing people's moods. I'm a little too much head-in-the-clouds. Always thinking about theories and experiments and not about people."

The same could be said about a lot of scientists or technical guys, as far as Zachary could tell. "How about the dinner conversation? Same topics as usual? Nothing out of the ordinary?"

Eddie considered for a moment, then shook his head. "I have no idea. No recollection of anything that was discussed at dinner. So, no, I would guess it wasn't anything out of the ordinary. If it was, I'd be more likely to remember it."

"And after dinner? You all had coffee and then… went your separate directions?"

"Same as usual, yeah."

"Do you remember the order people left in?"

"Alex was out of there like a shot, as usual. Logan stayed, of course. Karen was still there after me."

"Alex always left first?"

"Of course. He's the most important person in the world, you know. He has an important job he needs to get back to and important things he needs to do, even on what is supposed to be a night off." Eddie scoffed. "He still had the time to hang around the club that night."

"The club?"

"Professional club Dad belonged to. So we had privileges there by virtue of our familial relationship. I rarely spent any time there, which I guess everybody knew. That night, my car was making noises and I pulled into the parking lot at the club to talk to a mechanic and see if I should have it towed. Didn't want to break down on the highway. And Alex's car was there."

"You're sure it was his?"

"Sure. I know his car. I was sitting there a while, and he never came down to it while I was there. He was at the club for at least an hour or two. Mr. Big Shot, who could never stay once we were finished eating dinner."

"I guess he went to the club for another drink."

"Another drink…?" Eddie shook his head. "I don't think so.

Alex is always very careful about how much he drinks. A scotch before dinner, maybe a glass of wine, but that's it. He was always on at Dad for drinking too much. He wouldn't have had anything else after dinner. He must have been meeting someone at the club."

"Not just relaxing in the library or playing billiards?" Zachary tried to think what else Alex might be doing in the club but didn't have enough experience with such places to guess. He'd met with Bridget's partner, Gordon, at his club, and had questioned a suspect at one when investigating the disappearance of Pat's friend, Jose, but that was about it.

"Alex isn't a relaxed kind of guy, in case you haven't noticed. I don't think he uses the club much more than me. He takes meals there sometimes; it's not that far from his office. But none of us loved the place. He wouldn't have gone there for a meal after eating family dinner." Eddie shrugged. "Just ask him. I'm sure he'll tell you what he was there for."

"Yes. I'll need to do that."

19

Zachary double-checked the address Karen had given him with his GPS app and the number on the front of the house before getting out of the car to knock on the door. He had expected that it would be a nicer place. Two incomes, the daughter of a millionaire, with a good job as a nurse. He had imagined it would be a classy place, not a plain-vanilla split-level side by side with a hundred other houses that looked exactly the same.

After checking twice to ensure the car was locked and the security alarm engaged, he walked up to the house and knocked on the door. There was immediate yelling inside, young male voices shouting that there was someone at the door, shrieking back and forth about who would answer it. Eventually, the door was pulled open and a dark-haired boy of about eight checked Zachary out.

"Are you here to see our mom?" he demanded.

"Yes, I am. If your mom is Karen Godfrey."

"Camden," the boy corrected, "Not Godfrey!" He turned around and yelled back into the house. "Mom! That guy is here to see you!"

"I'll be down in a minute. You can let him in, please, like I told you."

"I needed to make sure who he was," the boy pointed out. He looked at Zachary. "What's your name?" he asked with suspicion.

"My name is Zachary Goldman. Would you like to see my card?"

The boy seemed to think that was a good idea. He nodded and held his hand out for it. Zachary pulled out a business card and handed it to him. It wasn't anything exciting, but it had a badge that made it look similar to the crest of the law enforcement officers in Roxboro. At a glance, it might be mistaken for a police-issued business card, but on examination, it did say *Goldman Investigations* in small caps underneath the large and bold *Zachary Goldman, Investigator.*

The boy examined it and looked back at Zachary with big eyes. "Are you a policeman?"

"I'm a private investigator," Zachary told him, which the boy could take whichever way he wanted. He looked back at the business card and breathed, "Cool!"

It wasn't very often Zachary was told that he was cool.

"You can come in and sit down," the boy finally told him. He opened the door the rest of the way and ushered Zachary politely into the living room. The boy pointed to the couch and told him to sit down. "Can I get you a glass of water?"

"Sure," Zachary agreed. "That would be great. It's pretty warm out."

The boy darted into the kitchen in the back of the house, behind Zachary. He could see the doorway if he twisted around, but only that. He couldn't see into the kitchen to watch the boy's progress.

Zachary instead looked around the living room. It was comfortable. Not so clean and tidy that he felt like he couldn't sit down or touch anything. But not overgrown with the boys' toys and dirty dishes, either. Zachary startled when he noticed a face peering around an easy chair at knee height. Karen's other son. Zachary decided not to speak to him. The boy wanted to remain hidden while observing this stranger who had come into his home.

It would be better if Zachary waited until Karen was there and introduced them.

The older boy returned with a glass of water, watching the surface carefully while he walked it slowly into the room to ensure it didn't slosh over the rim. He transferred it to Zachary's grip.

"I would have got you a coffee," he advised. "Only I'm not allowed. I'm only allowed to bring water, in case it spills."

Zachary nodded understandingly. "I'm sure you'll be allowed to bring other drinks as you get older."

"Yeah. That's what Mom says. You need to learn to walk before you can run. Only, you're not allowed to run with hot coffee, so I don't know why she said that."

Zachary wasn't sure he felt up to explaining that one. He didn't have to, as Karen's footsteps were on the stairs and, in a moment, she was in sight, awkwardly carrying a large box. Zachary jumped up. "Let me help you with that."

"I've got it," Karen advised. "Don't do anything to upset my balance."

Zachary helplessly watched her take the last few steps down to floor level. He blew out a sigh of relief that she made it without tripping or slipping. Karen pushed the box toward him. "This is for you."

"Oh," Zachary took it with surprise. It was heavy.

"It's Dad's papers," Karen explained. She hesitated. "Some stuff from the house and some from the office."

"Okay, thank you. I'll take a look through it. Did you see anything that you were concerned about? Anywhere in particular that I should start?"

"No… I didn't look at much. Just grabbed up everything I could before anyone else could touch it. There are notebooks, journals, that kind of thing. His datebook. I don't know whether any of it will be any help, but you can look through it and find out."

"That's very helpful. It will give me a better idea of his frame of mind and if something was worrying him lately."

"I don't think he wrote anything the night he died. So… nothing like that."

"That's fine," Zachary assured her.

"Finn, go play with Wally upstairs," Karen told the older boy.

He looked at her. "Wally isn't upstairs."

"Where is he, then? Wally?"

Finn pointed to the head hovering close to the floor, beside the easy chair.

"Wally, what are you doing over there? You boys go play," Karen ordered.

Wally didn't move. He continued to stare at Zachary.

"Wally!"

He still made no move to obey. Karen marched over to the easy chair and bent down to pick the skinny boy up. Wally let out a shriek of protest and kicked and squirmed, his arms and legs pinwheeling around as he struggled to escape. Karen pinned him against her body. "Wally! Stop that! Mr. Goldman and I need to have a private conversation. And it will be very boring. You and Finn go upstairs and play."

He bellowed in wordless protest, body flopping like a landed fish while he tried to work himself loose from his mother's grasp. She was strong, clearly having fought this battle before, and unsurprised by his reaction.

"I don't mind the company," Zachary offered. "And I don't think we will be discussing anything gruesome that will disturb him. Just boring, grown-up stuff."

Karen looked down at the squirming, protesting child and gave in. She dropped him unceremoniously onto the easy chair. "If you want to stay here, you need to sit quietly on this chair and behave yourself. If you can't sit still, you can go play with Finn."

Wally squished himself into the corner of the seat of the chair and wrapped his arms around his knees, making himself into as small a package as possible. Karen looked at him for a moment, but he didn't look at her or acknowledge her. He just sat there staring ahead, still and quiet.

"Fine," Karen sighed. She sat down in another chair. "This is Wally, and this is Finn," she said belatedly, introducing each of the children.

"Nice to meet you," Zachary said politely. "And I'm Zachary Goldman, you can just call me Zachary."

Zachary put down the heavy box and sat back down on the couch, selecting the end that was closest to Karen's chair.

"Sorry, this may not be the best place for an interview," Karen said. "My husband was supposed to be home with them today, but he took off and left me high and dry. Too late to get a babysitter."

"We're not babies," Finn intoned.

"I know you're not. That's just what they are called. Why don't you go upstairs and find something to do? Maybe Wally will want to join you later."

Finn obeyed, mounting the stairs. He had probably already figured out that Zachary wasn't such an interesting guy to meet. No gun. No real badge. And he could probably tell by the box of grandpa's paperwork and his mom's attitude that it wasn't going to be a fun visit.

"This is fine," Zachary assured Karen. "Let's just go with it. If we need to schedule something for follow-up, we can, but I'm sure it will be okay."

"You've seen Dad's room, and now you can look through his papers, too. You've talked to all of the guys." She stopped, waiting for confirmation.

Zachary nodded. "Yes, I've seen all three of your brothers."

"So now it's just me. And I guess if you want to interview any household staff, or people who worked with him, people who might have some insight… but my father was quite a private man, and he didn't do things with friends. Or confide in people at work, I don't think."

"What stands out to you about that evening? Anything?"

"I don't know. It was pretty much the same as any other family dinner. The same routine, same types of conversation. I don't think anything happened that was unusual. Other than Daddy—passing away that night." Karen's eyes went to Wally, but he didn't seem distressed by this.

20

"Who served the meal?"

"Mrs. Kennedy and Charlotte."

"They were the ones to plate the food and put it in front of each person?"

Karen nodded. "Yes."

"I gather from what each of you has said that Mrs. Kennedy has been there for a lot of years."

"Ever since I was a little girl."

"And Charlotte?"

"Hmm." Karen thought about it. "I don't know for sure. Two or three years, maybe? We haven't had any trouble with her."

"No issues that you're aware of?"

"No."

"Would you be? Or would that be handled by your father? Maybe without him mentioning anything to you?"

"It would probably be handled by Mrs. Kennedy."

"So you wouldn't know anything about it."

"She talked to me about staffing issues. I wasn't officially in charge of them—it was Dad's household—but after Mom died, I kind of took it over. Made sure that everything was running smoothly. Let Dad know if something had to be changed or addressed. Mrs. Kennedy and I would take care of any minor matters and, if there was something bigger, I would go to him and present our suggested resolution."

"So Mrs. Kennedy is in charge of the full staff, not just the kitchen?"

"She was aware of everything that went on in the house. It might not be her official job but, yes, she manages things for Dad."

If Charlotte had been there for two or three years, she probably had nothing to do with poisoning John. Not unless there had been an incident that Karen didn't know about or wasn't telling Zachary. An undisclosed assault or relationship between John and the maid.

"And at the table... there didn't seem to be anything wrong with your father? He didn't complain about... heartburn or indigestion? Feeling indisposed? Wanting to head to bed early?"

"No, nothing like that. Do you think that was when he was poisoned? Do you think he was feeling sick and didn't say anything?"

"No one has said anything to indicate he wasn't feeling well. Other than being grumpy or agitated throughout the evening."

"So you think it could have happened before we even ate? Before drinks in the study? Or *in* the drinks in the study?"

"I don't think anything yet. Still investigating all possibilities. You poured a drink for your father in the study."

"Did I?" Karen shrugged. "I might have. I often do. It would have been automatic. I don't remember specifically."

Zachary studied her for signs of deception. "Would he have asked you to get one, or would you just have done it without being asked?"

"I'd probably do it without being asked. If his glass was empty or almost empty and he didn't sound like he was already under the influence. It was pretty routine."

Zachary nodded and made a note of this. "Was everyone drinking the same thing?"

"No, we wouldn't have been. Dad and Alex had scotch. Eddie prefers wine. I like wine or gin. I think I had wine that night. Logan jumps from one thing to another. I don't remember specifically what he had. Probably the scotch because that was what was being poured. Maybe a couple of beers."

"So two or three people were drinking the scotch."

"Yes. And Alex and Logan are fine. So I guess if Dad was poisoned, it had to be before or after that. Or else someone slipped it directly into his drink rather than into the bottle of scotch. Oh—" Karen looked at Zachary. "That's why you wanted to know if I gave him a drink. Because I could be the one who slipped him something."

Zachary nodded. There was no point in denying it. "You had the opportunity."

"But then, I had it at every family dinner. And other times in between. So why that night? Nothing had changed."

"Why do you think anyone picked that night? Had there been any changes in any of your circumstances?"

"We all have reasons for wanting to get our inheritances now… or to persuade him to give us some before he died. But most of those arguments had already been exhausted. Alex didn't need the money, though. Not like the rest of us."

But Alex did have his own reasons for wanting his inheritance. For wanting to get out from under his father's thumb and be able to make decisions for himself.

"Nothing had changed. You didn't need the money any more this month than you did, say, six months or a year ago."

Karen looked at Zachary, then looked around the room. Her eyes landed on Wally, still sitting balled up on the chair listening to them.

"We had certain needs that were evolving," she admitted. "But it wasn't like I had to have my share *right now*."

He waited to see if she would say anything more than this, then went on. "What happened after dinner?"

"We had coffee, like usual. People went their different directions."

"Where?"

"Home. Dad and Logan were already home. I guess they went to their rooms. John and Eddie went home. I came back here."

"Did you leave immediately?" She did, after all, have young children waiting at home. With either a babysitter or her husband, who was maybe not the best or most interested in taking care of them.

"Mmm… no. I stayed for a while. Helped with the cleanup."

"Wasn't that up to Mrs. Kennedy and the household staff?"

"To an extent, yes. If I hadn't stayed, then they would have taken care of it. But Mom always kept a hand in, and I wanted to stay on top of it and ensure there weren't any problems. I enjoyed helping out there. It was… nostalgic. Not like washing a sink full of dirty dishes here."

Funny how the same chore could be a burden in one place and comfort in another. Zachary liked to lend a hand when he was at the Petersons' if Pat would let him, but he remembered how bitterly he had fought having to help with dishes and chores when he had been in various foster homes. And how he put it off when he was living alone or had to push himself to do it now that he lived with Kenzie. The same job, with all kinds of different emotions attached to it.

Karen had probably enjoyed talking with Mrs. Kennedy, an old friend, and whoever else had been there to assist. Enjoying her childhood home and delaying returning home until she couldn't put it off any longer.

"Who else was in the kitchen while you were there?"

"Just Mrs. Kennedy and Charlotte and me. I don't know; others might have been in and out briefly, but I didn't register them. We were working together, chatting, getting everything cleaned up and ready for the evening."

"Your father went directly up to his bedroom?"

"I don't know. Probably."

"So his nightcap had already been prepared?"

Karen went still. "His nightcap… no. He would shower, change, read for a while. I took the decanter up while he was in the shower."

"*You* took it up."

"Yes. I guess I did. Do you think… that's where the poison was? I unwittingly delivered it to him?"

"We still don't even know that he *was* poisoned," Zachary reminded her patiently. "It was probably perfectly okay. Did you fill the decanter?"

"No. That was already done."

"Mrs. Kennedy?"

"Probably. But it could have been anyone on the staff. Everybody pitched in, and the whole household would know that the decanter needed to be filled and taken up to him before he could ask for it. Whoever had a moment would do it."

"But it wasn't you."

"No." Karen rubbed her knee. "But you probably can't prove that."

"There were witnesses. You weren't alone there, and someone will have to admit that they filled the bottle for him. If there was poison, it might have been in the bottle already. Or in the glass."

"If it only took a few drops," Karen admitted.

Zachary shrugged. A good amount of poison could have been hidden in a decanter before it was topped off with scotch by an unwitting accomplice.

"Did you leave immediately after taking your father his nightcap?"

"No."

Zachary was surprised. He waited for more explanation.

21

Karen shifted and looked around. "Do you want some coffee? Tea? I should have gotten you something. I'm a terrible host."

"No, I'm fine. Finn got me water."

"Well, that's good. I don't know about you, but I could use something with a little extra kick…"

"This is good for me, really." Zachary leaned forward, hoping to engage her and keep her on track. But Karen stood up and flitted out of the room, calling out to him as she got herself a drink.

"I'm sorry. I don't know what to think of all of this. It's just our imaginations, right? Active imaginations. It was just a natural death. No one… you know… did *that* to him. I don't know what we were thinking, deciding we needed a private detective to look into it. This really is ridiculous…"

Zachary didn't try arguing through the wall, but waited for her to finish whatever else she was doing while she banged around the kitchen. Eventually, she returned to the living room and sat down, a mug in her hand. It wasn't steaming, though. More likely a cold drink than a warm one. But in a mug so that either Zachary or

Wally wouldn't realize that she was drinking during the day. She held it in both hands to minimize the shaking of her hands.

"Are you okay?" Zachary asked.

She chewed on her lip. "I'm not cut out for this. The more questions you ask and the closer you come to the answers… the more scared I am and the less I want to hear. If it were up to me, I'd tell you to drop it. I know that's stupid after we went to all this trouble and got you on the case, but… I feel like the walls are closing in around me."

But not, Zachary didn't think, because she had done something and was now afraid she was going to be caught. But his gut instinct on the matter could not be trusted. He needed to keep digging and find the truth.

"I think you'll be relieved when I finish my investigation. No matter which direction this goes, you'll be relieved to know the truth. It will be a weight lifted from your shoulders."

She sipped from her mug. "Do you think so?"

Zachary nodded. "You need to know the truth."

She pressed her lips together for a moment, then nodded. "Yes."

"Can we continue, then?"

She shook her head slightly, as if she hadn't been the one who had paused the interview. "Of course."

"You stayed later, after dinner and the cleanup? After giving your father his nightcap?"

"Yes. He had finished his shower and came out of his bathroom in his dressing gown while I was leaving the scotch. I decided to stay and visit for a few minutes. Sometimes when we were little kids, if we were good, we could stay up an extra few minutes to see Dad before bed. He often worked late, and we wouldn't see him before bed. But now and then, as a special treat, one of us would be allowed to stay up late and talk to him."

"Something you remember fondly."

"When he was finished his day, done with all of the work and aggravation, and just ready to relax and have a drink or two before bed… Yeah. He was mellow. Not in a hurry to do anything. Not mad about anything."

"That sounds nice." Zachary's experience with a father who came home to drink was not nearly as idyllic. Berk Goldman had been a mean drunk, and his arrival home at the end of the day, whether the kids were already tucked into bed or not, did not herald a quiet and relaxed atmosphere. There was no peace for the family as long as he was drinking and still conscious.

Karen nodded. "It was." Her eyes went to her own son, hunched over in the easy chair, and her expression softened.

"So you decided to revisit your childhood and visit with him while he had his usual before-bed nip."

"Yes."

"What did you talk about? Anything that had gone on during the evening?"

"Not really. Just… families. How quirky they are. I talked about Wa—about my kids and how different they are from each other and from me. How individual. We have fun doing things together, but we're all very different. And that was true when we were growing up too. I don't know if Logan ever felt like he was a part of that, but the rest of us… well, we played together, went to school together, went on vacations together, had family dinner every night, whether Dad could make it or not. We teased each other a lot, got on each other's cases, but we did like each other and got along okay. You might not be able to tell now, but… we were a pretty happy family."

"Believe me, I've seen plenty of brothers and sisters who were just as likely to—" Zachary looked at Wally, "—to hurt each other as get along. Being siblings is no guarantee of being friends or even being able to stand each other. You and your siblings haven't run each other down or pointed any accusatory fingers. From what I can tell, you don't spend much time together, but you don't hate each other. You still get together for dinner every few weeks. A lot of families wouldn't do that no matter who was pulling the strings."

"I hate to think of the possibility that any of them did

anything. I don't think we really thought through how this would all work out."

"So far, there's nothing to indicate that any of you did anything. And maybe the fact that all of you agreed to hire me means that none of you had anything to do with it. Because if you had, you wouldn't have wanted me to investigate."

"Only… if one of us refused to okay it, then we would look suspicious, wouldn't we? And Alex and Eddie… well, I hate to say it, but if either of them had done something, they wouldn't believe that someone like you could catch them."

"Someone like me?" It was clearly not meant as a compliment.

"I just mean… well, like me too. Someone without a degree. Who wasn't on the same kind of track to success as they are. I'm sorry if I've judged by appearances or made assumptions, but… I'm assuming you're not a billionaire with multiple degrees who moonlights as a PI."

"No," Zachary agreed with a rueful laugh. "You're right. I had to work to support myself as soon as I was eighteen. I didn't have a father to pay for my education, or a place to live, or supportive family and friends. I was on my own. And I've done better than most of the kids who grow up the way I did. But I'm no genius, not a social climber. Just a PI."

"And you have the skill set that we need," she pointed out, in case Zachary was feeling like the utter failure that he was. "They don't. You do."

Zachary shrugged.

"To get back to it, then. You talked about family. Your family, old times, current needs?"

Karen couldn't help glancing again in Wally's direction. "Yes."

"And did you get anywhere? Any softening on possibly helping you out? Or considering the others' needs?"

"He said he'd think about it, but I didn't have any confidence that he actually would."

Another disappointment. And Karen alone in the room with her father, his nightcap and the decanter close at hand. Very easy to tamper with in a moment of distraction. And then… then she would get her money and could help her sons to get the education she wanted for them. And to pay off the mortgage on the house or move somewhere nicer. And to be able to separate from her husband and his paycheck, if that was what she wanted. Freedom was just one drink away.

22

"I didn't do it," Karen said. "I'm just not built that way. What did I decide to do with my life? I wanted to become a doctor. I became a nurse. You really think that I could ki—hurt someone? Especially my own father? I want to fix people. To make them well. Improve their quality of life. I couldn't do that, even if it gave me everything I ever wanted."

"How was he when you left? Do you know what time it was?"

"I don't know. Ten-thirty. Eleven. He was tired, said it had been a long day. I don't know what was going on at work," Karen looked at the box of his papers and notebooks. "Maybe a big case or a difficult negotiation. A long day, coupled with family dinner; he was probably exhausted. He was already closing his eyes, starting to drift off."

For a moment, neither of them said anything; then Karen's gaze snapped to Zachary's face. "You don't think… you don't think that he was *going* then, do you?" Her eyes were big and round. "Should I have noticed…? Were those his last breaths?"

It was possible that he'd expired by the time Karen left the house. That she'd waited just long enough to see that he was drifting away and then made herself scarce.

She was a nurse, after all. Who knew what kinds of drugs she had access to or what knowledge she had on concocting her own?

If she weren't the culprit, should she have noticed that her father was dying? Or had his death come later, long after she'd left the house?

"There was no way you could have known," he reassured her, even though he had no idea. "Don't blame yourself. He spent his last hours on earth with his family, enjoying your company, having one last drink together. I'm sure it was a nice time for him too. Whether it was natural or not, he at least had that time with you."

"Unless it was really painful when it kicked in," Karen said. "Whatever it was. It could have been, you know. A heart attack, some kind of seizure or terrible stomach pain. No one said that he threw up, so maybe it wasn't anything gastric but, just because he went to sleep peacefully, that doesn't mean he died that way."

"I'll know more once we have the medical examiner's report."

"How long will that take?"

Zachary didn't bother to tell her that his partner worked in the medical examiner's office and the report was bound to be expedited for him. "I'll have it soon. It takes time, but the family has a right to request it or authorize its release."

Karen nodded. "I know. It just seems like it's taking forever."

"It's only been a couple of days."

She sighed, slumping back in her seat, and had another sip of her drink. "I know I'm being too impatient, but it's hard not to be."

"You already know what it says."

"The big picture, yes. But you might find something in there that's wrong. Or something that points in a particular direction. I want this just to be over. I don't want it to be any of us, but I want it to be over and done, whatever happened. How are we supposed to be at peace when we think that one of us mur—did that to him?"

Karen wiped away a tear. Zachary wanted to tell her everything would be alright, but he knew it was a lie. He could promise her only one thing.

"I'm going to get to the bottom of this," he said firmly. "I won't rest until we know who did this and why. I promise you that much."

As Zachary prepared to leave, Wally uncurled from his balled-up position on the easy chair and stood on it, where he was eye-level with Zachary.

"Mommy, I want to say hi to him."

Karen looked surprised at this. She nodded her encouragement. "You may," she agreed. "Thank you for asking before talking to a stranger."

The little boy leaned toward Zachary. Zachary waited to see what Wally had to say.

"You're helping my mom?"

"Yes. That's right."

"About Grampa?"

"Yes. You heard what happened?"

"He died," Wally intoned. "And dying is forever. Forever we can't go back to see him again."

"Yes, that's right."

"But Unca Logan is still at the house. So we can still go back there to play."

Zachary nodded.

"And Grampa won't be there."

"No. You won't be able to see him there again." Zachary admitted.

"Do you have a Grampa?"

This was something that Zachary had wondered about before, but he had no idea if either of his parents still had living parents or if they were dead and gone years previously.

"No," he told Wally. "I don't think so."

"My other Grampa, my Grampa Camden, he isn't dead."

Zachary nodded politely. Death was a lot for a kid to be working through. It might seem like it was all cut and dried to an adult, but kids were still figuring out permanence and what it meant to be alive.

"You're helping Mommy," Wally repeated.

"I hope so," Zachary agreed.

Wally held his arms out to his mother, and she picked him up. He nestled his head into the hollow of her neck. "I'm sorry, Mommy."

"It's okay, honey. It will all be okay."

Zachary shoved the box of files and notebooks into his car and took them home. Even though the police investigation had not revealed anything, he was eager to read through John's private papers and find out if there were something that the police had missed. If everything looked like a natural death at the scene, and the medical examiner said it was a natural death, then the police investigation would have been minimal. There was no point in wasting police hours and resources on something that was pretty clearly just an old man dying in his sleep. It wasn't the kind of thing that they put their energy into.

The box was heavy, and his arms and back were aching by the time he got to the front door. He grimaced and wished he had been more diligent about taking care of himself. He had been working on walking and spending more time outside, enjoying nature and taking pictures, but that didn't exactly strengthen the upper body. He should be doing something to improve his overall strength as well. He would never have the catlike ninja moves of a TV private investigator, but he could definitely improve on the current state of his health.

He set the box down briefly while unlocking the door before picking it up again and pushing it inside the house and down the hallway. He then took a moment to look around the yard and street, making sure no one was watching him or lurking around the house. No one sitting in a car or van on the street watching the house. Satisfied that there was no sign of anyone but himself and

Kenzie having been there, Zachary closed and locked the door before entering his security code into the burglar alarm to clear the *Door Open Event.*

He made himself a cup of coffee before sitting down with the box in front of him. He took a few moments just to look at it, wondering what secrets were hidden within its contents. Taking a deep breath, Zachary opened it slowly and began sorting through its contents. He had no idea what he was looking for or what he might find inside. It could be hours of tedious reading through dusty files to find absolutely nothing.

Or it could break the case.

23

Zachary pulled himself out of the piles of paper when he heard the garage door opening. He looked outside and then at the time on his phone. He hadn't realized that so much time had passed; he had been so immersed in John Godfrey's papers.

Kenzie parked her little red sports car—her "baby"—in the garage and, a moment later, opened the door into the kitchen. She peered through the doorway to the living room and smiled when she saw Zachary on the couch with all of the work spread out around him.

"Hey, sorry to be so late. Things were really hopping at work."

"That's a little scary to imagine."

She grinned at him. "Yes, dead bodies hopping around might be a little bit disconcerting. But we do have a few living people in the office too."

"Ah. Of course."

Kenzie took off her shoes and put down her purse. She rolled her shoulders stiffly, which probably meant that she had been bent over the autopsy table for a few hours that afternoon.

"Anything interesting?" he asked her.

"Hmm. All pretty routine. I don't think there was anything that you would find that exciting."

Zachary started to gather up his stacks of notebooks and papers so that they would be able to sit down and relax during the evening. He probably should have started his project in the home office so that he could leave things arranged the way he wanted to overnight and resume in the morning, but he liked the comfortable surroundings of the living room.

"What have you been working on?" Kenzie asked, looking at all of the paperwork.

Zachary stacked them back into the box and joined Kenzie in the kitchen. "John Godfrey's private papers. Journals, files, other records. His daughter gave them to me today."

"Looks like you've been busy. Finding anything interesting?"

Zachary nodded. "I need more time, but there was definitely something going on."

Kenzie washed her hands in the sink and started to look through the cupboards and fridge to decide what to make for supper. "Something going on?"

"Something."

"Something like what?"

"He was getting threats. Thought he was being watched. And I'm not sure about his financial records. I'm not the one to ask about creative bookkeeping, but there's something strange about his company accounts."

"Hmm." Kenzie pulled a bag of salad out of the fridge and handed it to Zachary. He opened it before getting out the bowl to put the salad in, which was the wrong order and he ended up spilling part of it on the counter while he tried to juggle the open bag and get the bowl out at the same time. He eventually dumped the salad into the bowl and picked up the bits he had spilled.

Kenzie shook her head after watching this process. "In the beginning, you didn't think that there was very much to the family's suspicions that he might have been poisoned. Does this mean you have changed your mind?"

"I still don't know anything. I can't say one way or another. But a couple of the adult children say that he was agitated the evening before he died. They both noticed him looking out the window like someone might be coming and being testier than usual. Although I gather he was pretty hard to get along with at the best of times. And that is supported by John's concerns expressed in his journal and other papers. He was concerned about a threat."

"But not a threat from the family, which is what they were initially concerned about."

"No. This would be an outside threat."

"Well… that should make them happy. To find out that they were not the ones who had targeted him. If there is any evidence that it was something other than natural causes."

"Any idea when I might get a copy of the medical examiner's report?"

"It's on Dr. Wiltshire's desk right now. He just needs to sign off on the request, and then I'll grab it for you."

"Or I can come by to get it tomorrow and take you out to lunch," Zachary suggested. "We said we were going to do something together."

He was eager to get the report as soon as possible, not to have to wait for Kenzie to return home with it. And lunch was the perfect time for them to pore over it and see if they could identify any avenues of investigation. As they had done with other reports. It was nice to have a girlfriend who wasn't squeamish about the deaths that Zachary occasionally investigated. Far from squeamish, she was always ready to jump right in and show him what he might have missed or to answer his questions.

Kenzie arched an eyebrow at him, clearly knowing he was impatient to come to get the report instead of waiting on her.

"We did say we were going to get together for lunch," Zachary repeated.

"Yes, we did, didn't we? And did you know that you were going to be requesting this file back then?"

"I don't remember."

She shook her head in amusement. "I feel used."

Zachary grinned, "But in a good way, right?"

24

Zachary dialed Detective El Garcia's number and waited for her to answer. He had woken up early in the morning and been unable to go back to sleep thinking about the case, so he had left Kenzie to sleep and gotten up to continue his review of John Godfrey's papers.

He rarely slept more than a few hours a night and, even though all of the health articles said that this was very bad, and he should do what he could to get a minimum of eight hours of sleep a night, it just wasn't practical. High-dose prescription sleep aids helped if he was unable to get to sleep. He didn't want to end up like he had when Bridget's twins had been born, and he had been unable to sleep for several days over his anxiety for her and the tiny babies—even though he and Bridget had broken up a couple of years earlier and the twins were Gordon's. However much he tried, he couldn't turn off his feelings for Bridget, and he had always had a soft spot for babies. He had helped to take care of his younger siblings, and that had apparently left him with a life-long concern over every helpless infant that entered his sphere, related or not. Not being able to sleep when the twins had been born had pushed him into a crisis, and he'd had to check himself into the hospital.

Kenzie was always concerned about his lack of sleep and

pushed him to take the sleep aids that he had been prescribed during that hospital stay. But Zachary hated how they made him feel in the morning, as well as the feeling of being out of control of his own body. And how could he be counted on to wake up in the night if Kenzie were in danger if he were drugged to sleep?

He had been overmedicated at one of his foster homes and, when his social worker had found out he had been so drugged that no one was able to wake him up, she had been pretty upset about it. Zachary hadn't understood how serious it was. They had told him that he needed drugs to sleep, and he knew that he couldn't sleep without them, but he hadn't realized how deeply they had put him under or how dangerous that was. "How would you be able to wake up if there was a fire?" Mrs. Pratt had demanded, which, of course immediately sent Zachary into a flashback to the house fire he had been trapped in less than a year earlier.

He tried to avoid mentally connecting deep sleep with house fires now, but it was a losing battle. He knew that if he slept too deeply, especially on a sedative, that he might not be able to wake up when there was an emergency. And he wasn't going to leave Kenzie unprotected, even if she was the one who was pushing him to take the sleep aid.

"Hello? Is anyone there?"

Zachary became aware that someone was on the other end of the phone, and he had become lost in his memories and meditations on nighttime meds.

"Oh, sorry. Someone was talking to me," he lied. He tried to remember who was on the phone and took a moment to reorient himself to time and place. Not in foster care or in the hospital. Not having a serious discussion with Kenzie about the need for him to get enough sleep. Investigating the death of John Godfrey. Trying to get ahold of the detective on his case. "Uh, Detective Garcia."

"Yes," she agreed impatiently. "Who is this, please?"

"Zachary Goldman. I talked to you before; I'm a private detective—"

"On the John Godfrey case. A case that is closed."

"Yeah..."

"Did you get your copy of the medical examiner's report? Are you satisfied that it was thorough and that he died of natural causes? Or are you still milking that poor family for more money?"

That poor family? Not exactly.

"Actually… I have been looking through some of Mr. Godfrey's papers, and they brought up some questions and concerns…"

"What papers?"

"His daughter gave me some personal papers—files, journals, notebooks, stuff like that. And looking through them, I started to wonder if the family was right and there *was* foul play."

"That's convenient, isn't it? You keep feeding them a line and they keep paying you."

"No. It isn't about the money. It's about finding the truth."

"And the truth is, John Godfrey had heart problems. He died in his sleep. Natural causes. There was no violence, no poison. Just a grieving family that isn't willing to let him go yet."

"I called to see if you wanted to look at what I found."

"I don't have time for crackpot theories."

Zachary took a deep breath. Mario had warned him that El Garcia was a tough broad. She wasn't going to take any nonsense from him. As far as she was concerned, he was just a citizen looking to draw the case out past its natural conclusion.

"John Godfrey had received a number of threats to his life."

There were a few beats of silence as Garcia considered this. "From who? Members of his family?"

"No. An outside threat. He was apparently used to getting threats, but he'd had a couple immediately before his death that he took seriously and was worried about. The evening before he died, more than one of his children noticed that he was agitated and watching out the window like he was expecting someone to show up."

"No one said anything like that to me. And I specifically asked about his behavior that night."

"There were threats. That isn't something they could have just made up after the fact."

"Do you have copies of these threats?"

"I have a file with several that don't appear to be from the same party. I'm not sure which he found to be of concern, and which were not. He may have made a police report…"

"There were no open police cases that referred to John Godfrey."

"Then I guess not. But he was taking the threats seriously, and so was his own security team."

Garcia sighed. "I am going to need copies of this information. The originals, actually." She cleared her throat. "I think a trip back to the house is warranted. The police need to keep a hand in here and see if anything needs to be followed up. And to show the family that we're aware of what is going on. I don't want some private eye messing up the evidence or leading them on a wild goose chase."

Zachary wasn't unaccustomed to this attitude from the police force. He'd developed a pretty thick skin to it over the years. "I'm sure they'll be glad to hear from you and know that the police still have an interest in what happened to their father, even if the medical examiner has already ruled on it. Maybe they'll confide in you about their concerns."

"You want to meet me over there, then?"

Zachary was taken aback. He had occasionally experienced cooperation from the police force. A sergeant who prodded him in the right direction, a detective who listened to what he had to say about a suspected serial killer, the cops who had helped rescue Bridget when she had been kidnapped. But it was a hard and fast rule that cops did *not* work with private investigators. Ever.

"Uh… you want me to meet you there?"

"To give me the papers. If Miss Camden could be there to verify where they came from, that would be helpful too. I would like to know about anything that has been discovered or disclosed outside of police purview."

In other words, she wanted him to tell her everything he had done and what he had discovered so far. Zachary wasn't sure he could tell her everything he knew or suspected, but he could show her the papers he had read and how he had interpreted them. He considered everything he had heard from the family private and confidential. Still, he didn't have anything like lawyer-client privilege or any other protected relationship so, if pressed, he would reveal what he had learned.

"Well, okay. I can meet you there," he agreed. "What time did you want to go?"

"I have some time this morning. Are you free now?"

He hadn't been expecting her to take immediate action and was flustered. It could be hard for him to change his plans at the last minute. He tended to get a little stuck, and pulling himself out of the mire was difficult even if he wanted to.

"Yes… if you could give me an hour? Would that work?"

"An hour until you are out there or an hour until you leave?"

"Uh… an hour until I leave."

"Where are you coming from? Would an hour and a half from now work? To be at the house?"

"Sure. I can do that."

"I may get there ahead of you. Just ask for me when you get there."

"Will do. See you soon."

He hung up the phone and pulled his thoughts back to the present. He had been so lost in his own head that he was slightly disoriented, unsure what time of day it was. He tried to get his brain into gear. There was work to be done before he met Detective El Garcia.

25

Zachary knew he was late leaving the house and wouldn't get there exactly when he said he would. He was sure that Garcia would understand; people weren't always able to get there when they said they were and, as a cop, she had probably dealt with her share of witnesses or interviewees who didn't arrive at the arranged time. But he still didn't like to be late and was pretty heavy on the gas pedal on the way to the mansion to make up some of the time.

It would serve him right to be pulled over by a cop because he was speeding on his way to see another cop.

But he never got pulled over for speeding. Or almost never. And his luck held this time.

He hadn't made up all the time but, hopefully, it was enough that Garcia wouldn't decide that he was unreliable and not to be trusted. He wanted her to see him as a professional like she was. Maybe not like her, because a cop would never see a private investigator as being on the same level, but he hoped she would at least see him as another professional, someone to be respected.

He lugged the box out of the car and put it down at the front door. The last time, Logan had escorted him into the house. He rang the doorbell and wondered how long it would take one of the servants to run across the house to answer it if no one was close. He didn't think he would enjoy being part of the staff in a house like the Godfrey mansion.

The maid who opened the door for him must have been close, because it didn't take her long to respond to the bell. She looked at him expectantly. "Yes?"

"I'm here to see Detective Garcia. She said she would probably get here ahead of me."

"Yes, she is here." The young woman shook her head, frown lines appearing between her eyes. "You could wait for her in the great room." She gestured to the big, heavy furniture around the room. "I will let her know you are here to see her."

She looked down at the box at Zachary's feet. "What is that?"

"Some documents I am passing on to the detective. She'll want to take it back out, so there's no point in lugging it around too much. Maybe I'll just put it inside of the door here?" He gestured.

The maid pursed her lips and nodded, though she didn't look too pleased about it. A maid probably wouldn't like anything to be out of place. More potential work for her. But Garcia wouldn't be leaving the box of papers at the house.

Zachary put the box in the house and entered. He selected a chair that would not leave him with his back to the door, but he still felt uncomfortable sitting down. The chair was huge and made him feel like a child, small and vulnerable. He was alone in the room; anyone coming through would wonder what he was doing there. He decided to walk around the room instead, disguising his pacing by looking at the various pieces of art around the room. None of it was cheap, he was sure.

It was some time before Detective Garcia came down the stairs and walked into the great room, her heels clicking across the hard floor.

"Mr. Goldman?"

Zachary nodded and took a few steps toward her, putting his hand out.

Mario had been right about her being both beautiful and intimidating. Maybe part of what made her intimidating was that the hard look she gave him was in such a beautiful face. Her hair was pulled back into a bun, leaving her cheeks and neck clear, and she could have been a runway model. She was taller than he was, with a slender figure accentuated by the tailored suit of her detective "uniform."

"Detective Garcia, good to meet you."

She looked him up and down, showing little interest in what she saw, and looked around. She spotted the box at the doorway. "Those are the personal documents?"

"Yes."

"This may not be an office, but let's sit down and look at them here anyway. I'd like you to take me through what you have discovered."

"Okay." Zachary retrieved the box and put it down. They both sat down on a couch, and Zachary pulled out the various files and books that he had tagged and laid them out on the coffee table. "It's not well-organized," he apologized. "That's not me; this is the way he kept it. He didn't put all of the information on this stalker in one place. It would have been a lot easier to put together if he had."

Zachary looked over the records, trying to figure out the best place to start. But there wasn't a clear logical order to follow. He picked up a hardcover notebook. "This is his journal. Or one of his journals. He didn't write a lot, and he didn't write every day. But you can see several mentions in here."

He turned to pages he had flagged, skimming to find key phrases on each page.

Followed from the office. Kept driving around downtown until I lost them

Security reports man asking for me at office but wouldn't give name. Who is this guy?

Another in the mail today

Garcia frowned. "Another what in the mail?"

"Another threat, maybe. Not a letter bomb, or the police would have been told about it. Or it could be a picture that was being used to blackmail him. Hard to know from just that phrase."

Garcia agreed. She leaned in close to Zachary to examine the journal without picking it up. A subtle perfume wafted through the air. He tried to ignore it, to ignore the closeness of Garcia's face to his and just focus on what to show her or tell her next.

"There were a few notes. I don't know if he only kept the ones he thought were legitimate, or if that's all he got." Zachary pulled away from her to shuffle through the papers in the box. He pulled out a slim folder and opened it before placing it on the table in front of Garcia. Garcia looked through the pages, touching only the corners with her fingernail. "Are your fingerprints going to be on these?"

"I used gloves when I saw what they were." Zachary motioned to the journal and the box. "I didn't use them for everything. But when I saw threatening letters… I didn't want my prints to be on them."

"That or you wiped them clean."

Zachary didn't see any need to dignify that with a response.

Garcia decided she'd better be gloved too, and pulled one over her right hand before slowly reading and turning over each page.

26

They're all different," Garcia observed, grimacing.

Zachary nodded. "I know. Different handwriting, different paper and ink, different writing styles."

"Different people threatening him. Different threats."

"But something must have happened to make him think one of these might be a credible threat."

Garcia nodded slowly. She indicated the journal, which had been covered up by the folder of threats. "If he realized that he was being physically stalked, he would want to know who it was—if he didn't know already—and why. A letter would provide the answers."

Zachary shook his head. "Most of these do not have names or signatures. And they're all pretty vague in their accusations. Some of them make clear threats and some do not."

"So how is he supposed to know who is making the threats?"

"I don't think he was. Most of them are probably just venting. Telling Godfrey that they're going to take their revenge, but not actually intending any follow-through. They wouldn't want Godfrey or the police coming after them, so they make it as anonymous as possible."

"Making it impossible for Godfrey to identify who it is coming from."

Zachary nodded. "If the accusation was too specific, then he might know who it was from that."

"It's too bad when the criminal actually has the sense to keep his mouth shut. Or pen capped."

"Yeah."

"If John Godfrey was taking this seriously," Garcia made a circling motion to indicate all of the paperwork. "Then why didn't he go to the police? Why don't I have any kind of file, not even a single complaint, from him?"

"I have some thoughts… but it gets into the realm of speculation. No… it is *rampant* speculation." Zachary shrugged apologetically. He rifled through the box and brought out a few papers that he laid on the table for Garcia to view. "What did John Godfrey do?"

"What did he do?" Garcia looked around her at all of the opulence. "I don't think anyone has identified it more specifically than 'businessman.'"

"I thought he was a lawyer. I don't know if someone told me that, or if I just assumed. His firstborn, Alex, is a lawyer, and John paid for his education, pushed him to make partner younger than anyone in the firm ever had, and gave him more attention than the other three children. Alex figured if he messed up on anything, John would disinherit him. I don't know if that was true or just what he believed."

"But John wasn't a lawyer."

"No. Nothing that I've come across says he's a lawyer. And I checked with the bar association. He wasn't a member. I checked Alex's university, because I figured he probably went to his father's alma mater. But John does not have a degree issued by them."

"Interesting. But why is it important that he wasn't a lawyer?"

"Well, for one thing… it would have given people a reason to hate him and threaten him."

Garcia chuckled. "Yes, I suppose that's true."

"I did some digging around. I'm a private investigator, so I have access to several databases and am pretty good at internet searches."

"Yes…?"

"He *might* have been an investment banker. Or something similar."

"But you're not sure."

"With most people… it's out there. They list their position on all of their social media. Maybe they have more than one job, or it's outdated, but you at least have some idea of what they do or where their expertise lies. Mr. Godfrey… not so much. He clearly works in the financial arena, helps people get funding for their ventures when they need more capital. He's some kind of troubleshooter. And he handles large amounts of money, obviously." Zachary flicked a hand to indicate their surroundings. John Godfrey clearly had plenty of money. Or at least a way to make it appear he had a lot of money. Some people looked rich even when they were in debt up to their eyeballs. Zachary hadn't been able to get a credit check on the man, which was unheard of.

Garcia nodded thoughtfully.

"I haven't seen his office, have you?" Zachary asked.

"Downtown? No. I've seen his study here, but only briefly. There really wasn't anything to see."

"I don't even know if he worked at a firm or if he ran the company. Or if he was on his own. He definitely had security staff, so you would think that there must be a pretty large company to go with that. But I can't even find a company name associated with John Godfrey."

"That sounds like it might be something for the police to look into," Garcia said, pulling out her notebook and jotting it down. "If a PI can't find it, there's something going on."

Zachary indicated the papers that he had laid out on the coffee table. "There were some financial records mixed in with the papers that Karen gave me. Not very much, and I'm no forensic accountant, but… it doesn't look right."

"What doesn't?"

"This is some kind of client ledger." Zachary indicated the first one. "If he was an investment banker, or a backer, or whatever you call the investment that he did, then why have all of these clients suffered a loss?"

Garcia looked across the rows of figures, which clearly showed that all of the people or companies listed were in the hole. "Well, maybe rather than investing in companies and some of the ventures failing and others succeeding, he was just making straight loans. So every client owed him money until it was paid back, and then they didn't show up on his ledger anymore."

Zachary nodded. "That could be. And since there are only a few of the financial papers here, and not full books, I could be wrong on this…" He pointed to a number company on a payment ledger. "Here is a payment by one of these clients." He found the name on the ledger showing the amount of money owed by each client and kept his fingers on both names for a moment before withdrawing and letting Garcia examine the correlation.

At first, she shook her head. "Yes, so they made a partial payment on the fifteenth. I'm not sure what you're trying to show me."

"If these are both from this year, then compare what was owed, what was paid, and what the indicated balance was following payment."

Garcia frowned as she looked at the numbers. She found a couple of other clients who were shown on both ledgers and repeated the comparison. She sat back and looked at Zachary.

"They owed almost as much—or sometimes more—after making a payment. That doesn't make sense."

"It does if they are almost all interest, with no payment toward the principal. Or, in some cases, not even the full interest payment they were required to make."

"So he was a loan shark."

"Looks that way to me. But I'm not an accountant," Zachary said with a self-deprecating shrug.

"Neither am I. We'll have to turn these over to the forensics department for examination. They'll be better able to tell us what we are looking at."

"And if he was a loan shark, and maybe involved in other criminal dealings, then that would explain getting multiple threats of revenge from the people whose lives he had ruined."

"And needing a security detail even if he was just a one-man business or only had a few men working under him."

Zachary nodded his agreement.

27

Garcia sat back, rubbing the space between her brows. "If this guy was a loan shark and possibly involved in other criminal enterprises, that puts a whole new perspective on the possibility that he was murdered rather than having died in his sleep of natural causes."

"Yeah. It doesn't mean that it wasn't natural causes, of course, but there were a lot of threats. And at least one person was trying to get to him. Following him. Requiring more security than usual. There are a number of security reports here." Zachary pulled out a much thicker folder than the one holding the threats. "And they are all along the same lines. People trying to talk to Godfrey at the office when he didn't want to see them and having to be ejected. Someone following his car. Even some reports of people hanging around the house here." Zachary looked around. They couldn't see much out the windows and, of course, if John Godfrey had been murdered, his killer wouldn't still be hanging around the property, especially in broad daylight.

Garcia followed his gaze and nodded. "Yes, this does put a different spin on him being agitated and watching out the windows the evening before he died. If the children are telling the truth about that."

It could, of course, just be cover. They had just told Zachary that John had been agitated to misdirect him. Point to an outside threat rather than to someone in the family. But they had already indicated that they knew they were suspects. That, in fact, they suspected each other. They could have pointed to an outside enemy right from the start, but they hadn't. They had painted targets on their own backs.

"I obviously need to talk to the children again," Garcia said. "In fact, I haven't ever talked to all of them. Mostly I interfaced with Miss Camden. Who, of course, would make herself a suspect if she had indicated to me that she thought her father had been murdered."

Then why come to Zachary and do just that?

He shifted uncomfortably, wondering, not for the first time, if his recruitment was only for show. To make it look like they had pursued all possible avenues of investigation when they didn't believe that he would be able to identify the killer. After all, a PI had far fewer resources than the police. Maybe the killer believed there was too great of a danger of the police figuring out who he (or she) was. But someone like Zachary—a solo operator who had some notable cases but mostly handled minor matters—could never crack it.

"Mr. Goldman."

Zachary looked back at Detective Garcia. "Sorry, what?"

"You've talked to all of the siblings?"

"Yes."

"And what are your feelings about them? Do you think they're being open and honest? Is it possible that one of them poisoned Godfrey? Or do you favor an outside threat, based on these?" She indicated the papers.

"I was just thinking about that. I think… right now, I would be more inclined to follow the outside leads. They look credible to me. In my interviews with the family… they do all have motive, but none of them stand out ahead of the others, and they would have known that they were the prime suspects."

"They all want the money."

"All of them have reason to want it early for one reason or another. And none of them had a good relationship with him."

"But you don't see any of them actually stepping into the role of cold-blooded killer?"

Alex, driven and a perfectionist, was desperate to please his father and keep everything he had been promised. Yet despite his best efforts, his father threatened to disown him and take away everything.

Eddie, a scientist with knowledge of both biology and chemistry, kept an emotional distance from their father. His analytical mind could look at the situation objectively without a personal bias.

Karen, the mother of the two boys, wanted nothing more than the best for her sons but was denied what her younger child desperately needed. As a nurse, she had access to medications and poisons that most wouldn't even know existed and which wouldn't be included in routine tox screens done by the medical examiner.

Lastly, there was Logan, unable to finish school or get the kind of job his father would have wanted. With no means to support himself if John had decided to kick him out, Logan would have been homeless. Although he had expensive tastes, he had no way to support himself.

Each of the four siblings had personalities that could have driven them to commit cold-blooded murder. Each person's character traits may have been what ultimately led to John's demise.

"Mr. Goldman?" Garcia prompted again, impatient. He would have thought that as a cop, she would have learned to wait for answers.

"It's Zachary," he said, "You can drop the mister. I actually don't have any problem seeing any of them doing it. But I don't think any of the family dynamics have changed lately. I don't think any of them have reached a crisis point. I could be wrong, but I think that when it came to weighing the choice between waiting for him to die and getting his money, and the risk of getting caught and thrown in prison, they all chose to watch and wait. But the outside threats seem to have escalated. At least one of them had

John running scared. Expecting the avenger to show up at his house."

Garcia looked surprised at this. She leaned back into the couch, studying him. "Okay. So you know people."

It seemed like an odd thing for her to say. Of course he knew people. How could he make a living as a private investigator if he didn't? However, he had witnessed firsthand the darker depths of human nature that some were capable of descending to. He wasn't naive enough to think that only the darkest minds could ever turn to murder as a solution.

"Most people have the capacity to murder, given the right circumstances," he admitted.

"Everyone," Garcia corrected.

There were true innocents out there. Zachary still believed that there were people who did not have it in them to kill, no matter what. But they were few and far between. He shrugged and didn't argue. It was a philosophical point that they didn't have to agree on.

"Let's focus on the outside threats, then," Garcia said, looking back at the papers spread out on the table. "What do you know from what you found in that box?"

Zachary cleared his throat. He hadn't expected to have to explain his theories to anyone. He figured she would just take the box of papers and run with it. Let her forensics team analyze everything and return to her with a profile of the person who might have killed Godfrey. Read through them herself and come to her own conclusions. Cops did not consult with PI's. He shifted uncomfortably in the seat, wanting to get up and pace as he reviewed his thoughts. He needed to get into the flow, but felt blocked sitting down.

"We don't know which threat is real. I mean, they are all real, but which one of them actually took action, if that's what happened?"

He stopped. Garcia nodded and waited for him to continue. It was obviously only his opening, not his conclusion.

Zachary's stomach was tight. He was holding tension all

through his body and could think of nothing other than releasing it. He shifted again in his seat on the couch. "Do you mind if I walk?" he asked. "Move around a little while I talk?"

She raised her eyebrows. "By all means."

With relief, Zachary got to his feet. He paced the length of the room and back again, taking deep breaths. Then he stayed closer to Garcia, fidgeting and pacing in smaller circles.

"There are similarities in the complaints. But they fall into two camps. Those who were angry at Godfrey specifically and saw him as the reason for all of their problems, and those who were angry at the world, and he was just one more problem. The straw that broke the camel's back."

"And do you see one group as being more likely to carry through with murder than the other?"

Zachary waved off the question. "Then there is a separation between those who saw him as someone who had taken advantage of their vulnerability and those who saw him as crooked. Not just doing what the law let him do, but a thief who had stolen from them."

"And if they saw him as being above and beyond the reach of the law, then they would be more likely to take independent action. Something more permanent."

Zachary nodded. That seemed obvious. He approached the coffee table and tapped the folder containing the threats. Garcia obliged and put it on top of the other paperwork. She was still wearing gloves, so he motioned for her to turn the pages over, looking for the one he wanted.

"That one," he said, stopping her. He wanted to push his finger down in the middle of the page, but refrained, knowing he couldn't get his fingerprint on it. He thumped the table with his index finger instead, stabbing into it with force. "Read that one."

He paced away while Garcia read through it. He gave her lots of time, not just to skim it, but to really read and take it in, and maybe to read it a second time.

"What is it about this one?" Garcia asked.

Zachary was surprised she didn't see it. He walked back over to her. "He's not just saying that Godfrey ruined his life."

She looked at it again, squinting a little while concentrating on it. "Okay… the sender says that he ruined someone else's life. Why does that make it worse? Shouldn't that make it better that it wasn't the writer himself?"

Zachary shook his head. "From the wording of the letter—'you took everything from him and what happened is your fault'—I would say that the consequences of Godfrey's actions weren't just that 'he' was left penniless or in dire straits. I think it was worse than that. Maybe the victim committed suicide."

Garcia nodded slowly. "It's a stretch. You're reading something into it that isn't actually on the page."

"As a private investigator, that's part of my job. Guessing. Filling in the holes. Following my instincts. If I only ever followed the hard evidence and didn't speculate about where to look next, I wouldn't be very effective."

"I suppose the same is true of police work," she conceded. "We like to think that we only deal with cold hard facts and that 'following your gut' is just something from TV. But when you are interpreting evidence, you have to speculate to some degree. Brainstorm, connect it as much as you can to what you already know, and go with your best guess as to the direction to investigate next."

Zachary nodded. "Godfrey is supposed to know when he reads that who the writer is talking about and what happened to the victim. And it isn't just what happened *to* him, but what happened *next*, which suggests that it wasn't just circumstances beyond his control. Ending up on the street or sick. A choice that led to something even worse."

"It doesn't say what he *did*, either," Garcia pointed out.

"No. Which suggests that the writer doesn't blame the victim for his choice; he blamed Godfrey. It's easier to strike out against an outside force, someone you don't love, to blame him for whatever happened. Avenge his life."

"Maybe exchanging a life for a life." Garcia's voice was low, musing.

Zachary paced. “Yes. Exactly. I think we’re looking for a suicide.”

28

Zachary expected to be dismissed by Detective Garcia once they had finished going over the key items in the box of files and discussing the possible scenarios. While there was still no evidence that Godfrey had been poisoned or killed in some other way, there was enough of a suggestion that someone had truly wanted to kill him for Garcia to entertain the possibility and gather further evidence.

But she didn't thank him and tell him to go home and stay out of her way as most of the cops he knew would have. Even cops he knew well, like Campbell, would have sent him on his way and not allowed him to hear anything from the investigation. But she allowed Zachary to shadow her as she spoke to the house staff and got their perspective on everything that had happened the evening before John Godfrey had died.

Not that there was anything particularly enlightening to find. The staff had been more removed from the action than the family members had been, so their observations were even less helpful. They walked through the events of the evening, going from room to room to discuss where everyone had been standing or sitting, what their movements had been as far as the staff had seen or that Zachary had discovered in his interviews with the family members.

Garcia also took a walk around the house looking for any signs that someone had been outside the house that day, watching the family and waiting for their opportunity to strike. But it had been a couple of weeks and, if there had been any evidence of a stalker, they did not find it. Zachary took a few pictures of the exterior of the house and the grounds, but it was mostly hobby photography, not anything that he expected to be able to use for the case.

"You wear that thing everywhere you go?" Garcia asked, indicating the camera on a strap around Zachary's neck.

"Pretty much, yes," Zachary admitted. "Although if it needs to be concealed, it's in my pocket."

"Tools of the trade."

He nodded. "And something that I enjoy doing. It was photography that got me into being a private investigator rather than the other way around."

"Really?" Garcia continued to walk around the house, looking for anything dropped in the gardens or around the trees, peering into dark corners and recesses, and checking the outside frames of windows that were close to the ground. "How exactly did that happen?"

"My first foster father got me interested in photography when I was a kid. Gave me an old camera for my eleventh birthday. It was the first birthday present I can ever remember getting. I didn't stay there for long, but I kept in touch with him, and he helped me to develop my film over the years. Before digital photography. When I got older… I happened to take some pictures that helped the police to solve a robbery and kept the person who was wrongfully accused out of prison."

Garcia gave him a brief smile. "And that set you on the path."

"I didn't really think anything of it. I was proud of myself, but I was dealing with some pretty tough stuff and didn't see the long view. But Mr. Peterson pointed out to me that that was what private investigators did, and suggested I pursue it as a career. It was a way to make money with the one thing I was good at." Zachary nodded to himself, remembering. "So… I decided to give it a try."

"Do you still keep in touch with him? Is he still around?"

"Yes. I visit him for dinner every couple of weeks. Phone calls in between. For decades, he was the only family I had."

"You have kids now?"

"No." Zachary swallowed. "One day, maybe. But I've been reunited with my siblings. And found out that I have a number of other half-siblings that I never knew about. And I'm in a relationship. So… more family than I've ever had before. But Mr. Peterson —Lorne—and Pat, they're the ones who were there for me through all the years when there was no one else."

They had reached the back of the house, halfway around from where they had started, and Garcia stared into the orchard across the lawn. There were enough trees growing densely together to provide a good screen for anyone who wanted to watch the house. If it had been Zachary, he would have mounted a couple of cameras in the orchard to provide him with all the information he needed about the family's usual routines before attempting to breach security. Infrared cameras would give him even more information about what was happening inside the house when people weren't turning lights on and off or walking past windows.

"And since that first case, you've always interfaced with the police on your cases?" Garcia asked.

Zachary thought about that. He hadn't connected his diligence in informing the local police whenever he was investigating a case with that first case when Ivy, a young woman living on the streets, had been fingered for holding up a convenience store. He remembered the exultant feeling of proving to the cops that they had jumped to conclusions in arresting her for the robbery. They had judged her by her circumstances and a general description and then tried to make it stick. Confirmation bias had proven them right. Until Zachary's photography provided her with an alibi.

"Maybe that's part of it," he said slowly. "I just… I respect what the police do. They helped me more than once as a kid, and I was never really scared of them or resented them like a lot of the other foster kids who had been in trouble. I think we can find the truth and see justice done more often if we share information—if I share information with law enforcement—than if we work separately and are opponents."

"Yup." Garcia gave a brief nod. "If citizens worked with the police instead of against them, I think things would work a lot better."

Zachary agreed. They continued to walk around the house. Eventually, they reached the front again. Garcia looked at her watch. "I need to get back to my office. I'll grab the box, and I'll let you know if I need anything else from you." She paused with her hand on the doorknob of the front door. "And you'll let me know if you come across any other information about who made the threats or might have been involved in this. If anyone." She raised her brows. "We still don't have any evidence that it was a poisoning. Just because people made threats or had a motive to kill him, that doesn't mean that anyone did. We'll need some evidence, including a second look by the medical examiner."

"Oh." Zachary looked at his own phone and found that a number of hours had passed without his realizing it. "I still haven't seen the original report."

"Well, he may be back to the drawing board now. You may as well wait until he's had a chance to review the case."

"I've already asked for a copy. I'll take a look just in case there is anything that jumps out at me. Sometimes I can work things out."

Garcia frowned at him. "You have a medical background?"

"Uh, no. Just a bit of experience in reading coroner's reports and some friends with experience that I can tap when I need to. You never know. There might be something there."

He thought it best not to tell Garcia that his partner was in the medical examiner's office. She might think that there was some kind of conflict of interest.

"It was not an extensive autopsy. There was no reason at the time to think that there had been any foul play."

"Right," Zachary agreed, keeping his tone casual and nonchalant.

"All right. Thank you for this information," Garcia opened the door and picked up the box of papers. "I guess I've got a bit of reading to do."

Zachary nodded and bid her farewell, then returned to his car. It was only a couple more hours until Kenzie got home, and he had a number of things that he hoped to get done before then. If she brought him the medical examiner's report, they could go over it together to see in what direction Zachary should direct his investigation.

29

When Kenzie got home, Zachary was finishing up with some billings and sending them out via email. Pretty early in the evening for her. She often ended up working late on one thing or another. He smiled a greeting.

"Hi, Kenz. How was your day?"

She looked at him for a moment, then dropped a large envelope onto the kitchen table with a slap. Zachary's gut tightened. He did not like the expression on her face. She was pretty good at masking when she was upset about something, but that very mask told him that there was something wrong. He stood up from the couch and walked into the kitchen to be closer to her and show his support.

"What's wrong? Did something happen at work?"

There was an infinitesimal headshake that gave him the answer before she managed to get any words out.

"Are you okay?" Zachary went on immediately, his mind jumping to the kidnapping and how jumpy she had been even though several months had passed. Had something happened to trigger a memory? To scare her? Had someone made a threat or tried to hurt her? He hated that her name was still on the official

Medical Examiner's Office website, even though they had finally gotten around to taking her picture down. People could still see her name and figure out who she was. Get her picture with a web search, social media, or an internet archive. He grasped her by the shoulders, looking into her face to try to discern the slightest change in expression, halfway to a comforting hug, if she made any move toward him.

Kenzie jerked back from his hands, and he didn't attempt to re-initiate contact. He might have triggered something by touching her, and he would leave it to her to decide if she wanted any contact. She ignored him, took off her shoes, and put down her bag. Zachary waited.

"I'm going to have a shower and change," Kenzie told him curtly, and brushed by him, heading toward the bedroom.

Zachary watched her go, his mouth open to ask her another question, but he was not sure what to say. Needing a shower immediately after work might mean that it had been a more physically demanding day than usual and she had been sweating. Or that she'd been dealing with a particularly pungent corpse and needed to get the smell of decomp out of her hair.

Or it might mean that she was stressed about something or angry with him, and she didn't want to look at him until she'd had a chance to work things through.

Zachary sighed and looked around the kitchen. It would be best if he had something ready to eat when she got out of the shower. If she was just sweaty, it might only take her a couple of minutes. If she was upset, it could be an hour or more. Make something too soon, and it could be cold by the time she got out. Take too long, and she could be hungry and irritated that he hadn't bothered to start on anything.

After some waffling, Zachary ordered from their favorite Thai restaurant, got out a bagged salad and bottles of salad dressing, and started cutting up some fresh vegetables to add to the salad. He had learned that while a bagged salad was adequate, he got more points if he added something to liven it up a bit.

If she had a two-minute shower, the salad would be almost ready to eat and she could have some while they waited for the takeout. If she took an hour, then the Thai food would be there, still warm, and she could have salad to go with it, which would not suffer from being too cold. If she wasn't in the mood for salad, it could be sealed up and put away in the fridge, and he still got brownie points for trying.

When the Thai food arrived, Kenzie was still in the shower.

Zachary sighed. He put plates and forks on the table, filled a jug with water, and lowered the lighting. A few flickering candles—electric, not real flames—hopefully set a comforting, romantic atmosphere that would make her more likely to forgive him for whatever he had done.

Eventually, the shower was turned off and Kenzie put in an appearance, skin flushed pink, dressed in a t-shirt and shorts set that she used as pajamas in the summer. She looked around at the food and candles and didn't smile. She folded her arms in front of her, displaying typical "closed" body language.

"This is nice. What's the occasion?"

"I just… You seemed like you could use a break tonight. Something nice, intimate… a chance to relax."

She stared at him, waiting for more, but Zachary didn't know what else to add.

"And… you have no idea what I'm upset about."

He had been hoping against hope that it was something to do with work or her anxiety following the kidnapping. Not something that he had done. But her tone and her question and everything else about her that evening told him that it wasn't. He was in the doghouse.

"I'm… sorry…"

"For what?"

"For… being so dense about this. I did something wrong. I missed or forgot something." He mentally checked the day of the week to make sure that he hadn't missed couple's therapy. But there hadn't been any messages or missed calls on his phone from Dr. B indicating that he had missed an appointment.

Kenzie snorted and sat down at the table. She started to dish up, reaching for her favorite noodles first. Probably no salad today. Zachary could put it away for another day. Kenzie sighed heavily and got up again to get a couple of glasses out of the cupboard.

"Sorry, I could have done that," Zachary apologized again. It wasn't the first time he had flaked out when setting the table and missed something vital. It was more common than not, if he were to admit the truth.

She settled back in at the table, and Zachary made his way tentatively over to his chair and sat down. She wouldn't want him hovering over her, or refusing to eat when she had decided to. They were quiet for a long time. Each time one of their forks clinked or scraped along the plate, Zachary gritted his teeth. He could usually ignore the noise. When they were talking or doing something else, it was more muffled. But not when the room was dead silent.

"You look like you're in pain," Kenzie snapped. "What's the matter?"

"Nothing. Everything is fine."

"Everything is not fine."

They continued eating. Zachary looked around the kitchen for things to distract him from the lack of conversation and the noise of their cutlery. The flickering candles, which looked real behind their frosted glass or cut crystal cups. Kenzie's shoes, misaligned where she had dropped them when she came in. The large envelope was still on the table. Homework? She usually tried not to bring anything to do at home. Once she got there after work, it was her time for relaxation and unwinding. For spending time with Zachary or by herself.

He realized that his name was written on the front of the envelope in Kenzie's neat printing.

Then everything fell into place.

What else would she bring home from the medical examiner's office for him but the medical examiner's report on John Godfrey?

The report that he had been so eager to get from her that he had said he would come by the office to get it instead of waiting until the end of the day.

That he would take Kenzie out for lunch so that they could go over it together.

Thinking back over the day, Zachary was pretty sure he hadn't even eaten lunch. He had certainly not gone to the medical examiner's office and taken Kenzie out.

Instead, he'd spent the day with Detective El Garcia and hadn't even called Kenzie. Then acted oblivious when she got home, looking for brownie points by ordering in, just aggravating matters by either thinking he could make up for his mistake by buying her supper or remaining clueless that he had done anything wrong in the first place.

Zachary swore.

Kenzie looked up from her meal and followed his gaze to the envelope. She shook her head. "You really had no idea."

Zachary smacked his forehead with the heel of his hand. "Kenz, I'm so sorry! I completely forgot that we were going to get together for lunch. The whole thing slipped my mind. I am so sorry."

"Where was your head? I thought you were all into this case and couldn't wait another minute to get your hands on that report."

"I was. I mean, I am. I was working on this case. I just… the whole day got away from me. I was with Detective Garcia, and—"

She leaned back in her chair, eyes closing partway as she studied Zachary. "Detective Elena Garcia?" she asked.

"Uh… I guess so. She was introduced to me as El Garcia. I thought it was short for Ellen."

He knew that her name wasn't the point.

"You spent the day with her."

Zachary nodded. "Yes. I needed to go over those papers with her…" Zachary motioned to the living room where they had been the previous day but were no longer. "And then, there were interviews with the staff and reconstructing the evening, and a security sweep outside…"

"She's very pretty, hey?"

Zachary swallowed, recognizing the trap. If he said she was pretty, he would be in trouble for noticing. If he said he hadn't noticed, she would know he was lying and be angry about that. There was no right answer.

The fact was that Garcia *was* a very attractive woman, and he had enjoyed working closely with her and admired her face and figure when she wasn't looking in his direction. He was not supposed to notice how beautiful she was?

"It was work," he told Kenzie firmly. "And it's pretty rare to even find a cop who will talk to me, so I wasn't going to turn down the chance to work with her on the case."

"She was very accommodating, was she?"

"It was work," Zachary insisted. He licked his dry lips. He did not want to be having this discussion. He had no desire to have an argument with Kenzie or to fight over anything that had happened or not happened that day. He hated arguments, and a fight with his girlfriend was the worst kind of all.

He almost preferred his ex-wife Bridget's screaming, swearing, and imprecations to Kenzie's quiet, civilized words. She would act as calm as if they were just discussing the weather. A polite, even, understanding voice. Like it was any other day, having any other conversation. But it wasn't just any conversation.

"You can call her and ask about it," Zachary told her. "It wasn't anything inappropriate. We were just going over evidence together. Working a case. There was nothing else involved."

"I'm sure there wasn't," Kenzie agreed. "Not on her side. But that doesn't mean you weren't hanging all over her like a dog begging for a bone. Making puppy dog eyes and admiring her high cheekbones and sleek black hair…"

Zachary's cheeks burned and he knew his face was getting red. "I wasn't attracted to her. I'm not interested in anyone except you. You work with other men all day, but I don't worry about you flirting with them or starting something. I know it doesn't mean anything."

"You don't worry that I might be flirting with Dr. Wiltshire?"

Kenzie demanded. "Or George? I'm so glad, Zachary. You must really think a lot of me."

Zachary tried to remain focused on the actual issue and keep his emotions under control. "I'm sorry I forgot we were getting together for lunch and didn't even call you. I completely forgot to even eat."

30

Great. Well as long as you are sorry, all is forgiven."

"Can I take you out for lunch tomorrow? I know that doesn't make up for forgetting about our date, but..."

"No." She shut him down. "I'm busy tomorrow."

"Okay. Is there any way that I can..."

She shook her head. "It's nothing. I know by now how you can get hyper focused on a case and forget everything else. It would have been nice to have had a call warning me that you wouldn't be able to make it, or even to have you remember when I got home, but I guess I can't compete with Detective Garcia for your attention."

"It wasn't anything to do with Detective Garcia."

"You spent the day with her. You can't tell me it was nothing to do with her."

"Not with her personally. It was to do with the case. The case that I'm working on at a higher-than-usual billing rate. The case that Dr. Wiltshire decided was natural causes, but his family thinks was murder and there were written threats against his life. People following him around. Maybe someone on the grounds that night."

Kenzie tilted her head slightly, taken aback by this. "What?"

"Detective Garcia will be talking to Dr. Wiltshire tomorrow. She wants him to take another look at it."

Kenzie frowned and twirled noodles around her fork but was no longer eating. "She thinks there was reason to believe that he might have been murdered? There was no violence, so is she thinking poison?"

"That's the standing theory, until we come up with something better."

"Routine tox screens were done, and nothing came up."

"But it could easily have been something not on a routine tox screen. There are a lot of things that you wouldn't test for unless you knew to look for them."

Kenzie nodded her agreement. "We take the lead from the police on the case. We can't know what to look for without their direction. If there aren't signs on the body, I mean."

"Would there be anything? If he was poisoned?"

"In a lot of cases, yes. Vomiting, cyanosis or other changes in color, scratches or other signs that he was in pain or distress. But in other cases, no. Some can act very quickly and quietly. You know about insulin. It could be a paralytic, succinylcholine or botulinum, batrachotoxin, tetrodotoxin, plenty of things that wouldn't leave any sign unless we knew to test for them. Or it could have been something that should have been there, but they gave him too much. Digitalis can be toxic, but I would expect vomiting with an overdose. We'll need to know any prescriptions or non-prescription medications he was on. It could have even been an interaction. Two drugs that should not be taken together."

"I have that," Zachary told her. He pulled out his phone and unlocked it, then tapped and swiped through his phone until he found the pictures of the drugs in John Godfrey's medicine cabinet. He handed it across to Kenzie. She zoomed in and slowly panned through the rows of medications in each picture.

"Some of these could be dangerous if someone double-dosed him. Or they can't be taken with Tylenol or alcohol."

"He had been drinking. He shouldn't be taking those with alcohol?"

"It's a risk factor, for sure. He might be able to get away with a glass of wine with dinner a few hours before, but severe liver damage could result if he was mixing them."

"He had at least three scotches and a glass of wine in the hours before bed. Probably double that, if I'm not mistaken."

"I'll check his BAC levels. I remember there was alcohol in the blood but not how much. Send me these pictures. I'll make sure they're logged into the file. We'll need to look for signs of an overdose or toxic interaction. He wasn't jaundiced, which is a good thing," she mused, more to herself than to Zachary.

"Yellow?" Zachary verified.

Kenzie looked at him briefly, and nodded. "Yes. That's the word that means that he had too much bilirubin in his blood, which would make his skin and especially the whites of his eyes look yellow."

Zachary nodded. He was relieved to have her focus on the case and what they had found so far instead of on his failure to show up for lunch that day. If he kept her talking about medical stuff, she might forget her ire and give him a break.

"Do you mind if we go over the medical examiner's report?" he asked tentatively.

Her eyes went to the envelope and her irritation at him returned. "No, not tonight. It's useless anyway, with this new information. A revised report will be issued after Dr. Wiltshire has a chance to look at the new information and order more tests."

"You still have the body?" Zachary asked. "I thought it had been released to the family."

"It was. But we kept fluid and tissue samples. So we can still do some more testing. And I assume that if the family is intent on finding out what happened to him, they will not object to an exhumation of the body if we need to do further tests."

"It's kind of morbid, but I guess they would agree to it. They all want to know what really happened to him, more or less. And if it turns out that it was not someone inside the family, they'll be even happier."

"They think it was a family member?"

"That's why they came to me. They thought one of them might have done it to get their inheritance faster."

Kenzie shook her head. "That would be hard. Most families would have just let it go and lived with the suspicions. It's easier to keep secrets than to expose a family member and send them to prison. Most siblings have been raised to be loyal to and support each other. Protect each other from bullies and other outside sources. When something like that happens inside a family, they just keep following that principle, protect the family, instead of going to the police to seek justice." She gave a nod to Zachary. "Or to a private investigator. What were they going to do if you discovered it was one of them? Go to the police? Or put him on a plane to some non-extraditing country?"

Zachary considered. "I assumed that they would go to the police. But I'm not sure any of them ever said that. I guess they might have intended to take care of things their own way. They're not *really* close, but they are family."

Kenzie stood up. "You can look at the report yourself if you like. The basics are there. But you're not going to find anything in there that points to poisoning. And there were no needle marks so, if it was poison, it was consumed, not injected. You'll have to wait for the revised and updated report like everyone else."

With that, she strode out of the kitchen and to her bedroom. Zachary heard the door shut firmly, but quietly. No door slamming. She wasn't that angry anymore. But he was still in the doghouse.

He tried to remain focused on the task at hand as he cleared away the salad and the leftover Thai food and put the dishes in the dishwasher. He tried to do everything right, the way she would have wanted it, so she would see that he cared about her and wasn't completely oblivious to her needs. Normally, they cleared together, or Kenzie ended up doing it because Zachary was too absorbed in his work to notice what was going on around him. This time, it was his turn.

After loading the dishwasher, Zachary sat down again at the table and opened the large envelope. It might not be the final report, but he still might be able to get something out of it. Something that Dr. Wiltshire and Kenzie had missed. Something that his investigation into the case informed him was wrong or out of place.

Melancholy over the fact that Kenzie had shut herself in the bedroom and they would not be spending a pleasant evening together as usual, Zachary opened up the medical examiner's report on John Godfrey. He started to skim over the headings and pictures.

31

Zachary spent a miserable evening alone. Before he had moved in with Kenzie, he had been used to that. He liked to be alone. He was an introvert and working with people often exhausted him, and he just wanted to be alone. He had grown up without any family of his own and was used to isolating himself.

But it was different now that he and Kenzie lived together. They spent every evening with each other, even if they were doing separate things. And usually, they did not work on separate things. They set time aside to be with each other visiting, watching TV, cuddling, going for walks, or even going over medical documents together. Dr. B had encouraged them to spend time focusing on their relationship, putting work aside—other than if they were discussing an interesting medical case, which both of them enjoyed—and doing relaxing and relationship-building activities before bed.

He'd gotten into the habit of spending that time together, and it was painful knowing that Kenzie was on the other side of the bedroom door, deliberately keeping her distance from him. He tried to focus on work, and when that became impossible, he turned on the TV and tried to find something to occupy his attention. But he was too distracted to follow the storylines and couldn't even have said what shows he had watched later.

It was late when Kenzie's bedroom door opened, and she came out to talk to him in her bare feet and pajamas.

"Come to bed."

Zachary longed to, but he didn't want to rush into anything or make her feel like she was compelled to ask him back in after what he had done. He swallowed. "I can use the guest bedroom if you like. If you need some time and space…"

"No." Kenzie sighed. "So you forgot lunch. It wasn't the first time by any means, and it won't be the last. That's just part and parcel of your ADHD, and you can't be blamed for that. And as far as spending the day with the lovely El Garcia…"

"Maybe I could ask for an ugly guy to be assigned to the next case I investigate."

She laughed. "Yeah, I'd appreciate that. Okay, I understand that you had a job to do and that included working with Detective Garcia on the case. I don't understand why you had to be there for so long or why she would want you there. But it *was* work."

Zachary nodded. Kenzie nodded to his camera, sitting on the laptop table. "You'd better not have any pictures of her on that camera," she teased.

Zachary's mouth was dry. He picked up the camera and handed it to her, not touching any of the controls, so she couldn't accuse him of trying to delete anything. Kenzie shook her head and didn't take it. "It was a joke."

"Look," Zachary insisted. "I was there with her most of the day with the camera. So if I was so entranced with her, then her picture must be on it."

"Unless you already downloaded and deleted it."

He gazed at her steadily. "I didn't. Take it to a cop and get them to check the memory card."

Kenzie shook her head. She took the camera from him reluctantly and clicked backward through the stream of pictures. She held it close to her face, studying the images on the small digital display.

"It's quite the place," she observed.

Kenzie's family came from money, so Zachary was sure she had probably seen similar properties before, or even bigger and more luxurious. But the Godfrey mansion was still impressive. Kenzie kept clicking back through the photos until Zachary thought she should be well past the ones he had taken that day, but she kept going. He must have taken more than he had realized.

Eventually, Kenzie put the camera back down on the laptop table. "Come to bed," she invited again.

Zachary nodded and stood. They went through their usual evening routines, with Zachary brushing his teeth and taking his meds in the main bathroom while Kenzie completed her night routine in the bedroom en suite.

He still felt a little anxious entering the bedroom, tiptoeing as if she were already asleep and he didn't want to disturb her. He knew that the discussion about his mistake would not continue in bed. Kenzie had admitted that it shouldn't be such a big deal, and they had a rule about not arguing in bed. Anything that important could wait until morning and, often upon waking, they found it was not that important in the light of day after a good night's sleep. When Kenzie finished in her bathroom and joined him in bed, he pulled her to him, craving the warmth and comfort of her body. She stiffened for just an instant, then snuggled into him, and they were both still and quiet, waiting for sleep to descend.

As usual, Zachary awoke before Kenzie and could not get back to sleep. But he lay there with her for a long time, just listening to her breathe and savoring the closeness of her body to his. But he couldn't lie still and he didn't want to wake her up early so, eventually, he slid close to the edge of the bed and eased off of it, hoping not to jolt her when he did so.

"Are you up?" Kenzie murmured.

"Shh. Go back to sleep."

She turned over and mumbled something else, then her

breathing lengthened and she was asleep again. Zachary sighed in relief and left the bedroom, shutting the door quietly behind him so as not to wake her.

He had plenty of work to do, not having expected to be busy with the Godfrey case for most of the previous day as he had been. There were other cases that he needed to push forward, and he needed to think about everything he had found so far on the Godfrey case too. The papers that Karen had brought provided some enlightenment, but he wasn't sure that he had processed everything that he had read. He had also taken pictures of some of the documents he hadn't had a chance to study so that he could still refer to them after giving the originals to Garcia. And he had made notes during his discussions with Garcia and listened in on the interviews she had conducted with the staff. And he wanted to review the pictures he had taken for anything he might have missed. There was a lot of information still to be considered.

When Kenzie got up, she walked into the living room, rubbing her eyes. "What time did you get up?"

"I'm not sure." Zachary glanced at his system clock. "I didn't look."

"It's been a while, though. I think I remember waking up for a minute."

He nodded. "You asked me if I was getting up. I'm glad you got back to sleep."

She nodded. "Coffee?"

Zachary looked around to see if he had made any. His travel mug stood on the side table nearby, away from his computer. "I think I just made a cup. If I made a pot, it's been sitting on the burner too long and you'll want fresh anyway."

She nodded and went into the kitchen to make herself a cup. She returned, still blinking, trying to wake up for work. "You make any progress?"

"Not much. Just looking at what I've gathered… not making much out of it."

"Sometimes there isn't very much to find. Just a lot of stuff that doesn't mean anything."

"Yeah. I'm sure you find that with autopsies too. Plenty of stuff that looks normal. Some stuff that doesn't look normal, but wasn't the cause of death. Unrelated ailments and mutations."

"Yup. Sometimes you open someone up and wonder how the heck they ever had a normal life. Other times, you can't see any reason for their death."

She sat down to look through her phone while she drank her coffee. "Did you look at the autopsy report?" she asked without looking at him.

"Looked through it, but nothing jumped out at me. It wasn't a very in-depth examination."

"No need for it at the time. A man with diagnosed heart disease dies in his sleep. Nothing suspicious at the scene. No signs of violence on the body. No needle marks. Clear tox screens."

"Alcohol in his blood."

"And you know he was drinking, so that isn't surprising. His BAC is noted in the file."

"But nothing else."

She shrugged. "None of the top recreational drugs or household poisons."

"What else can you test for?"

"Hundreds of things. But only if you know what you're looking for. We only have so much fluid and tissue to run tests on."

"Unless we exhume him."

"Hmm. I checked with the funeral home last night to find out if he'd been embalmed and buried. Sometimes families don't hold the funeral right away and just keep the body cold until they're ready."

"And he was already buried?" Zachary guessed from her tone of voice.

"Even worse. He was cremated."

Zachary raised his eyebrows, thinking about that. "Well… that surprises me. The family didn't say anything about having him cremated. I think most of these upper-crust types would be very traditional about having a burial rather than a cremation. Unless Godfrey asked for a cremation."

"In this case, they have a family crypt. But it's full. There is only space to add cremains, not full bodies."

"Oh. Well, I guess you're stuck with the samples you took, then."

"Yep." Kenzie nodded. "So we won't want to do a lot of testing unless we have a pretty good idea of what it is we're looking for."

32

After Kenzie was off to work, Zachary sat at his computer again to see what he should tackle next. He kept an eye on the time, but was still startled out of his work later by the alarms he had set.

While he knew it wouldn't make her feel any better about his forgetting lunch with Kenzie the day before, he wanted to do something nice for her, so he arranged for a pickup from her favorite pizza place—not Thai two days in a row—and took it over to her at the medical examiner's office.

He had ordered an extra-large so that there was enough for anyone who happened to be in the office that day. It wasn't a big office, but he wanted to ensure he was covered if a couple of extra people were there.

Kenzie's eyes got big, and she shook her head, smiling. "You know this doesn't make up for forgetting."

"I know."

"But it's nice," she admitted. "Come on; we'll put it out in the boardroom. The kitchen counter is too crowded."

Zachary put down the pizza box, opened it, and set out the plates and napkins from the pizza place while Kenzie walked around to inform everyone that there was pizza. By the time she finished making her rounds, a couple of employees were already helping themselves. Zachary didn't know everyone in the medical examiner's office, but recognized George, a large man who helped with transportation and preparing bodies for autopsy. And probably some other duties that Zachary was unaware of, since that would not keep him busy most of the time.

George lifted a slice of pizza to his mouth to take a bite, and then addressed Zachary as he chewed it.

"So what did you do?"

"What did I do?"

"Well, pizza isn't exactly anniversary fare, and I've never seen you bring it before, so what did you do? You're in the doghouse for something, aren't you?"

Zachary rolled his eyes. He was supposed to be the detective, not George. "Yes. Missed a date we had set up. Was at a client's and lost track of time."

"Lost track of time?" Kenzie repeated, helping herself to a slice.

"Lost track of time and forgot all about it," he admitted.

George chuckled. "Not a good way to keep the girl, Mr. Goldman."

"I know. That's why I had to do the pizza thing."

"Lucky for us," George approved. "It should be mandatory that we get pizza in at least once a month."

"As long as it's not on my dime. Or because I'm in trouble."

Zachary sighed and stretched as he got out of the car at the house. He would hold himself tense all day until Kenzie got home, worrying that she was still upset with him, unless he paid attention and made an effort to relax his muscles.

He had done what he could to make up for his mistake, and it was up to Kenzie to decide whether he had done enough. And, of course, he would have to avoid any further major mistakes, or he would be right back where he had started.

There was an envelope sticking out of the mailbox, and he

grabbed it before stepping into the house. He locked the door and cleared the burglar alarm, then ripped the envelope open without more than a glance at it to see that it had his name on it. Sometimes clients mailed or dropped off checks rather than using e-transfer. Older clients, mostly.

He opened up the trifold notepaper, but there was not a check sandwiched inside of it. It was just a handwritten note. Zachary stared at it, not understanding. He flipped it and looked at the back. Nothing on the back. He took it with him into the living room and sat down, studying it.

Somewhere along the line, he had miscalculated.

Zachary patted his pockets until he found his phone, and then put a call in to Detective Garcia.

It wasn't long before she showed up at the house. He hadn't been sure when to expect her. She surely had cases other than John Godfrey's death to deal with. Cases that they actually thought were murder and had some leads on.

He was watching out the window, so he opened the door before she had a chance to knock, and disarmed the burglar alarm so they could go in and out without tripping it.

"Where was this letter?" Garcia demanded.

"In the mailbox," Zachary pointed. "The envelope was sticking out. He would have had to lift the lid to put it in. There might be fingerprints. Or there could be some on the doorframe, if he leaned against it to stabilize himself while reaching over." Zachary mimed how reaching from the steps to the mailbox might make a person unstable.

Garcia nodded. "Don't touch anything. And we'll need your prints for elimination."

"Sure."

"Some techs will be by to dust for fingerprints. How about the letter itself?"

"Come in." Zachary led her to his laptop desk and pointed to the letter where he had put it down after realizing what it was. "I'm sorry, I touched it without considering that it might be evidence. I thought it was just a client check."

"A check? Who pays by check these days?"

He smiled, acknowledging how archaic it had become in just a few years. "Some of mine still do."

Garcia stood looking at the note.

I will bring the curse of a father's sins upon even the second and third generation

She grimaced. "It is the same handwriting and notepaper."

"I think so," Zachary agreed. He had thought so right from the start, but had pulled up pictures he had made of the threats and compared them. The threat he thought was the most likely to be the killer's was an obvious match. There had not been any attempt to disguise the writer's handwriting or to use a different kind of paper. Did that mean he didn't care if he were caught? He had obviously not expected Godfrey to recognize his writing. Unless, of course, Godfrey was supposed to know who the threat had come from. But then why not sign it?

"There were no scriptural verses on the original threat," Garcia said.

Zachary frowned, looking at it. "Is that what it is? I thought maybe it was Shakespeare."

"Bible. Old Testament. Don't ask me for more than that; I'm afraid I'm not as well-educated as my mother would have hoped after all of those years of Sunday school. I do know it is a misquote, though. It should be the third and fourth generation, not the second and third."

"So maybe it doesn't have anything to do with the Godfrey children..."

"Oh, no. I'm sure it does." Garcia straightened. She pressed her mouth into a thin line, not looking happy. "And that means that John Godfrey's children are at risk."

"Whoever this is, they obviously breached security at the

mansion once. They could do it again. Or reach the children in their own homes."

"Their homes might be more secure."

"Logan is at the mansion. I've been to Karen's house, and there's no security. Just standard locks on the doors and wooden frames. Easy to pick or kick in. I haven't been to Alex's or Eddie's houses, but I don't imagine they are that different. Eddie was tight on cash. Probably lives in an apartment building. Alex, I don't know. I'd have to search up his address."

"No need, I'll just ask him for it and conduct a security review. They'll need to take steps to protect themselves. We certainly don't have the resources to protect them in any meaningful way."

"Even knowing their father was murdered and the same guy is now after his kids?"

"We still don't know that. It could just be someone using the coincidence to their advantage. Claiming credit for killing Godfrey when they did nothing of the kind."

"I suppose. But do you really think so?"

"No. I don't."

Zachary looked over the line again. "The second and third generation."

"Well, luckily, we don't have multiple generations of family to protect. Just one."

"And their children. What about Karen's kids?"

Garcia sighed. "I forgot about them. How old are they?"

"I'm not sure. Elementary school. And one of them is… has challenges."

"And those are the only grandchildren?"

"No… Eddie also has children. They don't live with him and probably this person has no idea that they even exist, but if they happen to know…"

"He has children?"

"A couple of 'youthful indiscretions,' according to him. I don't know if there is the possibility of more. I suppose if there were two, there could be more. And for that matter, Alex and Logan could both have children out of wedlock that they didn't bother to tell me about. I didn't ask. In Eddie's case, it just came up as an explanation of why he was short on funds—paying current and back child support. Garnished from his wages. His brothers might have children, either that they know about or that they don't know about."

"If they don't know about them, then they are safe. There is no way that someone outside of the family would know any differently."

"In this age of ancestry DNA tests… I wouldn't count on it," Zachary said, remembering Tyrrell finding half-siblings that they had never known about. "Anybody could know anything. Or the mothers could have told a mutual friend. Or Godfrey himself might have found out, with the mothers asking for child support. Someone who had been to his office might have overheard a conversation or seen something they shouldn't have."

"I'll ask them," Garcia growled, taking out her notepad to write down a few thoughts.

Zachary stared at the note. It seemed so innocent. Just a quick, handwritten note, the kind a person might send to a grandmother or friend they hadn't seen for a while. But instead, a threat not just to John Godfrey's children, but also to his grandchildren. And for what? Vengeance?

What could justify threatening innocent children?

33

Various techs were taking fingerprints and any other forensic evidence they could. Zachary had given one of them his fingerprints, pressing his fingers to the glass of a mobile scanning unit. Much easier and less messy than the old ink method.

The note had been taken into evidence and would be examined for both fingerprints and DNA. The envelope had a self-sealing flap, so there was no saliva to collect, and the note was short, so the writer might not have had their hand on the paper enough to leave any skin cells or sweat behind. But there was always the possibility.

They would also need to do handwriting analysis to make sure that it was the same person as the threat Zachary had given to Garcia. Maybe she had someone she could call on for a behavioral analysis of the words in the original threat, which was much longer, and could tell them more about the motivation of the killer or other aspects of his personality. That kind of thing always worked on TV, but Zachary knew that wasn't quite the way it worked in real life.

Even though there wasn't a lot of evidence, they would do whatever they could to identify the sender and try to stop him from taking any action against Godfrey's children or grandchildren.

Zachary thought of Wally, curled up in a tight ball on the chair, listening to every word they said, and the other boy, Finn, acting so grown up and opening the door for Zachary. He couldn't bear the thought of either of them getting hurt. He'd barely met them, but he'd always had a soft spot for children.

He heard the familiar noise of the garage door opening and whipped out his phone to look at the time. He hadn't realized so much time had passed and that Kenzie would be arriving home. But looking at the phone, he realized it wasn't that late; she was a couple of hours early. His stomach clenched. He wasn't yet past the last goof-up with Kenzie, and now she was going to land in the middle of a forensic team processing her house.

He swallowed and looked at Garcia, who seemed to sense that he was not happy about something. He shoved his phone back in his pocket and walked away from her before she could ask him what was the matter. He was in the kitchen when Kenzie walked in from the garage, screening her from the rest of the activity in the house and ready to give her an explanation before she could get upset about it.

"Kenzie, I wasn't expecting you home so soon. I—"

"Was hoping that all of the cops would be gone by the time I got here?"

Zachary licked his lips. "Uh… yes."

"You didn't think that maybe you should call me to let me know what was going on? Haven't we been through this before? I want to know what's going on from you, not someone else. And not hours or days later. When there's a problem. When it happens."

He wasn't sure what to say to that. The police weren't there because he was in trouble or because he was in danger. Did she really want him to call her at work to tell her that a threatening note had been left for someone else in the mailbox?

"Sorry." An apology was the best course of action in any argument. "I didn't think it was something that you would want to be bothered with. I'm taking care of it and thought it would all be out of the way by the time you were home."

"Somebody leaves a threatening note in my mailbox, and you don't think I would be bothered by it?"

"Well… it isn't a threat to you or me, so… I would have told you about it. I just didn't think there was any reason to interrupt your day with it."

Kenzie shook her head irritably and removed her shoes. She looked past Zachary and saw Garcia standing there, watching.

"And I see Detective Garcia came out in person."

It seemed natural that she should, since it was her case. Zachary didn't bother trying to justify her presence to Kenzie. Kenzie felt threatened by Garcia working closely with Zachary. But once she realized it was just business, he was sure she would relax.

Kenzie walked into the living room to greet Garcia. At least she wasn't going straight for her "rival's" throat.

"Detective Garcia, I don't know if you remember me…" Kenzie offered her hand. "Dr. Kenzie Kirsch. With the medical examiner's office."

Garcia shook hands. She sent an amused look at Zachary. "You have friends who can help answer questions about the coroner's report?" she teased.

Zachary's face flushed. He tried to look casual, as if he weren't embarrassed to have his own words thrown back in his face. Now Kenzie would think that he'd been trying to cover up the fact that she was his girlfriend, when really he had just been trying to avoid the appearance of a conflict of interest; that she might be using her position with the medical examiner's office to help her boyfriend.

He gulped, licked his lips, and tried to come up with the proper response. "I didn't want to use Kenzie's position to influence you."

"Right." Garcia winked. Zachary hoped Kenzie wouldn't take it as flirting. "You just didn't want me to know where you get all of your medical knowledge. Show off."

Zachary laughed weakly. "I don't want to get Kenzie tangled up in anything."

"You're such a gentleman."

Kenzie bristled at that. "Zachary *is* a gentleman. I've never known a guy who shows as much care for his partner."

"I'm sure he is," Garcia laughed. She shook her head. "I don't care whether the two of you are together or not. It makes no difference to me one way or another. I don't think law enforcement should be giving information to private investigators, but the medical examiner's report is available to the next of kin, and he's working for the next of kin, so there's no breach of policy there."

"The request *was* made by the next of kin," Zachary clarified. "They're the ones who signed the form and released it to me. We followed the proper protocol."

"Of course you did. From what I've learned from you, Mr. Zachary Goldman, you are very careful about things like that. Things to keep yourself out of jail," she clarified.

Zachary had to admit that he didn't feel like spending any more time behind bars than he already had in the past, between institutions he'd spent time in as a child and occasional run-ins with the police when he had been working a case. He'd learned pretty quickly to stay out of the way of the local police when he was working an investigation.

"I'm sorry about all of this," he told Kenzie. "I didn't want to disturb you, but I wasn't trying to hide it."

She looked at him, her face serious and lips pushed tightly together. "You received a threat to your life and you didn't want to bother me with it?"

"No! No, it wasn't a threat to my life." Zachary blew his breath out in a puff and clutched Kenzie's arm to reassure her that he had never been in any danger. "It was a threat against the Godfrey family, not against me."

"Why would someone deliver a threat against the Godfrey family here?"

"We figured it is probably because they didn't want to take the chance of being seen at the Godfrey mansion. They got away with murder once, but they don't want to push their luck. Figured it would be easier to drop it off with me."

"And how did they get your address?"

34

"It would have to be someone who knew that I had been retained by the family," Zachary said. "Not many people would have known there was a relationship between us."

"Yes," Kenzie agreed. "But how did they know you live here?"

The question gave Zachary pause. His name was not connected with Kenzie's home on any public records. His mail went to a post office box or, if someone had an old address, to his old apartment, which Tyrrell rented from Zachary. He had never given anyone Kenzie's address, not even his friends. He didn't meet clients or friends there, but always picked a neutral location. The utilities, mortgage, and everything else were in Kenzie's name, as it was her house.

There were people who knew that the two of them were a couple and that he lived with Kenzie. He couldn't help that. But how did the killer know that Zachary was in a relationship with Kenzie? That was just as disturbing as the thought that he knew Zachary's unpublished address.

"I don't know," he admitted. He looked at Garcia, frowning. "My name isn't published with this address anywhere. I haven't given it to anyone."

"You've probably written it down on something without even thinking about it. Or posted on social media with a picture of the house and enough information for them to find it."

"No. I'm careful. I… had a suspect show up at my last apartment. And…" He trailed off, deciding not to tell her that his apartment before that had been set on fire by yet another suspect. That might be a bit too much. "I'm very careful not to let that happen again."

Not for a *third* time.

Garcia looked from Zachary to Kenzie, studying them both for how much she could trust the assertion. People said things like that all the time—*I never gave my key/password to anyone*—When they had given it to multiple people.

"We both have good reason not to want people coming here because of Zachary's work," Kenzie confirmed.

Her father was the one exception that Zachary could think of. Obviously, he knew where Kenzie lived, and that Zachary lived with her. Zachary should have listened to Kenzie and not taken his case.

Garcia turned this information over in her mind. "So… your address is unpublished. Your relationship with Kenzie is not generally known?"

Zachary shrugged. "To our friends, yes. But my clients? No. And I don't post to social media," he advised before she could attack it from that angle.

"Whoever left the note for you knows you are working on the case. And probably followed you home."

"That makes it a very small circle. The Godfrey children, the house staff… the only other people who know I'm working on the case are Kenzie and you."

And whoever each of those people had talked to, of course. Spouses, friends, coworkers? Gossip could spread quickly. But who in the Godfrey circle was closely connected with the person who had killed John Godfrey? Did that point back to it being one of the children? But why would one of the children have sent a threatening note to John Godfrey about how he had ruined someone's life? Why would they threaten the other children and grandchildren?

"You haven't talked about the case to anyone else?" Garcia asked.

Zachary shook his head. "I keep client names confidential. A lot of the time, even when I talk to Kenzie, I don't mention any names. She knows in this case because I requested the medical examiner's report. And *you* didn't know my address or that I was connected with Kenzie until I called you today."

She scowled at this. "*I'm* a suspect?"

"You knew I was on the case. I don't know if you mentioned it to anyone else. But if you did, how would *they* have my address?"

"We're back to someone following you home."

Zachary shook his head. "I *watch* for tails. I'm a private investigator!"

"Then it's someone who is very good. Or else you were distracted."

Zachary glanced at Kenzie, who could testify many times over to his distractibility. But not when he was driving. Not when he was returning home and wanted to ensure Kenzie's safety.

"There must be another way," he said stubbornly. "But I don't know what it is."

"Okay, well, it goes on the list of unanswered questions." Garcia took out her notepad and added her scribbles to it with a flourish.

Zachary evaluated their security. Both of them were careful not to leave the burglar alarm unarmed, even if they were in the house. It was directly connected to the security company, who both of them could attest had a faster response time than the police. They would be there in minutes in the case of a break-in. But could someone get into the house without setting off the alarm? Zachary couldn't think of one, other than Zachary or Kenzie letting them in. And he would not be letting any client or anyone related to the case into the house. Or any unexpected pizza deliveries, flowers, or utility company employees.

One of the forensic techs approached and stood hovering near Zachary's elbow, waiting for his attention. There wasn't much more Garcia could help with, and he and Kenzie wouldn't be able to settle down and work things out until everyone else was gone, so Zachary turned to him, raising his eyebrows to find out what he wanted.

"You have an outside camera?" the tech asked, jerking a thumb in the direction of the front door.

"Oh… we do!" Zachary agreed. It had been one of his additions to the security system Kenzie already had in place. Not a cheap doorbell camera, but a good external camera with light boosting and good definition. He went to the couch and sat down at his laptop to access the cloud drive where recordings were sent. He narrowed the timeframe to when he had been out of the house and scrubbed the video to find the picture of the person who had approached the house. How had Zachary forgotten the existence of the camera? Here they were focused on fingerprints and DNA, when someone that close to the Godfrey investigation was probably easy to identify on video.

He stopped as a figure in an oversized, shapeless hoodie walked up the sidewalk. Kenzie, Garcia, and the tech crowded around him to watch the screen.

The deliverer of the note was not only wearing a hoodie, but also a baseball cap. He kept his head tucked way down and to the side, so that the baseball cap and hoodie blocked any view of his face from the camera mounted above the door. He tucked the envelope into the mailbox and walked back the way he had come. There was no sign of the vehicle he had driven there in. Off-camera somewhere a few houses down. Maybe even public transit, since all he had to carry was an envelope.

Zachary swore angrily.

"I know you can't see his face," Kenzie said calmly. "But what about the build and the body language? Does it remind you of anyone, even vaguely?"

Zachary closed his eyes, reviewing the various people in the Godfrey family and household.

"No." He backed the video up and watched it again. And again. And again. He would, he knew, probably replay it a hundred or more times in the next few hours looking for any minute thing he had missed. When he got stuck on something… he just kept on it long after he should have given up. Sometimes that persistence bore fruit. Sometimes it just made him feel like he was going crazy.

"What about you?" Garcia asked Kenzie. "Does that look like anyone you know? People at your office will know where you live and that you live with Zachary. And maybe that he requested the file on the Godfrey case."

Kenzie frowned, staring at the screen at their poison-pen writer. "You can hardly tell anything, even whether it is a man or a woman under that sweatshirt. Too loose to guess much about their build. Average height for a man, on the tall side for a woman."

"How about the gait?" Zachary asked, as she had been able to guess correctly in other surveillance videos they had watched.

"Sorry, not sure of this one. The way he walks hunched over and turned away affects everything else."

"Right." Zachary nodded. It was a covert, crablike walk, approaching the house slightly sideways. Maybe someone in the neighborhood had noticed the visitor's suspicious behavior.

"Will you be doing a canvass of the neighbors?" he asked Garcia.

She nodded. "I'm not sure it will give us anything, but we'll see if anyone noticed him, if anyone has doorbell or surveillance cameras that might have caught him. If we're lucky, he might lead us to his vehicle with a license plate on it."

That would be helpful. So it probably wouldn't happen. Zachary wasn't making any bets about the case being cracked so easily.

Especially since they didn't have confirmation yet that there had even been a murder. And the letter with the scriptural reference couldn't be proven to be a threat. It wasn't anything to do with Zachary. But he had no way to prove that it was intended for the Godfrey family, either.

What was the letter-writer's motive? His expectation? He was, Zachary assumed, expecting Zachary to pass the letter on to the Godfrey siblings. To scare them. And then what? Just sit back and enjoy their anxiety and any steps to tighten security?

Or to actually attack and harm one of them or their children?

35

By the time that Kenzie would normally have been home, the police and the techs were gone, and Zachary and Kenzie had the house back to themselves. Zachary sat on the couch in front of his computer, rubbing his temples and forehead. He had a killer headache after all of the drama. He didn't know how much longer he would be able to hold things together and not give in to the knot of anxiety and dread tightening in his stomach.

"You okay?" Kenzie asked.

Zachary nodded without looking at her. His eyes were closed and he didn't want to have to take in any more sensory input than he had to. It was like hiding in the dark under his covers as a scared and overwhelmed child. Shutting out everything he could until it was all over.

"How did you know?" he asked, thinking back to Kenzie's early return home. "Who told you?"

"One of the guys upstairs heard that Garcia got called out to my place. Mostly a bunch of speculation on whether we'd had another break-in. I asked around and got enough information to know that you hadn't been attacked, that it had just been a threatening letter. But you still didn't call me."

"You could have called me," Zachary pointed out. "I would have told you that it wasn't anything to worry about."

"Maybe," Kenzie grunted. He felt her sit down on the couch next to him. "Or maybe you wouldn't have told me the truth. Maybe you would have tried to deflect, even if you had been attacked and hurt."

He would like to be able to say that he wouldn't ever do that, but he knew it would be a lie. Of course he would do his best to shield Kenzie from anything upsetting and had done so in the past. Not by lying, but… he might shade the truth or deflect, as she had suggested.

She laid her hand on the center of his back, a firm, even pressure that she hoped would not startle him while he sat with his eyes closed and head down. Zachary didn't flinch or pull away, and she rubbed his back in slow circles, trying to help him to relax. It was warm and soothing. Zachary sighed and cupped his hands over his eyes.

"Thanks."

"Let me get you something for your head. Then I'll pull together some dinner. You weren't going to eat over at Mario's, were you?"

"Oh…" The knot in Zachary's stomach tightened. He couldn't deal with socializing after everything that had happened. "Is that tonight?"

"It's Friday night, right?"

"Yeah. It's supposed to be pizza and the game. I'll tell him that something has come up and I can't do it tonight. We'll have dinner together."

"No." Kenzie moved up to Zachary's shoulders, kneading them. "You go have your guys' night with Mario. You need some relaxation. It will be good for you to go out and take a break from this."

"I'll be worried about you."

"Why? I've got the burglar alarm, and why would somebody come here? They'll want to stay as far away as possible, in case the police set up surveillance."

"But…" Zachary couldn't think of an argument for that. "I

really don't think I can. I need to see if I can make a break in this case. I have so much to do."

"You're more likely to have a breakthrough if you get away from it and let your subconscious work on it. Obsessing over it isn't healthy."

As if he wouldn't obsess over it if he went to Mario's.

"He won't mind if I reschedule."

"Come on. You and I will spend time together tomorrow. Tonight, I want you out of the house so that *I* can relax and not worry about you."

"You're just saying that," Zachary countered.

"Why?"

"What?"

"Why would I 'just say that'?"

"Because… you don't want me to work on the case tonight. You want me to go out and enjoy myself instead."

"That's exactly what I want you to do. Give yourself a break. It's the best thing for your mental health."

"I don't feel like doing anything with Mario. I don't feel like leaving the house."

"Maybe that's when you need it the most. You won't know until you try it and see what the results are. Mario has been looking forward to it all week; don't disappoint him."

Zachary grumbled into his hands.

"You lived with the guy for months," Kenzie pointed out. "You can relax and be yourself there. You don't have to put on a show. He's seen you when you let down your guard."

At least she hadn't said, "seen you at your worst," as Zachary had thought she was going to. Because he hadn't been his worst at Mario's, not by a long shot. He'd initially been in pretty bad shape, but he'd been climbing out of the hole at that point, not sinking more deeply into the darkness.

But he wasn't at his worst now, either. It was summer. He was in pretty good shape. It had just been a stressful day. And there were worse things than hanging out with a friend and having a couple of slices of pizza together.

"Fine," he mumbled. "What can I make you for supper? If I'm having pizza, you should have something nice."

"No. You go take a pill for your head and have a hot shower. I'll eat whatever I feel like."

"Ice cream isn't dinner," he teased her.

"It might be tonight."

Zachary had to admit that he felt a lot more relaxed when he got out of the hot shower. Since he couldn't stay home and work on the case through the evening, he would have to put those worries aside and pick them up again tomorrow. He called Mario not to cancel, but to confirm that he would be on his way shortly. Mario seemed quite pleased by this. Zachary was glad he hadn't canceled as he'd been inclined to.

"You're sure you'll be okay?" he asked Kenzie.

Even though he knew her answer, he wanted to hear it again. He needed the reassurance. "I'll be just fine. I lived on my own for years before you were around, you know."

"And you'll leave the burglar alarm armed and won't let anyone in."

"Of course."

"Are you sure—"

"I'll be fine, Zachary. Get out of here."

He opened his mouth, and she nudged him playfully toward the door. "Go, or I'll kick you out for good. No more arguing. No more asking if I'll be okay. Out."

He let the momentum carry him out the door. He stepped down onto the sidewalk and turned to wave to her and offer one more goodbye.

"Shoo." Kenzie waved him off. "Go away."

Zachary followed the walkway to the curb where his car was parked. When he looked back at the house, the door was shut and the burglar alarm armed. She would be fine there without him. As she had said, she'd lived for years on her own. He probably brought her more danger by being there than by leaving.

36

Zach, come on in," Mario invited heartily. "I'm glad you made it! Pizza has been ordered, and the game just started. Perfect timing."

"Thanks." Zachary allowed himself to be hustled into the familiar apartment. He had stayed there for several months and was surprised to find that it still had the feeling of home. Rather than feeling foreign and empty because he no longer lived there, he felt warm and comfortable. Like he was in a place where he could let down his guard, as Kenzie had suggested.

It was a bachelor apartment. Not fancy, decorated with too much sports memorabilia. Not dirty or neglected, but not exactly the tidiest either.

He settled into what had been his favorite spot on the couch, settling into the slight hollow and sighed.

Mario took his seat in the easy chair with a good view of the generously-sized TV. "I was afraid that you weren't going to come."

"Well..." Zachary didn't know whether he should say that he had considered not coming. "We made an appointment, and I like to follow through on my promises."

"After what happened today, though...I thought you would want to stay home with Kenzie."

"I did, but she kicked me out," Zachary told Mario with a grin, knowing he would appreciate that.

"Good for her. Probably didn't want you moping around there all night ruining her fun."

"Exactly," Zachary agreed.

He watched the game on the TV without any real interest. His mind echoed back what Mario had said.

"How did you know what happened today?" he asked, straightening up a little and looking at Mario with a frown.

"You know I've always got my ear to the ground. Do you think I wouldn't know that my buddy had been threatened?"

"Well, it wasn't exactly a threat..."

"Wasn't it?" Mario challenged, looking back at Zachary with his eyebrows raised.

"Well, it was a threatening letter, but I wasn't the one being threatened."

"Who, then? Who would threaten Kenzie?"

"Not her either. It was directed toward one of my clients."

Mario shook his head slowly. "Why would someone leave a threat for one of your clients in your mailbox?"

"That's one of the things we're trying to sort out," Zachary sighed. "Along with who it was."

"You don't know? I wouldn't think it would be too hard for the great Zachary Goldman to figure it out."

"Maybe it was you," Zachary teased, "maybe you actually didn't want me to come over tonight and were looking for a way to scare me off."

"Yeah, that was it." Mario sank back into his chair, grinning.

Mario did, after all, know that Zachary was working on the Godfrey case. He was the one who had looked it up for him to see which detective was working on it. And of course he knew that Zachary was living with Kenzie and what her address was. Mario was always tied in to the latest gossip and often knew things way before Zachary heard about them.

"You *did* know what case I was working," Zachary said aloud.

"What?" Mario didn't look away from the TV.

"Which case I was working. You knew that."

"Sure," Mario agreed. He picked up a beer can from the table beside him. "That, uh, millionaire. Goddard."

"Godfrey."

Mario snapped his fingers. "Right."

"You haven't talked to anyone else about it, have you? About me working on that case?"

"No." Mario stared at the TV for a moment, then looked at Zachary. "What's that?"

"You didn't tell anyone else I was working on the Godfrey case? That I was representing the children and they believed that he had been murdered."

"No, why would I?"

"I don't think that you would... but someone knew who shouldn't have. No one who had anything to do with the case knows where I live."

Mario chewed on this for a moment and took another sip of his beer. "Well, someone did."

They didn't talk much more until halftime, when Mario got up to put what remained of the pizza into the fridge and get himself more beer. Without asking, he tossed Zachary a bottle of water. Zachary managed to catch it cleanly and nodded to him. "Thanks."

Mario took a long pull on another bottle of beer, leaning against the doorway between the living room and the kitchen. "So, what did I tell you about El Garcia?" he asked, giving Zachary a knowing nod.

Zachary thankfully didn't blush at this, but just shrugged. "You were right about her being beautiful," he admitted.

"Right? I don't know how that woman ended up in law enforcement instead of on a runway somewhere. Man. Even coming off of a two-day shift without any sleep, she still looks like something that walked out of a dream. But she's no bimbo."

"No," Zachary shook his head emphatically. He would never say anything negative about Garcia's intelligence. She had clearly earned her position as a detective. "She's brilliant. I just wish we could turn this case around and figure out what's happening."

"Is there even a case there? I mean, the medical examiner said that it was a natural death, didn't he?"

Zachary nodded. "Garcia is going back to him on it. More evidence now. He might dig deeper and be able to find something else. The guy was… not well-liked. Not by his family or anyone else. They all had motive to kill him, and now with this threatening letter showing up…"

"But you said it was against his family, so it's obviously not one of them."

"Unless it was a double bluff… a way to make it look like it couldn't be someone from the family."

"You and I both know that most criminals are dumb as hammers. And the killers… they're usually right in front of your face. It isn't like on TV where there is a whole twisted plot and the criminal is a mastermind that the cops would never have suspected."

"It usually is the most likely suspect," Zachary agreed. "Except when it isn't."

Mario laughed and pointed his bottle at Zachary. "Right you are, Zach, my man."

"If Godfrey was poisoned, then whoever did it was careful enough to avoid detection so far."

"And it would have to be someone in the home. Because he died in his sleep, right?"

"Some poisons take a while to act, there is the possibility that he was actually poisoned hours earlier, but I don't think so. I think that he was poisoned that night. Most likely by someone in the household… but they didn't have great security. I think that anyone who was determined could probably get in."

"Without leaving any sign of a break-in?"

That was a good question. They had not found any sign of tool marks indicating that a pry bar had been used on any of the windows or doors, so an outside killer would have had to pick a lock or be let in. Unless a patio door had been left open or something equally as inviting.

"If somebody let them in…" he mused.

"Then you're still looking at someone in the family being involved."

"Yeah. But maybe not directly. Maybe just a door left open for somebody. Or someone had a key." He thought of Logan's girlfriend, just walking into the house. And the rest of the siblings and their spouses or friends—How many people had keys or were used to letting themselves into the house without planning or announcing their intentions?

But did he really think the threats had come from one of the family members?

They knew who he was and that he would suspect someone in the family and, as much as Zachary would like to say that there was no way one of them could have followed him home, he couldn't explain how whoever had dropped off the note had known where he lived. That letter could be explained, if he were to admit that he could have been distracted one day and not noticed a tail.

But what about the original threat? The one that had been penned in the same handwriting on the same paper. They were obviously a matched pair. Why would one of the children have sent their father a letter like that at work? If they had an issue with him, they would have discussed it at home or through other personal communications. Not by a letter to his place of business.

And that first letter had not spoken about an aggrieved child who needed money but had been turned away, or a child who'd been verbally abused and mistreated. It wasn't a letter that spoke of the grievance of the writer, but of a wrong that had been done to someone else. A third party. He wondered how Garcia was coming along in her review of suicides that had taken place in the previous few months.

It had definitely been a good thing for Zachary to get away from the investigation and spend some downtime relaxing with Mario. In the end, he was glad that he had set a date to get together with Mario as he had. It had been too long since they had done anything together, too long since Zachary had done anything social. He needed to remember to take time out of his schedule for things other than work or Kenzie. While he loved to be with her, he probably smothered her by being there all the time. She might like some time on her own too. Or time that she could go out with friends of her own.

She was one to talk to him about working all of the time with the hours she put in at the morgue.

So maybe they were both guilty of putting too much time into work and not enough into recreation or things that could help them relax and recharge.

As Kenzie said, Zachary needed to take a break from his cases now and then to gain perspective and do something more relaxing to maintain his balance and mental health.

After this case was solved.

37

Kenzie was reading a book in bed when Zachary returned home. When she looked up as he walked in the bedroom door, she smiled and lifted her brows.

"How was it?"

"You were right."

She laughed. "Of course I was. Tell me all about how I was right."

"I had a good time there. It was relaxing. It wasn't bad to be there with Mario. I felt… at home there."

She nodded. "Good. I'm glad. You seem a lot more relaxed now."

"Definitely." Zachary looked back toward the living room, but knew that he wouldn't be able to escape to get back to the case tonight. But tomorrow… he was going to tackle it and he was going to move it forward.

"Not tonight," Kenzie warned, reading his face.

Zachary shook his head. "No, not tonight," he agreed. As much as he felt refreshed and like he would be able to make a breakthrough on the case if he looked at it again now, he knew that he had to go to bed and get the sleep he needed. He got little enough as it was. If he stayed up all night, there would be trouble.

"I'm ready for bed, so hurry up and join me," Kenzie prodded.

For once, Zachary did what he was told.

In the morning, he was more than ready to tackle his notes and thoughts on the Godfrey case again. He forced himself to start with his email and task list to ensure he wasn't falling behind on anything important. Heather would help keep him on track and let him know if something was getting too stale or needed an answer right away, and she helped with his billings, which was a godsend, since Zachary was decidedly *not* good at the financial side of things. She also helped with skip tracing and some of the lighter, computer-based PI work, which she loved. After so many years of being "just" a mother and housewife, she had enjoyed breaking into the work world and being able to help Zachary with his business for a small salary. He should probably give her a raise. She was the one keeping his business operating leanly and efficiently.

After doing his duty and making sure he wasn't letting anything too big fall through the cracks, he turned to the problem of who had left the envelope with the threatening note.

He should be able to recognize the person who had dropped it off. It had to be someone he had talked to about the Godfrey case. Putting aside the problem of how they had known his address or managed to follow him in a moment of distraction, only someone he had talked to on the case would know that he'd been retained by the family and what questions he was asking. His questions had prompted the additional threat. Until Zachary was hired to investigate the case, things had been quiet. No one in the family had been threatened. The killer had expected the murder to go undetected and for Godfrey to be cremated, and then he could go on with his life. But then Zachary had shown up on the scene, requiring an additional threat to be made.

Why?

Was the family supposed to fire Zachary? Was that why the note had been left in his mailbox? Were they supposed to take steps to protect themselves? Did the killer want them to live in constant fear? Was he sitting back somewhere he could watch what was going on, enjoying it?

If he really wanted to take revenge on the second and third generations of Godfreys, why announce it? No one was expecting anything. He could have worked in the dark, for at least a while. Until enough of the Godfreys had died that they knew something was going on. Maybe that would just take one death, and maybe it would take more but, until the letter-writer dropped off the note, no one had been on guard.

He wondered whether Karen had kept her kids home from school. And how could she keep them home from school and safe while she still worked to earn an income as a nurse? She needed the money from the estate, and then she could stay home and still be secure.

He watched the video again, thinking through every person he had talked to about the case, looking for familiar features, attitude, or body language, but he kept coming up dry.

Zachary wasn't sure how much time had passed before Kenzie got up and headed straight for the shower. He looked at the clock and saw that she was running quite late. Should he have woken her up earlier to make sure she had time to get to work?

It wasn't until she had been in the shower for forty-five minutes that he realized it was Saturday, and that was why she wasn't in a rush to get to the morgue. While she often worked on a Saturday to get caught up on some of the backlog, she didn't need to be there at a certain time. The office was closed and she could be there whenever and for however long she felt the need.

The late start meant that she didn't have much to get caught up on, or she still would have gone in fairly early. Zachary enjoyed a nice, relaxed Saturday when they were only apart for a few hours. And tomorrow was Sunday; they had planned a trip to see Lorne Peterson, his old foster father, and Lorne's partner, Pat Parker. Zachary's chosen family. The men had been there for him through thick and thin and were always happy to see him, no matter what shape he was in.

He went back to watching the video of the letter delivery until Kenzie pulled him out of it.

"Hey!" She bent down to kiss his head. "Get off the computer and have coffee with me before I go in."

"Sure, I'll just be a min—"

Kenzie firmly pressed the lid of the laptop shut, so Zachary had no choice but to stop watching the video and transfer his attention to her.

"You're stuck," she told him.

Zachary stretched his sore muscles and stood up. He knew he had been watching it for too long, but that was how he worked. Sometimes it seemed like a case would never get cracked, and then something simple like the number of pictures on the wall suddenly brought him the fresh insight needed.

"I'm going to find something on that video."

"Your eyes are as red as tomatoes. Have you blinked once in the last three hours?"

"I just need to rest them for a few minutes."

"You need to put in eye drops, and then use an ice mask for an hour. If you don't, they'll be so swollen and sore you won't even be able to open them tomorrow."

Zachary grumbled, but she was usually right about things like that. He did spend too much time staring at his computer screen. And he knew it wasn't good for his eyes, would give him a headache, and wasn't good for his mental outlook.

"You should get outside, too," Kenzie advised, echoing what Zachary had just been thinking. A walk and some fresh air in the afternoon would help him to reset.

"Yeah. I will."

"And eye drops and ice?"

"I'll go put eye drops in right now."

While he hated the cold compress, he knew that he would end up compromising and putting it on. For a shorter length of time. Not an hour, but maybe ten minutes. Just enough to constrict the blood vessels and bring down the swelling and burning.

They both sat down with coffee and Kenzie had her usual slice of toast. Zachary opened the cupboard that held his snacks and selected a granola bar. He stayed turned away from Kenzie and tried to tear the wrapper open and remove it as quickly as possible with the least amount of crinkling. Since his med change, the sound drove him nuts, like fingernails on a blackboard. But he refused to use a pair of scissors or let Kenzie open it for him while he was out of the room. He would not give in to the horrible, teeth-grinding feeling, sure that if he just pushed through it, he would eventually become accustomed to the sound again and the pain he experienced upon hearing it would go away. Avoiding it would just allow it to continue. Or to grow.

It was getting better. He could almost open it without visibly grimacing now.

He tossed the wrapper into the garbage, took out a plate to catch the crumbs, and sat at the table to eat.

Kenzie did not comment on this ritual. She had challenged him on it several times, insisting that if his meds were causing the misophonia, he should get his prescriptions switched again, but he wasn't about to try. Med changes were a big deal, often resulting in unexpected side effects. As irritating as it was, the sound sensitivity was relatively minor compared to others he had experienced. Better than insomnia, increased suicidal thoughts, or constant nausea. If he had to pick a side effect, misophonia was something he could live with.

"You *will* put ice on your eyes?" Kenzie asked.

"Yes. Later, after you go."

"If you put it off and forget about it, you're going to regret it."

Zachary nodded. "And a walk. I will."

"Good. I don't think you're going to get anything else out of that video, other than a headache."

And she didn't have any idea of the number of times he'd already watched it.

"I'll do something else when I get back. Call Karen Godfrey and see how they are all doing today."

"That poor family, I can't imagine what they must be going through right now, wondering about whether they are in danger and about their children." Kenzie shook her head. "Why would anyone think it was okay to take vengeance on the children and grandchildren of the person who wronged them?"

Zachary shook his head. "I guess if you think it's okay to take revenge on people instead of involving law enforcement or letting natural consequences follow, then you're already putting yourself above society's usual rules of engagement."

"I suppose so."

"I don't know how anyone could threaten children either," Zachary admitted. "But people do. People do all kinds of things to hurt children or the people who love them. I never could understand it."

Kenzie gave him the soppy smile she always did when he started talking about taking care of his younger brothers and sister.

38

It was the summer, so Zachary couldn't argue that it was too cold to take Kenzie's shiny red convertible to the Petersons. In fact, since they used his car for the trip all winter, she would argue they should use hers all of the summer.

And using Kenzie's car meant she was driving, because no one else was allowed to drive her baby. Zachary loved the peace and calm he always felt driving on the highway. He wouldn't want to miss out on that all summer. He had to let her trade off every other trip if he wanted to be able to drive to the Petersons in the summer at all.

"Let's go," Kenzie encouraged, as Zachary looked over the laptop case he had packed to take with him. They weren't staying overnight, so he would only be using his laptop in the car during the drive. He could even manage with just his phone.

"I just feel like I'm missing something…"

Kenzie sighed. She looked around while she waited for him. "Keys, wallet, phone, power cables, photography…"

"Oh, I had some photos." Zachary went to the home office and thumbed through a series of file folders, looking for a couple of pictures he'd wanted to give to Mr. Peterson. Photography might seem like a very tenuous thing to base a relationship on, but it was what had held them together all of those years as Zachary was passed from one foster home or facility to another. And in the decades since. At some point, it stopped being about photography, but photography was still something that they shared and held on to.

He eventually made it out to the car, where Kenzie impatiently revved the engine, waiting for him to settle in and close the door. Once he pulled it shut, she backed out of the garage.

Zachary ended up not even opening his laptop. He just sat back and watched the highway ahead and let the wind blow by them.

The flower borders at the Peterson house, planted and nurtured faithfully by Pat, were a riot of color. The house rivaled any other in the small town with its clean, freshly painted trim and landscaping. Zachary remembered the brown, cluttered yard that had been outside of the Peterson house he had moved into when he was ten, just released from Bonnie Brown, a care facility that had been like a prison for unwanted kids. At that time, Mr. Peterson had not been with Pat yet, but with his former wife, and life there had been very different.

They had tried. That hadn't been the issue. Mrs. Peterson attempted to keep everything in the house and their foster children's lives in calm, orderly paths. Mr. Peterson had been a warm light in their lives, showing his kindness and caring at every opportunity. The outside of the house and yard had been his responsibility, though, and had been sadly neglected, maybe a reflection of his relationship with Mrs. Peterson, a partner who did not suit him. Zachary's problems had been too much for them to handle, and he had not been there long.

Mr. Peterson opened the door as Zachary and Kenzie walked up the sidewalk. Smiles wreathed his round face and he pulled Zachary into a tight hug. "How was the drive? Isn't it a beautiful day?"

"It's gorgeous, Lorne," Kenzie agreed, waiting until after Zachary had been released to claim her own hug. "I love these summer days. And driving with the top down…" She tried to pat down her wild, curly, windblown hair, "It's just so perfect."

"Well, you two both work so hard; you need the break. I'm glad you could make the time. Come in, now, come in. Pat has fired up the grill, but we have cold soup to start." He rolled his eyes. "I still can't get used to the idea of serving soup cold. But it's strawberry, and it's very nice. I try to think of it as 'smoothie in a bowl' instead."

He ushered them directly to the table that had been set for their arrival, and Mr. Peterson pulled the bowl of strawberry soup from the fridge and put it in the middle of the table.

"They're here," he called out through the screen door. "I'm putting out the soup!"

In a minute, Pat was there, his broad chest covered with a BBQ apron that said: "Kiss the Cook." He grinned at both of them. "Well, it took you long enough."

"We're not late—" Zachary started to protest.

"I just put the steaks on the grill," Pat assured him with a laugh. "You're right on time."

They started with the cold strawberry soup, then a spinach salad that Zachary did the best he could with, but he wasn't a big fan of greens, and he took the smallest serving he deemed polite. By the time they were finished eating these appetizers, Pat had returned with a platter of grilled steaks that were cooked to perfection. They both admired the presentation before digging in.

"So, tell me about your current cases," Mr. Peterson suggested. "You said you were busy, so you must have something bigger on the go right now."

Zachary nodded. "A wealthy man who died, and his children hired me to find out which one of them killed him."

"Which one of them?"

Zachary nodded. "They don't believe it was a natural death, and figured he must have been poisoned. They all have motive, but don't know which one of them it was that killed him. Unless they're all gaslighting me and already know who the perpetrator is."

"That must be a very unusual case to work on."

"It has been," Zachary agreed.

"And do you favor one of them over the others?"

"Well, things have progressed, and it looks as if it might *not* have been one of them, but another party. An outside one."

"You're kidding."

"No. Threatening letters have been received, and it doesn't look like they came from one of the children. In fact, the letters threaten not only them, but their own children as well."

Mr. Peterson's eyes widened in alarm. "I hope the police are taking this seriously!"

"Oh, the police," Kenzie snorted. "Yes, the police have a great interest in the case *now*."

"Well, that's good. Isn't it?" Pat looked at Kenzie, his brows drawn down. "If they weren't taking it seriously and those children were in danger, that could be a tragedy…"

"Of course," Kenzie agreed. "They have to take an interest in the safety of their citizens. It is just their interest in *certain* citizens that bothers me."

Mr. Peterson and Pat both followed Kenzie's gaze to Zachary. They looked curious, but neither asked what Kenzie meant. Zachary's face warmed. "There is nothing inappropriate going on. Detective Garcia hasn't shown me any more interest than anyone else. We've just been working the case together."

Kenzie put down her knife and fork. Which Zachary appreciated, because maybe it wasn't the best idea for her to have a steak knife in her hand while she was getting aggravated about Detective Garcia all over again.

"And does that go both ways? You haven't had any more interest in her than in any other law enforcement officer either?"

"No," Zachary agreed. "I haven't. I don't. She's a cop. When I get the opportunity to interface with the police on a case, I take it. Most times, it is hard to get them to pay attention to anything a private investigator has to say. So I'll take what I can get."

She looked at him and didn't remind him again that he had spent the day with Garcia Thursday and forgotten his promise to take Kenzie out to lunch. He had thought Kenzie had forgiven him. Maybe she was testing the waters and trying to decide whether Lorne and Pat would be on Zachary's side or hers. They were Zachary's family, after all.

There was a period of silence. Everyone looked down at their plates and ate without making eye contact.

"I have a blackberry pie for dessert," Pat offered, "so don't stuff yourselves! No need to be part of the clean plate club here."

Pat was used to Zachary's small portion sizes. Meds that suppressed his appetite or made him nauseated kept him thin and meant that he didn't eat much at a time. Or even remember to eat every meal. It had been better since the last med change. Even so, he wouldn't have room for pie if he finished his steak. And like a kid, he preferred the sweet berry pie. He took another bite of his steak, then pushed the plate away from him slightly and laid down his fork. Pat chuckled.

"Now what would you do if it was a choice between garlic bread and pie?"

Garlic bread was one of Zachary's favorite treats. Even when he wasn't hungry, he could wolf down half a loaf in a sitting. "That would be a hard decision. Couldn't I have the garlic bread for dinner and the pie for dessert?"

Pat laughed. "Of course you could!"

39

"So, what's going on between you and Kenzie?" Lorne asked as he and Zachary sorted through a stack of photos. "Is there a problem?"

"I don't know. I don't think so. I mean, I think it will go away once she cools down a bit. She thinks something is going on between me and Detective Garcia, but there isn't. Nothing at all. I'm just working with her on the case."

"Kenzie's reaction seems extreme, if that is the case."

"I missed a date with her. Because I was working with Detective Garcia and got wrapped up in what I was doing. So… she thinks I chose to spend time with Garcia over her."

"Ah." Mr. Peterson nodded. "And I assume that Detective Garcia is good looking?"

Zachary sighed. "Very."

"Yes. That could present a problem."

"And I thought we were through it, that she wasn't worrying about it anymore. But then when this letter came to the house… and Garcia showed up for the investigation… then Kenzie came home early from work to find Garcia there at the house."

"Ouch."

"Just handling the investigation. There were all kinds of techs and other law enforcement around. It wasn't just her and me sitting on the couch or something like that." Zachary's throat heated up when he mentioned sitting alone on the couch, remembering meeting with Garcia at the mansion to go through the papers, sitting close to her so that her perfume tickled his nose.

"But still. Garcia was in Kenzie's territory," Mr. Peterson pointed out, "And you hadn't warned her beforehand that Garcia was there?"

Zachary shook his head helplessly. "No. Why would I?"

"Because, like it or not, Kenzie sees her as a rival. And you can't invite her rival into her house without her being there and not expect her to react."

"They aren't rivals. I don't have any interest in Detective Garcia."

"That's good. And it's fine to say it, but you have to show it too. And you have to keep showing it until you're way past it."

Zachary opened his mouth to object that they were already past it, that it was Kenzie who kept bringing it up again.

"*Way* past it," Lorne repeated. "Right now, you're talking about something that isn't even a week old. Of course it is still a sore spot. Sometimes stuff like that can fester for years."

"Years?" Zachary's stomach clenched at the thought of being punished for years for something he hadn't even done wrong.

"I'm sure it won't be that long for you and Kenzie. You're taking couple's therapy. You're actively working on the relationship, and you can talk about it with your therapist. Most people try to avoid the issue and never talk about it. So it is never resolved in any way."

"But I didn't do anything. All I'm doing is pursuing a case."

"I didn't say you'd done anything wrong. But you need to understand where Kenzie is coming from. Forget about what you did and think about how she is feeling."

Zachary frowned. He was used to Dr. B asking him to put himself in Kenzie's shoes, so it wasn't an unfamiliar exercise. He had told Kenzie he didn't feel jealous about her being away working at the morgue all day with Dr. Wiltshire and the other men working there. But how would he feel if he knew that a hot new morgue attendant had started working there? That she was alone with him, working closely together, every day? And what if he came home to find the man there, even if he had only stopped by for something legitimate, like dropping off a report or picking up some papers that Dr. Wiltshire needed from Kenzie right away? How would he feel about having his home invaded by a very attractive young man he suspected of being interested in Kenzie?

His heart pounded at the thought and, even though he knew that he had only invented the scenario himself, he still felt his anger and anxiety rising at the thought. It was ridiculous and would never happen, but he had to admit that, put into the same position, he probably would have reacted more aggressively than Kenzie.

He ran a hand over his face, closing his eyes for a moment and trying to compose himself. "In her place… I guess I would feel jealous and betrayed."

Mr. Peterson nodded. "Even if nothing was going on. Even if she didn't flirt or give any sign she even noticed your rival. As sophisticated and advanced as we think we are, we are still primitive creatures. We react in an instinctive, territorial way."

Zachary paged through a few photos, snapping them down on the desk as he looked at each one.

"You and Pat don't seem to have any problems. You have other friendships. There don't ever seem to be any tensions."

Mr. Peterson chuckled. "You only see the outward, idealized life. You are an experienced enough detective to know that what happens behind closed doors can be a very different picture." He held up his hand to forestall any questions or comments. "Pat and I are just fine. You don't need to worry that things are falling apart. But yes, there are occasional twinges of jealousy or times when I don't want him to go out somewhere, but just to stay home with me. And times when I want to go out to an event that he isn't interested in, and I have to either push him to come with me or go by myself or with other people. Neither one is ideal. But that's just the way things are in relationships. You dance, you compromise, you try to let the other person know that they are all-important to you."

"She is. Kenzie is, I mean. I don't feel any temptation to sneak off somewhere with Detective Garcia."

"Don't forget that Kenzie has had to deal with Bridget too."

Zachary did not like to be reminded. Even with how loyal and committed he was to Kenzie, the thought of Bridget could still send his heart skipping. If she called him for help, he would still go. He would never get back together, even if she were free and single, but the fantasy was still there. The memories of their life together. The good times, the excitement, the thrills of getting together with such a beautiful, sophisticated woman. The love and longing, even when he was with her, to be one unit instead of two separate people. To have children and raise a family and grow old together.

No matter how often he told himself that the relationship was old and defunct and that he didn't care anymore, it was a lie. He still wanted to watch her, be close to her, and know what she was doing all the time. The old obsession was still there. He kept it at bay with medication, regular therapy, and the strategies Dr. B gave him. But he was afraid that it would never really be gone. And he was afraid that one day it *would* be gone, and part of him would be lost forever.

Kenzie had handled the Bridget situation well. Amused at first at Bridget's moods and rages, then irritated and impatient. Angry when Zachary talked about her or had contact with her, yet remarkably understanding when Gordon had hired him to investigate the parentage of Bridget's twins and he had ended up falling down that rabbit hole again.

"This is nothing like Bridget," he told Mr. Peterson.

"And maybe that's why she feels freer to confront you about it. We're not talking about a relationship that existed long before she ended the picture and the fact that she can't change what happened in your past. This is a current, late-breaking situation. This is her future with you."

Zachary sighed and nodded. "So what do I do? I already told her that nothing is going on between Detective Garcia and I."

"You keep letting her know that you're not interested in this other woman. And that your relationship with Kenzie is important. Take the time to make it important. Be home when Kenzie gets home. Don't spend your evenings investigating this case or talking to Detective Garcia. But do keep Kenzie updated on whether you are meeting or talking to Garcia. Don't hide it."

Zachary scratched the back of his head, nodding.

40

They said their goodbyes to Mr. Peterson and Pat and headed home so they could get to bed in good time. Kenzie needed her sleep to be alert for work the next day. She always said that Zachary needed his sleep too, but he had functioned on so little sleep for so long that he wasn't sure it was true. Certainly, there had been a couple of times when he had been so sleep-deprived that the situation became critical, but that didn't happen very often.

Zachary watched the road, hoping that it would calm his brain. Not as much as if he were driving himself, maybe, but to at least calm him a little.

They had been driving for a while when Kenzie spoke up. "I'm sorry about bringing my issues up in front of your family," she said with a sigh. "That was completely inappropriate, and I'm embarrassed I behaved that way."

Zachary turned his gaze to her, surprised. "You didn't do anything wrong." It was true, he had been embarrassed by Kenzie bringing her jealousy up in front of Mr. Peterson and Pat. But she hadn't made a scene like Bridget would have. And Pat and Lorne had seen some doozies from Bridget.

"I should have saved it to discuss with you privately. Or

rather… we had already talked about it privately and I shouldn't have ambushed you in front of them. I think we should talk it out during our next couple's session."

He hated to bring it up in front of Dr. B when, as he'd told Mr. Peterson, Zachary hadn't done anything wrong. And Kenzie hadn't either. She was just following her heart. They could get past this little bump in the road themselves.

"If you like," he agreed neutrally.

Something in his voice or manner gave him away, because she looked aside at him, frowning. "Why wouldn't we go to her with something that is stressing our relationship? Isn't that the whole point of the therapy?"

"I just… didn't think it was that much of a problem."

She was silent, staring straight ahead as she drove. A wave of frustration washed over him as he realized he had once again said the wrong thing. Zachary thought back to the scenario he had pictured when Mr. Peterson had said to put himself in Kenzie's place. What if she brushed off his feelings of jealousy as meaningless or insignificant? That would just make him angrier and more suspicious that she was interested in her handsome coworker.

"That came out the wrong way. I didn't mean… that your feelings don't count or it wasn't important. I just mean… I felt like we had already discussed it and put it to bed."

"Well, I think it is pretty obvious that we have not."

It was evident that she had not, anyway.

"Okay. Will you remember to bring it up when we're at Dr. B's next?"

"I don't think I'm going to forget it."

Zachary nodded. He sighed and watched out the window. He could get his laptop out and do some work. If he buried himself in work, then Kenzie would know not to interrupt him with any talk. But he was trying to spend time with Kenzie and not do work on Sundays. It was the one day that they set aside for each other.

His mind wandered to Karen Camden. She hadn't told him much of the situation between her and her husband, but he gathered that she was not very happy and was just waiting until she was wealthy enough to escape from the marriage. Not a great situation to be in. But then, no one in the family had been in a particularly happy relationship, from what he had seen. Maybe Logan. He'd been holding hands with his girlfriend and had seemed like he was pretty comfortable with her. She came and went from the house without any apparent worry about whether she would find him there with another girl.

Eddie had a trail of youthful conquests, and gave no indication of whether he was seeing anyone now. Zachary doubted it. He got the feeling Eddie spent nearly all of his time at the office. Maintaining a serious relationship while working those hours or being that wrapped up in his job would be pretty hard. Alex hadn't mentioned a wife or children. He too was working too hard, trying to make partner as his father wanted him to. He might have a girlfriend in the wings somewhere, some arm candy that he took to firm events or a purely physical relationship that he didn't have to put any time or emotional effort into. Or maybe he had no girlfriend, just the occasional hookup when he clocked out of work for a few hours. If he didn't fall asleep the moment he relaxed.

And their relationships with each other were no better. Mr. Peterson had talked about the time and effort needed to put into a relationship. He wasn't just talking about Zachary's relationship with Kenzie, but other types of relationships too. The way that he and Zachary had stayed in touch over the years despite being in very different places in their lives and separated by circumstances that made it very challenging to keep in touch. After separating from his wife, Mr. Peterson had not lived in a very good part of town, making it dangerous for teenage Zachary to go over there on his own. And the case worker that he'd had for his last few years in foster care had been convinced that allowing a teen boy to visit a gay man was just asking for trouble.

Zachary liked to think that if he had grown up knowing where his siblings were, they would have kept in touch and been very close. They were close now after being reunited. Or at least, he and Tyrrell and Heather were. Even with how close he thought they were, he had still been shocked to discover the multitude of secrets Tyrrell had kept from him.

He suspected that the only time John Godfrey's children had ever gotten together was for those family dinners. And now that he was gone, would they keep going on? Or would they drift apart without him to pull them back together?

What secrets were each of them keeping?

41

Detective Garcia called Zachary Monday afternoon. It was a low-energy point in Zachary's day, and he was happy to take her call and just sit back and close his eyes while he talked to her. He had been studiously avoiding watching the video of the envelope being delivered to the house. However, he had given in to the compulsion to make sure that nothing new was in the mailbox several times.

He wasn't as anxious as he would have been if Kenzie were home and he'd felt the need to protect her from the writer of the threatening letters, but he was still jumpy and dreading the possibility that the killer might return with an additional warning or proof that he'd done something else violent. He was haunted by visions of shows and movies he had seen where children had been snatched away and the vicious kidnapper had sent a body part to the parents as a warning of the lengths they were willing to go to. He did not want to find any more surprise packages in the mailbox.

"I was wondering whether you have talked to any of the Godfrey siblings since we informed them of the letter?" Garcia asked after exchanging a few of the expected pleasantries.

She didn't say what she was hoping to hear from him. It was an open-ended question, and Zachary wasn't sure how much to say.

"I've talked to each of them on the phone," he said. "But I haven't gone to the house since I discovered the letter."

And he didn't want to, worried about leading anyone back to Kenzie's house, even though that was ridiculous. The killer already knew where he lived. Was he afraid there were *more* killers in the wings? Was he afraid that one of the Godfrey children would find out where he lived and come after him? If they didn't want him working the case anymore, they could fire him.

Though he *had* been known to stick to a case even after he'd been fired. Sometimes, he just needed to know the truth that much.

"How are they taking the news that there have been threats made against them?"

"Better than you would think. I guess they think that it was just words. Nothing serious. It's easier to believe that someone is just blowing off steam and there isn't really a danger."

He could see Garcia in his mind's eye, nodding sagely at this. "People prefer to live in their own comfortable little worlds."

"Karen said that she would keep her kids home from school, but I doubt if she'll do that for more than a day or two. It isn't a long-term solution. The others just shrugged it off and said they would go about their daily lives like usual, but would keep an eye open for anything suspicious. I don't understand how they can be so relaxed about it when they think that their father was killed. Do they think the threat against the next generations is just a joke? Hot air?"

"Pretty much the same responses I got from them. I was hoping that they would have more to say to you about it. I don't know. As a cop, I'm trained to take action. I don't just sit around on my laurels if I think there is a threat or there is something I can do about the situation I am in. But a lot of people seem to have a block… they get overwhelmed and shut down. And there is a problem with wealthy families who think… that everything should be done for them. If there was a real danger, we would provide them with police protection."

"And you won't?" Zachary laughed. He already knew that the police department didn't have the resources that the cops on TV always seemed to have available. Twenty-four-hour surveillance, several teams of cops to guard the family inside and outside the home. Safe houses, federal marshals or FBI agents. There was always plenty of manpower to go around. "Why don't they just hire private security?"

"They seem to have inherited their father's opinion that the home doesn't need to be guarded that closely. It's safe because it is isolated. It isn't listed, so only their friends will know where they live."

Zachary was aware of the gentle tease. He, too, had thought that people would not be able to find him.

"But they know that the killer has already been to the house. *Into* the house. So that doesn't exactly follow."

"People are not always logical. In fact, they rarely are. We adapt to our environment by trial and error, not because we know intellectually what the right behavior is."

Zachary grunted his acknowledgment. He wanted to believe that people were innately logical and would make the best choice, but experience had taught him otherwise. Not just his experiences in dealing with other people, but also watching himself make a choice that he had just told himself didn't make sense or was dangerous. Following a compulsion, knowing it was the wrong thing to do.

"Well, I have evidence," Garcia announced briskly.

"Evidence? What did you find?"

He didn't believe that Garcia would share anything she knew about the case with him. He was a civilian, and she had already said several times that she did not work with private investigators.

"There was DNA on the letter in your mailbox."

"Recoverable?" Zachary was blown away. There hadn't been any visible spots from tears, a greasy palm, or any other fluids likely to be on the letter. He knew sometimes the police could recover DNA from fingerprints, but it still seemed like a future technology, not something that a small Vermont police force was likely to have for another forty years.

"Yes. Enough to sequence. And I told you that we are on a pilot program that allows us to use rapid-processing technology and matching."

"Against the Vermont DNA database?" Zachary didn't think that Garcia could possibly have turned around a request already.

"As it turns out… against the other DNA we have collected on the case."

"What other DNA?"

"The DNA of various people who might have touched items in the house."

"The family?" Zachary was finding it suddenly difficult to breathe.

"We have the family, the staff, you…"

Zachary's exhilaration deflated. "You found my DNA on the letter? I already told you I opened it without gloves. That was supposed to be an elimination sample."

"I didn't say that we matched it against you. I'm just mentioning what DNA samples we've collected on the case so far."

"It wasn't mine?"

"No."

Zachary's brain kicked into high gear, and he tried to figure out which member of the family or staff it could be. Was somebody working at the family home a danger to all of those who came there? If so, why was Garcia chatting on the phone with Zachary rather than hurrying over there to make an arrest?

"I should say," Garcia went on, "that it was a half match."

"A half match? What does that mean? To who?"

"To Logan Godfrey."

"Logan!" Zachary immediately tried to figure out how Logan might have been involved in his father's death. He could certainly have administered the poison. He had been there. But why would he send a threatening letter? And how did he know where to send it? Zachary's address was not on any of the documents that he had signed with the family. They only included his post office box number. "I don't understand. You think he's the killer? And what does a half match mean? That you don't have enough points of comparison?" There must not have been enough DNA. It had not been a high enough quality sample to get a full match to Logan.

"No, not to him. To a relative."

If the killer was a relative of Logan's, then he must be a relative of all of the other siblings too, but Garcia had not said so. Could it be a child of Logan's? Someone who carried half of his DNA? "But Logan was too young to have a child old enough to write or plot to kill someone." Zachary's mind tried to make sense of it.

"Not his child," Garcia agreed.

"But how could someone be related to Logan and not his siblings? Oh—" Zachary got it suddenly. "He was adopted. Maybe he wasn't even told that he was."

But why would the couple adopt a child so late in life? Karen and Logan had made it clear to Zachary that Logan had been an "oops" baby.

Maybe that, too, was a lie. A child adopted later in life might be a grandchild rather than a child. Maybe Logan was Alex's child. Or another of Eddie's. Even Karen's, if she had gotten pregnant very young, maybe as the result of a sexual assault. But if Logan were the child of one of his supposed siblings, then the killer's DNA would not only have matched Logan's, but his biological parent's as well.

"We're still working everything out," Garcia told Zachary, taking pity on him and helping him to understand what the testing had shown. "But Logan is only a half-sibling to the others. They share a mother, but not a father."

"Their mother had an affair?"

"Apparently so."

"And the killer is not related to *her*, or he would show up as related to all of them."

"Bingo," Garcia said. "Got it in one. That was pretty quick."

Zachary's brain was still whirling as he tried to follow through with all of the implications of this information. "So the note was written by someone related to Logan through his biological father. A man Mrs. Godfrey had an affair with."

"Or a sperm donor," Garcia said. "If she wanted another baby and he was shooting blanks, then it might be as simple as that. Unfortunately, she is not around to ask."

"And the letter writer is… can you tell what the relationship was to the father? Or to Logan? How close of a familial relationship is it?"

"From what the experts tell me—and I guess I'd better believe them—the writer and potential killer is Logan Godfrey's half-brother."

42

When Garcia informed Zachary that she was going back to the Godfrey mansion to interview Logan again, she didn't word it as an invitation, but Zachary took it as one. He wasn't staying home while she figured everything out without him.

"I'll be right behind you," he told her, immediately jumping to his feet. She could get out there with lights and sirens much faster than he could without, and she could be halfway finished the interview before he even got there.

He didn't stay on the line to hear Garcia protest that she hadn't invited him and he'd better stay home and wait for the news to break on the local media. *Millionaire's son arrested.* Only that wouldn't be the headline, because not only was the killer not John Godfrey's son, but Logan wasn't either. Had Logan and the others known it all along? Had they just been stringing him along, figuring he would never find out the truth? Without a little bit of DNA left on that paper, they would still be in the woods, with no idea as to the identity of the killer.

Zachary might have had his foot on the gas all the way out to the mansion, even blowing through a couple of intersections where the lights were not quite as green as they should have been. When he got there, he found that Garcia had not, in fact, used her lights and siren to get there and he had beaten her there.

He decided he'd better wait in his car. If he went blasting in there and started interrogating Logan about his parentage and long-lost half-sibling before Garcia got there, she would string him up and have him for dinner.

He was impatient, so it seemed like it took her hours rather than minutes. Zachary rubbed his brow line, trying to relax his facial muscles. He wasn't sure how much sleep he'd gotten the night before, but it was even less than usual. If Kenzie had known that, she would have had something to say about it.

There was a rap on his window, and Zachary's eyes flew open. He looked at the knocker, expecting it to be Logan, the one who had accosted him the first time he had shown up at the house without an invitation. Or maybe they had hired a security guard after all. To keep the house safe, if not its residents.

But it wasn't; it was Garcia. Zachary rolled down his window to talk to her.

"Don't tell me you've already been inside and gotten yourself kicked out with your intrusive questions," Garcia said, her face and voice somewhere between serious and sarcastic.

"No. I thought you would be here ahead of me, so I was hurrying. But when you weren't here, I thought I'd better wait to make sure I didn't get in trouble."

"Well, after some of the things I've heard of you doing on other cases, I'm surprised to hear that, but that was a good choice. Thank you for waiting. I just hope he didn't see you sitting here and bolt."

"Why would he? We know it isn't Logan."

"But we don't know who the killer is and if he is here or not. He could be on the staff."

Zachary mentally reviewed the various men he had seen working there. A butler, a gardener, a couple of others who were in and out from time to time. None of them had seemed suspicious to him when he or Garcia had talked to them. None of them seemed particularly close to Logan in age or looks, but he supposed they didn't have to. There were plenty of brothers who were thirty years apart in age or who looked nothing alike. He remembered how different he had thought all of the Godfrey siblings were. Did they all have the same father and Logan was the odd man out? Or did they all have different fathers? Maybe John Godfrey hadn't fathered any of them. Perhaps that explained his indifference toward meeting their needs.

Garcia gave a brisk nod. "Let's go."

She wasn't going to make him sit in the car while she conducted the interview, as Zachary had half-expected her to. He knew that he didn't have any standing to be there. If he was allowed to listen to the interview, he was lucky. More than lucky.

He scrambled out of the car to go with her into the house.

The butler answered the door this time. Zachary stood behind Garcia while she negotiated her way in, asking where Logan was and insisting that she had to talk to him. Eventually, they were escorted into the study to wait for Logan to put in an appearance. Zachary studied the spines of the books that lined the wall, the big globe that could spin on three different axes, the bottles of alcohol lined up on the sideboard. This was where they had all gathered the evening before John Godfrey died. Godfrey and his four children. Or three children and one impostor. But how many of them had known that?

Eventually, Logan put in an appearance. He wore white tennis shoes as if they had interrupted a tennis game. Maybe they had. He made a beeline for the drinks counter and poured himself one immediately. He looked at the police detective and obviously knew that she wouldn't drink on the job. He pointed at Zachary. "What can I get you?"

"Nothing for me, thanks." Zachary shook his head. "I'm good."

"If you've come here to interrogate and arrest me, the least you can do is have a drink with me first."

"I don't think anyone is arresting you right now. Certainly not me."

"Have a drink with me."

"I don't drink," Zachary reminded him. "It interferes with my meds."

He wasn't supposed to drink alcohol with some of them, but he hadn't taken anything that would preclude it. But after looking at the bottles lined up on that counter, he had already decided that drinking with someone who might have been involved in or the target of a poisoning was not the best idea.

"You had a Coke last time. I'll get you another."

Zachary forced a smile. "I'm not thirsty right now. Just barely finished a coffee. You go ahead."

Logan tossed down his first drink and poured another. He settled into one of the soft leather chairs, stretching out his lean form and holding the glass in a relaxed posture. "So, why are you here again? I thought you got everything you needed the last time?"

43

Some more facts have come to light that we wanted to talk to you about," Garcia informed him.

"You want to talk to all of us, or just to me?"

Garcia didn't answer immediately. The silence stretched out as she considered her answer. "I would like to talk to you first. What I do after that depends on the outcome of our discussion."

"I don't know what you could be here to ask about." Logan shook his head. "You have been pretty thorough. I don't know anything I haven't told you."

"No?"

Logan waited for Garcia to say something more, then shifted uncomfortably. "No, I don't know what this is all about. Is it more about the letter that Zachary got? I don't think there's anything to it. Why would anyone want to come after us? Or Karen's kids? It's just some nut job trying to get a rise out of you, and I guess they succeeded."

"If you believe that your father was poisoned, then you must have some idea how," Zachary pointed out. "And if you believe that he was poisoned at dinner, then you believe that there was someone inside the house who wanted to kill him."

"Well, yes. I guess that's the theory."

"If someone killed your father, what makes you think they would stop there? Why don't you believe they could come back again for a second time? The person who killed him could still be in the house or have easy access to it. You already know the security here is no good. That doesn't bother you?"

Logan shook his head. "What reason would anyone have to kill me or any of my siblings? If someone really did poison Dad, what does that have to do with me? If it was one of the others—Alex or Eddie or Karen—then how do they get what they want from killing me? Or Karen's kids? That's ridiculous."

Garcia, standing near Logan's chair, leaned toward him. "If you were to die, then where would your portion of the estate go?"

"I don't know. I don't have a will. I guess to the others."

Garcia nodded. "If you don't have a will, then your estate would go first to your parents and then to your siblings. And if you die within thirty days of your father, then the portion of his estate that was to go to you will go to whoever he specifies. According to the copy of the will that Karen gave to me, that would be to the rest of the siblings. So either way, if you die, your siblings will get a bigger piece of the pie."

"Yes, but…" Logan shrugged. "Does it make that much of a difference? Either way, they get enough money to set them up for life. And if Alex kills off Eddie, Karen, and me, it will look a little suspicious, don't you think? We can't go killing each other. An old man with heart disease dies; that's one thing. But you start murdering his surviving children, and someone might notice."

"There's nothing to say that it's one of your siblings, either. Whoever killed your father might have a reason to kill one or more of you. To get revenge on the entire family?"

Logan gave a bark of laughter. "For what? What did we do? Or what did Dad do that was so bad they have to take revenge on the entire family? That's ridiculous. You might just as well say that there is some loony on the loose killing people, because no one would have any reason to kill off the whole family."

"No one is saying that the killer's motives are logical."

"Then why even discuss them?" Logan had a swallow of his drink. "No one is coming here to kill me. It isn't going to happen. And there are enough people around here that I would have a warning that something was going on. Maybe we don't have security guards, but there are people around all the time."

"Which didn't help your father," Garcia pointed out.

"We are not in any danger," Logan insisted stubbornly. "If that's all you came here about, you might as well leave. I'm not going to debate it."

"That's not why I came here. You brought it up. I told you that we have new evidence."

Logan paused, considering this. He took a slower sip of his drink. "New evidence. Okay, what? You know who it was? Or what he was poisoned with?"

"We are not that far yet, but we have made some progress."

"What?"

"Before I get into details, I wanted to ask you about your relationship with your father. I know that you had diverging opinions about your education. Other than that, things were good? He let you live here, so I assume you still have a good relationship with him."

Logan grimaced. "I don't know about that. We never did get along well. But Mom would have killed him if he ever kicked me out, so I traded on that knowledge. I told him that I was dropping out and coming back here. That I'd need time to get back on my feet and decide where I was going and what I was doing next. He went through the whole 'if you're dropping out of school, you're not coming back here to sponge off of me' speech, and I told him flat out that I was coming back whether he liked it or not. If he kicked me out, I'd call the police, and it would be all over the papers. And Mom said I always had a place there, no matter what happened."

After what he'd heard from the others, Zachary was surprised that Logan would have dared to stand up to him like that. Even Alex was afraid to do anything John disapproved of because he worried he would be disowned if he crossed his father.

"That was pretty bold," Garcia observed.

"Where else would I go? It wasn't like things could get any worse if I stood up to him. I was dropping out of school with no skills or ability to make a living. I'd be out on the street. He wouldn't give me the money to support myself; I'd already seen that with the others. I had to come back here. So… I decided I would do whatever it took."

Garcia nodded. She wrote a couple of things in her notebook.

"So," Logan's voice was insistent this time. "Tell me about this new evidence. If that's what you came here for, why are you stalling?"

"What did you know about your father's business?" Garcia asked, not answering his question. "You said that you couldn't believe anyone who wanted to kill your father would want to take it out on the rest of the family. So you must know enough about his business to be able to make that assertion…"

"Well… no." Logan took a swallow of his drink. "I just mean that no normal person would want to take vengeance on the guy's entire family. Even if they wanted to kill him… everybody in his family isn't guilty."

"That doesn't answer the question. What do you know about what your father did?"

"Nothing." Logan shrugged. "I guess it was some kind of law, like Alex. Business law."

"Did he have a law degree?"

"Sure. I'd seen it in his office, on his wall. Juris Doctor. I remember asking him what it meant when I was a kid. Couldn't understand how he could be a lawyer when the certificate said he was a doctor. One of those things that kids just don't get."

"And he practiced law?"

"I don't know. I think he was sort of… a corporate lawyer. Troubleshooter. He helped to get businesses and individuals financing when they were starting a new business or product line, or when they ran into trouble. Law, finance, whatever. But he wasn't a doctor!" Logan chuckled.

Garcia nodded slowly. She leaned on one of the chairs but still didn't sit down. Zachary suspected that she preferred the power position. "So you didn't know that he was a loan shark."

Logan's eyes widened. He scowled at this and shook his head. "No. A loan shark? He was in finance. Yes, he invested in companies, but that's not the same as a loan shark."

"Loaning money to individuals and companies at usurious rates where they can barely afford the interest payments, if that? That's what you call a loan shark," Garcia told him.

"That's not what he did. You just don't understand the business."

"Your sister didn't give us many of his business papers to draw conclusions from. But from what we can see, yes, that's exactly what he did. Why do you think he got these complaints and threats? Why do you think someone was stalking him?"

"No one was stalking him."

"You know that he was concerned that night. That he was watching the windows and acting as if he expected someone."

"Stalking," Logan repeated, shaking his head as if the idea itself were ridiculous.

"There were threats made against his life. And then he died. And then there were threats made against your lives. Don't you think there might be something to that? I want you to think back to what you know of his business—what you know firsthand to be true—and tell me that I'm wrong."

Logan didn't even consider it. "No. That's nonsense. We have old money. He had a respectable job. He didn't do anything criminal or immoral. He was an upright citizen, and if I hear you slandering him in the press or blaming him for his own death, you will hear from our lawyers."

"No one is talking to the press here. No one is slandering anyone. I'm talking to you. Asking you to think about what you know about his business."

"I know he wasn't a loan shark," Logan said stubbornly. "And now, I would like you to leave my house. I don't need this from you."

"I thought you wanted to hear what I had discovered."

Logan stopped, his glass halfway to his mouth. "I thought that *was* your news."

Garcia shook her head.

"Well, will you get on with it, then?" he said in exasperation. "Explain this amazing news you needed to share with me."

44

"John Godfrey was not your father."

Logan just sat there, looking as if he hadn't heard what Garcia said.

Zachary supposed it was so shocking that Logan didn't know what to think about the news. He was processing it, parsing it out, trying to figure out what it meant to him. Whether it was potentially true.

That, or he was shutting down, unable to believe it.

Garcia sat down, pulling one of the other club chairs closer to Logan's. She gazed at him, their eyes now level.

"Logan. Did you hear what I said? John Godfrey was not your father. Not your biological relative."

Logan shook his head slowly. He drained his glass, but didn't seem able to get up and get himself a refill.

"We have compared your DNA with your siblings' and your father's, and you are not John Godfrey's child."

"I didn't give you permission to do that."

"You gave us your DNA. And when it turned out that the note writer was biologically related to you but not your siblings, we had to dig down deeper and investigate why."

"That's not possible. He might have threatened to disown me, but I know he was my father. My real father. My biological father. I don't know whose samples you've mixed up with mine, but there's been a mistake. You're not even supposed to be investigating me. That DNA was for elimination purposes. That's what you said. And you've obviously made some kind of mistake. You need to get it straightened out."

"We've double-checked our results. We will be doing more extensive testing, but we are confident about the initial results. John Godfrey was not your biological father."

"And the others? Was he theirs?"

"We haven't reviewed the others' results since they were unrelated to the letter writer. But I can tell you they do not share the same biological father as you."

"Are you telling me he was their father but not mine?" Logan demanded, his voice rising in outrage. He seemed even more upset at the thought that his siblings were John Godfrey's offspring than that he wasn't. Zachary supposed that if he knew that his siblings were not John's children, it would at least put the four of them back on the footing. As things stood, Logan was the odd man out. The illegitimate child, who they could now challenge for his portion of the estate.

"I'm not telling you anything about their parentage. Only yours. You never knew?"

"Of course not." Logan shook his head. His mouth twisted into a bitter expression. "Though I suppose it would explain a few things."

Garcia nodded encouragingly. "Like what?"

"Why I'm so much younger than the others. Why he had no interest in me. Why I didn't inherit any of his interests or abilities. I thought maybe my learning disabilities were because he was so old when I was conceived. I know with older mothers, you get kids with Down Syndrome and other stuff. Maybe with an older father, you get other disabilities. But if he wasn't my father, it would explain why I didn't inherit anything from him."

"But you never guessed that he wasn't your father. And he and your mother never said anything that might have indicated that they were aware of it."

"No. They never said anything around me."

"We'll need to take a look at your birth certificate. And find out whether she may have used a sperm donor. She might have if she still wanted more children and your father… wasn't able."

Logan looked at his glass, clenched between white fingers as if he were considering throwing it. But he didn't. "Do you really think that my parents would put another man's name on my birth certificate? Do you know the kind of scandal that would cause? And no, my mother did not use a sperm donor. She made it quite clear that they had thought they were finished having children and my coming along was a surprise."

"That might not have been true. That might have just been to protect your father's reputation."

"No. It wasn't."

Garcia didn't say anything else. Logan sat there brooding.

"What did you mean…?" Logan said finally. "You said that I was related to the letter writer. What letter writer? The threat? The second and third generation thing?"

"Yes," Garcia agreed. "You're related to the person who wrote that threat. And who wrote a previous threat against your father."

"Related how?"

"They are telling me that from the DNA you share with the letter writer, it would appear that you are siblings. Half siblings."

"Sharing a father."

"Yes."

"So somewhere out there, I have a half-sibling who just killed my father."

"The father who raised you. Maybe. We don't know yet whether he killed John Godfrey or for sure that he was, in fact, murdered. We are still trying to find signs of the kind of poison that might have been used or how it was administered. If it was poisoning."

"He? So it was a brother?"

"Yes. The Y-chromosome confirms that the letter writer was a male."

"And I've never met him before," Logan mused. "You have no idea what a strange feeling that is."

Having just met his first set of DNA half-siblings recently, Zachary could relate. It was a bizarre feeling to know that he had brothers and sisters out there who he had never met. And there were still more. Several that had been signed up with the DNA registry, and who knew how many others Berk Goldman had fathered who had not had their DNA tested and had no idea that Zachary and the others were out there?

"You can't tell any of this to the others," Logan said. "This is private medical information. You have to keep that confidential by law. I know that. You can't tell the others what you found out."

"I think it will probably get out whether we say anything or not," Garcia said. "These things have a way of coming to the surface. Especially with all of the ancestral DNA stuff available now."

"You can't repeat it to anyone."

"Unfortunately, I can't promise you that no one will be told. We need to pursue this investigation. We'll try to give you your privacy, but you need to understand that this is a key piece of information you can't keep to yourself. It may be one of the only leads we have on the identity of the letter writer. Who may, in turn, be the killer."

"I'll take you to court. You'd better not think you can get away with slandering my mother in this 'investigation' of yours."

"That is not my intention."

Logan shook his head, not sure what to say to this. He wanted assurances, but Garcia wasn't giving them to him.

45

Do you have any of your mother's old papers around?" Garcia asked. "Any personal correspondence, journals, photos..."

"You think I would give them to you? Knowing what you are going to be looking for? You're trying to smear her reputation. Speculate about who she might have been having an affair with. Who my biological father is."

Garcia nodded her agreement. "We need to learn everything we can about her life around the time you were conceived. Who lived here and was on the staff. Who she spent her time with when Mr. Godfrey was out of the house. I'm sorry if it sounds sordid. We're not looking for dirt. Just facts."

"My mother did not sleep with someone on the staff," Logan insisted, wrinkling his nose. "She was a lady! I can't believe you would even suggest such a thing."

"I didn't exactly say that. If anyone who was on the staff then is still around or you know how to reach them, they would be a very good source of information."

"Mrs. Kennedy was here then, wasn't she?" Zachary suggested, remembering the previous discussions. The kids had grown up with Mrs. Kennedy and she could probably tell them a thing or two about how the household had been run and who Mrs. Godfrey might have been seeing when the master of the house was away.

Logan sent a scowl in Zachary's direction. "I don't want you talking to Mrs. Kennedy. You shouldn't be bothering her with something like this. It's not right. You're sullying my mother's reputation."

"I had nothing to do with who she decided to sleep with," Garcia said firmly. "That was solely her decision, and with DNA technology as omnipresent as it is now, it would come out sooner or later. Someone doing DNA genealogy is going to figure it out. All kinds of family secrets that were safe, even ones that happened two or three generations ago, are being outed now."

"How could we have gotten ourselves into this kind of a mess? You can't control a technology like that." Logan shook his head. "It could disrupt everything."

Zachary hadn't thought about it that way. He had been interested in connecting with his siblings, that was all. And they had used DNA on Heather's case to figure out the identity of the man who had assaulted her. But other than that, Zachary didn't see it as any different from any other technology that allowed him to make connections between people.

But to Logan, it was different. Something that could prevent him from getting the money he was expecting. Maybe something that could set the whole structure of high society on its head when people made discoveries about infidelities that had been going on undiscovered for generations.

"I gotta hit the head," Logan said abruptly. He set his heavy glass down on a table with a thunk and got to his feet. "I'd ask you to show yourselves out, but I have a feeling you're not going to do that."

"I'm hoping you'll be able to provide us with some papers," Garcia said. "Maybe I should ask Karen. She seems to be the one who was saddled with looking after the paperwork in the wake of your parents' deaths."

"You are *not* going to talk to Karen about my mother's papers," Logan said firmly. He shook his head as he walked away from them to visit a nearby bathroom. Garcia waited until Logan's footsteps had faded and they heard the click of a shutting door before speaking.

"This is a situation that needs to be managed with some delicacy," Garcia told Zachary unnecessarily. "The police department has to deal with frivolous lawsuits all the time. We don't want to have to defend against one from such a prominent family."

"Well, as you said, you're not smearing them. You're just trying to find out the truth. To catch a murderer. The killer of their father. They can't exactly complain about that."

"Oh, they can complain about anything they like, believe me," Garcia said with a chuckle. "But I'm going to have to dig deeper despite any objections. If we are going to figure out who this half-sibling is, then we need to have some idea of who Mrs. Godfrey was spending time with at that time."

"Do you want me to talk to Mrs. Kennedy while you talk to Logan? I can get some names from her."

"You will not!" Logan said sharply, returning to the study through another door. "I told you; the staff won't know anything about this. If either of my parents had affairs, they would have been very discreet about it. They didn't go around flaunting their outside relationships."

"If it was with a staff member, then Mrs. Kennedy might have become aware of it," Garcia pointed out.

"Members of this family do not go around having affairs with the servants," Logan said primly.

He pressed his lips closed and proceeded to turn very pink. Zachary watched him change color, trying to read his expression and body language. Even though Logan's words had been angry and aggressive, his blush and body language suggested something else. Embarrassment over his mother's affair? Something that he had said that was not true? Maybe he knew that the blanket statement that no one in the family had affairs with the servants was false. If he didn't know about his mother's affair, then what? Was he thinking about an affair that John Godfrey or one of his siblings had indulged in?

Somehow, Zachary didn't think so. He had not acted that concerned about what his father or siblings might have done before. He was remote and unconcerned. The information about his mother had made an impact, but this was something different.

"Are you talking about *your* affair?" Zachary asked, keeping his voice level and neutral.

Garcia turned around and looked at him, her expression surprised. Then she looked back at Logan and the two of them watched his face get even redder. Logan spluttered and couldn't find coherent words at first.

"Which one was it with?" Zachary asked, mentally reviewing the staff members he had met or seen at work. There was no way to tell exactly who someone would be attracted to. While the default was someone attractive, reasonably close in age, of the opposite gender, that was by no means the only possibility.

But he had found that most people had types. Logan's girlfriend was nice-looking, blond, and close to his age. There was a good chance that if he'd had an affair with a staff member, she had been similar in most respects.

"Would that have been Charlotte?"

Logan's mouth hung open. He took off his glasses and smudged them with his shirt, putting them back on eventually and looking at Zachary with anxious, glistening eyes.

"There was no affair," he said flatly.

"Are you talking about your mother or you? Because I think you've pretty clearly answered the question about whether you had an affair with the staff," Garcia said, enunciating her words clearly, as if they were all separate instead of part of a sentence.

"I did not have an affair with Charlotte." Logan choked the words out, barely able to get them past his lips. It was clear that his body rebelled against such a blatant lie. He was fine with small social lies. But his relationship with Charlotte was much too important to him to be lied away.

All three of them knew that he hadn't managed to convince anyone of the veracity of his story.

"Is this affair ongoing, or was it only temporary?" Garcia asked.

"I told you there was no affair."

"And there clearly was. Or is. Which is it?"

Logan shook his head. "It isn't like that. I know she's staff, but… it wasn't about looks, or about me having power over the staff. It's not 'lord of the manor' stuff; she was attracted to me too. It wouldn't have mattered where we met or that we were on two different social levels."

"*Was* attracted or *is* attracted," Garcia persisted.

"Is, I guess."

"You still have a relationship with her?"

"Yeah. I guess so." Logan looked down at his feet, properly ashamed to admit it. He took his tumbler over to the drink station and poured another drink.

Zachary could see Garcia recalculating, seeing how this affected their case. He, too, was thinking about the various permutations. Logan's opportunities to poison his father had doubled, if another person might have dosed his drinks or dinner. Charlotte was the one who had served him at dinner time. She had been in the kitchen when Karen had been preparing John Godfrey's nightcap. But did they suspect a woman now? It had been proven that the threats had been penned by a man.

And yet the threats might not have come from Godfrey's killer. Someone might have just taken advantage of what had happened, or been trying to throw the whole thing into confusion.

"Did you ask Charlotte to take your father a drink?"

Logan's head snapped in Zachary's direction as if a switch had been thrown. "What are you talking about?"

"She didn't have any motive that we are aware of, but she did have access to him. You could have persuaded her to give him a drink. You might have told her that it contained something that would help him to sleep or be good for his heart. She wouldn't know the difference until he died. And then you could hold it over her head, prevent her from talking because you could point to her as the actual poisoner."

"I wouldn't do that!"

"You had reason to want this house to yourself. To have your piece of the inheritance. And you could convince yourself that she was helping you out of love." Zachary shrugged and went on. "Even though it had nothing to do with romantic feelings toward you. It was the fact that you were one of her bosses and could influence whether she kept her job or was let go."

"That's a lie!" Logan exploded. "She loves me. I am not influencing or corrupting her. And I never told her to put anything in my father's drink."

"She did that of her own volition? Because she figured that it was what you wanted?"

"She didn't do anything. She's a good employee. She does what she is told. She works hard. She's trying to get ahead. She wouldn't do anything dishonest or against the law. She's not a violent person."

"You also said that your mother would not have an affair. I don't think your judgment is that accurate."

"I know my mother. And I know Charlotte."

"You didn't know your father very well," Garcia contributed. "You didn't know the stuff that he was involved in." She looked at Zachary. "Maybe he's just one of those people who sees the good in everyone."

"Maybe," Zachary agreed with a nod. It was a good trait, being able to see the good in people. But it could lead to someone like Logan being naive about other people's motives and true nature.

46

We are going to need to talk to Charlotte," Garcia observed. "Logan, I want you to stay here while we talk to her. I don't want you to leave this room or the house. Do you understand?"

"You can't make me. I'm not under arrest." He took a gulp of his drink. "If I am arrested, then you have to read me my rights and all of that. And I want a lawyer."

"You are not under arrest at this time. I'm making a request. Do you want to be seen as cooperating with the police investigation or impeding it?"

"I'm not stopping you from investigating. You go ahead and investigate all you like, and you'll find out that I wasn't involved in any plot against my father, and neither was Charlotte."

"I hope so," Garcia said neutrally.

Zachary looked at Garcia, wondering whether he should stay in the study with Logan to keep an eye on him, or whether he would be allowed to go with Garcia as she asked Charlotte questions. It wasn't likely that Garcia would want him hanging around for that interview. He'd had the insight she needed on Logan, but he hadn't talked much to Charlotte previously and probably wouldn't be any help during Charlotte's questioning.

Garcia headed toward the door and gave a slight jerk of her head to invite Zachary along. He put his hands on the arms of his chair and started to rise, watching her to make sure that he had understood the gesture correctly. He still expected to be told to stay there while she went to talk to Charlotte.

But Garcia paused at the door and waited for him, so he followed her out of the study and into the hall.

"You want me there?" Zachary asked tentatively, not wanting there to be any misunderstanding.

"You may as well come along," Garcia agreed, but didn't give any reason for this or thank Zachary for his help with ferreting out the truth about Logan's relationship with Charlotte. But he would take what he could get. Being allowed to observe the interview directly was better than any words of thanks.

They went to the kitchen, which seemed to be the hub for the various staff members, and asked after Charlotte. Mrs. Kennedy, a large woman always busy with one thing or another, wiped her hands on a towel, studying them with a frown.

"She's doing the upstairs housekeeping. Do you really need to interrupt her? It will throw off the entire schedule."

"I'm sorry, we need to see her," Garcia apologized.

Mrs. Kennedy sighed. Her lips pressed tightly together as if she were holding back everything she wanted to say. She slid her hand into an apron pocket to find her phone and dialed. There was a pause of several seconds while they all waited for Charlotte to answer her phone, and then it connected.

"Charlotte, I need you downstairs. Please leave what you are doing for now and come see me in the kitchen," Mrs. Kennedy instructed firmly.

There was apparently no argument from Charlotte and, in a few minutes, she walked into the kitchen. Her eyes flicked over to Garcia and Zachary and then away again. She knew who they were, having talked to them previously about the events that had taken place the evening before Mr. Godfrey's death.

"You wanted me?" she asked Mrs. Kennedy.

"The detectives want to talk to you," Mrs. Kennedy said briskly, indicating Garcia and Zachary. "You can go with them to the morning room and answer their questions. When you are done, go back upstairs and continue with your work."

"I don't really want to…"

"Go on," Mrs. Kennedy insisted, shooing her away. "The morning room."

Charlotte's jaw was set as she led the two visitors out of the kitchen to a bright, sunshiny nook. Zachary could picture Mrs. Godfrey here, sipping orange juice and reading the morning newspaper, in a lacy but modest dressing gown.

He'd been watching too much TV.

They all sat down. Charlotte looked from Zachary to Garcia, wondering what was going on and which of them wanted to ask her questions. Zachary evaluated her, trying to identify anything he might have missed before. She was pretty. Not as young as he had thought the first time he met her. There were fine lines around her eyes like cracks in her makeup. Past her twenties. Older than Logan.

"We would like to talk to you about your relationship with the Godfrey family," Garcia said.

Charlotte's narrow shoulders lifted and fell. "They're good employers, I guess. It's a big house and we keep busy. There's a lot to be done."

"But you get breaks."

Charlotte frowned at this. She nodded her head. "Employment standards say they have to give me a certain amount of time for breaks and lunch. They do all that, if that's what you're asking."

"That's not what I'm asking."

Garcia used silence to her advantage, looking at Charlotte and waiting for her to grow more anxious and uncomfortable and fill the silence. Charlotte looked around the room, her face getting red under Garcia's focused gaze.

"What is it, then? I don't understand."

"Do you ever talk to members of the family?"

"Well, yes, when they're here. The only ones around most of the time are Logan, and Mr. John, before…"

"Before he passed."

"Yes." Charlotte nodded quickly, looking like a small bird pecking for bugs or seeds.

"Did you have much reason to talk to Mr. John?"

"No. Sometimes he would ask me to pick something up or to get him something. But usually, it's Mrs. Kennedy who gives me work. I try to stay in the background, unobtrusive."

"But you have talked to Logan."

"Yes. Of course I have."

"And you have spent time with him."

She swallowed and looked around the room. "I don't know what you mean."

"I mean that you were having an affair with him," Garcia said baldly, a sudden, sharp contrast to the open-ended, roundabout questions she had been asking until then.

Charlotte gave a little gasp. She looked at Garcia, then at Zachary, then back at Garcia again.

"I'm… I… whatever would make you think such a thing?"

"You're not going to say that Logan was lying, are you?"

"Well… I don't know what to say."

"You need to tell me the truth. I don't want to have to lay charges against you for obstructing an investigation. You should have told me this before when I first talked to you."

"You didn't ask," Charlotte pointed out.

Garcia stared her down. Charlotte looked away, her eyes shiny with tears.

"You know you should have disclosed that to me the first time we spoke. I've wasted a lot of time looking in other directions."

"But… Logan and I… that doesn't have anything to do with Mr. John's death. Or with anything else. It was… private. It wasn't anything to do with Mr. John."

"You know that Logan has a girlfriend."

"I guess," Charlotte admitted.

"Of course you do. You see her here all the time. And you know that affairs between staff and the family are prohibited."

"There isn't a rule," Charlotte said stubbornly.

"I think you're being disingenuous. You know very well that such a thing would be frowned upon by both Logan's family and Mrs. Kennedy. You kept it a secret."

"We needed to be discreet. It was private. But it wasn't… forbidden." She blushed more deeply at his, her body giving her away.

"Yes, it was. And of course you should have brought it up when we were talking to you about Mr. John's death. Quit giving me excuses. What I want are answers."

Charlotte looked meekly at the plush carpeting under their feet.

"You've worked here for what, three years?"

The young woman nodded. "About that."

"How long has this affair been going on with Logan?"

"It's not… I just…" Charlotte tried again to find something to say to explain or brush off her affair with Logan. Zachary felt sorry for her. While she and Logan were about the same age, Logan was her employer and was in a position of power over her. How was she supposed to say no to any approaches by him?

"How long?" Garcia repeated.

"A few months."

"Did Mrs. Kennedy or Mr. Godfrey know about it?"

"No." Charlotte's voice was tiny.

"You served him the night before he died."

"Yes."

"You could have put something into his food."

"I didn't!" Charlotte protested, getting her voice back. "I didn't do anything to Mr. John. I would never do something like that."

"You were also in the kitchen when his nightcap was being prepared, and you could have tampered with that."

"But I didn't. Why would I want to harm him?"

"For Logan. Because he was in danger of being disinherited after dropping out of school. He needed this house and his inheritance. And it would be so easy for you."

"No. I didn't want to do anything to hurt him."

"Now that he is gone, Logan is safe, right? He will get his share of the estate. Be able to live here until he decides to get a place of his own. Support himself. A wife and children." Garcia raised her brows suggestively. "You would like that, wouldn't you?"

"I wouldn't do that. Not for anyone. Not even Logan."

"You want him to be happy, don't you? You didn't want to see him kicked out of here."

"Mr. John wouldn't have done that."

"Is that what Logan told you?"

"No," Charlotte shook her head. She twirled a lock of hair around her finger until it tightened so much it made Zachary wince. "He didn't tell me anything about his father disinheriting him or kicking him out. He and his dad got along okay."

"Did they? I think there was probably a good amount of arguing going on."

"Men are like that," Charlotte dismissed. "Competitive. They yell and argue and complain, and then it's all over and they're fine."

Some families were like that, Zachary knew. Occasional blow-outs, followed by peaceful interludes where everyone seemed to be getting along just fine. But Zachary had also lived in homes where the fighting never stopped and he always had to be vigilant, watching for the anger and violence to come his way.

"Logan never told you that he wished his father was dead?" Garcia asked.

"No. No, of course not."

"And it never occurred to you that he would be better off if Mr. Godfrey was dead?"

"No!" Charlotte insisted.

Garcia studied the young woman closely. She kept her head down and away, so it was difficult to read her.

"We will need to search your room."

"Go ahead. I don't have anything to hide."

Garcia nodded slowly. "Fine. That's what we will do, then. You stick around here. I want to be able to find you again when I have further questions."

"Here in the morning room?"

"Here in the house. But stay away from your room until we have finished with it."

Charlotte nodded and made her way quickly out of the morning room, swiping at a tear in the corner of her eye.

Garcia was silent for a while, considering what they had heard. She eventually turned to face Zachary. "Well, I think we're going to need to talk to some of the others in the household. I don't think we're getting the full story here."

Of course not. Charlotte had picked out her position and was sticking to it. She had just fallen for Logan. Nothing sinister about that. Never mind that Logan already had a girlfriend or that they came from two different social classes. Zachary didn't believe it was the innocent romance of two kids that had just happened to fall in love any more than Garcia did. Logan had been looking for someone to do his dirty work. Someone who had easy access to John Godfrey's food and drink and could poison him while Logan was somewhere else with an alibi.

But then, why had they chosen the night of the family dinner to do it? It didn't make sense to do it when Logan was clearly in the house and had the opportunity to put poison in his father's pre- or post-prandial drinks. Why *hadn't* they picked a time when Logan had an iron-clad alibi? Was there something that had made the need for John's death more urgent? Or had Charlotte jumped the gun and done it before Logan had a chance to pick the time? Had Logan pressured her into it, or had she decided that it was something she would do for him without being asked?

47

Maybe others in the household would have more insight, as Garcia suggested. Zachary stood and he and Garcia returned to the kitchen. Mrs. Kennedy looked at them with a scowl on her face that was even more forbidding than the last time they had entered.

"You've come to make more disruption?" she demanded. "I have a household to run here."

Zachary wasn't sure how running a household for one person could be quite that demanding. But he supposed there was cleaning and other maintenance to be done whether one person lived in the house or ten. There were still just as many rooms and knickknacks. And there was still dinner to be made, unless Logan decided to go somewhere else for his supper, and other staff members to supervise and keep busy and coordinated.

"We're sorry," he said, covering himself and Garcia with the apology, even though he suspected she wasn't the least bit sorry. "But there are some things that came up… we just need someone who knows how things work around here to be able to answer them."

She looked at him with a frown as if trying to read his mind or find something in his manner that indicated he wasn't being sincere. Then she shrugged and turned back to the stove, where there was something unidentifiable cooking in the pot.

"I suppose I'm the one to ask, then. You're not going to find anyone else who knows as much as I do about this household and how it functions. I've been here since the children were young. Before Logan was even born."

"That's amazing. You must have felt very sad to see both Mrs. and Mr. Godfrey pass on."

She paused for a moment in her stirring. "I was quite close to Mrs. Godfrey," she admitted. "We worked together for a lot of years, handling all kinds of balls and parties and dinners. She was very good at it all, and she never had a bad word to say about the staff. You have to give her that. A very classy lady."

Zachary and Garcia both moved in closer. It was hard to know where to stand for the conversation, when Mrs. Kennedy's back was turned toward them. There was no way for them to watch her facial expressions or minute changes in her body language.

"Were you aware of anything going on between Logan and Charlotte?" Garcia asked.

Mrs. Kennedy stirred and worked over her pots silently for a while before turning partway around to look at Garcia.

"Going on between them?"

"Were you aware that they were having an affair?"

Mrs. Kennedy *tsked* and looked back down at her work. "They were discreet," she said. "I didn't know for sure. But… I did suspect."

"What was it that gave them away?"

"Oh, the looks when they were both in the same room together, even when Charlotte was just serving and there was no conversation. I warned her. More than once. I told her that no good could come from mixing between the family and the staff. It would only lead to a messy situation and heartbreak." She sighed. "And now we're here. With an even bigger mess than I anticipated."

"You knew it would come back to bite her," Zachary acknowledged. "But I guess Logan was more persuasive than you were."

"Do you doubt it?" Mrs. Kennedy laughed ruefully. "When

was the last time you saw a girl pay more attention to an old woman?" She turned her head to look at Zachary. "The opposite sex will always win."

"When did you notice something was going on?" Garcia asked. "When did you warn Charlotte not to get involved with him?"

"Oh, it was a few months ago, I guess. I noticed her paying more attention to him, lingering for longer when she poured him a drink, standing closer to serve him. Nothing that could be construed as inappropriate, but he couldn't help but notice her interest in him."

"You think that *she* was the one who initiated it?" Zachary asked in surprise. Like Garcia, he had assumed that it was the other way around. Logan pursuing Charlotte, flirting with her and pressuring her until she gave in.

"He was oblivious at first." Mrs. Logan tasted the sauce in one of the pots and put the used spoon in the sink. "I would like to tell you that boy is suave and sophisticated and could have his pick of the girls, but… I'm sure that you've noticed he's not the best catch. He's… *plain* would be the most polite way I could put it. And awkward. No Lothario. He has the lovely Amy, but you can bet that girl is nothing but a gold digger. If she ever found out that he wasn't getting any money, she would be out the door in an instant."

Zachary had wondered what Amy saw in Logan. Mrs. Kennedy was right that there didn't seem to be much to attract a girl other than his wealth and social position. As well as not drawing the winning combination in looks or urbanity, he had dropped out of college and had no employment prospects. His money was literally the only thing left to attract a girl. Unless there was some personality trait that attracted her or pastime they shared. That alone wouldn't hold a relationship together in the long term.

"But Charlotte was interested in him?"

"I was surprised," Mrs. Kennedy admitted, resting her hands on the counter for a moment. "When she started to show an interest in Logan, I mean. I eventually put it down to him being the only young man available in the house. But before that… she seemed like she was quite happy with the boyfriend she had. I wasn't expecting her to dump him for the likes of Logan Godfrey."

"I guess maybe she saw herself getting that money too," Garcia said. "She worked here, served him, might as well get the benefits that went with it. She could remake herself as a society lady."

Mrs. Kennedy shook her head. "She was never going to be a society lady. Even if she was able to get Logan… he would never be a prize. He isn't interested in parties or causes or business. I don't think he will ever attain anything like what his mother and father did. The other children may do better, but Logan… will always be the black sheep."

"He has disabilities," Zachary pointed out. "It isn't just because he chooses not to be successful."

She shrugged. "The other children do just fine. He has the same genes, the same upbringing. Why should he be any different?"

Zachary opened his mouth to correct her, but saw Garcia's sharp look and stopped himself.

"What else can you tell us about their relationship?" Garcia asked. "You said you didn't have any proof, but you seem pretty observant and intuitive. Was there anything that may have concerned you? Other than a pairing between the family and the help?"

Mrs. Kennedy stirred slowly. An older man came into the kitchen, and she gave him instructions. It sounded like he was the gardener or landscaper. Eventually, the man left. Zachary waited for Garcia to ask the question again.

"There was one day," Mrs. Kennedy said with slow deliberation, "I overheard the two of them talking. Just a fragment of conversation. I don't stand at doors listening." Garcia nodded, acknowledging this and encouraging her to continue. "This was before Logan dropped out of school. And Charlotte was… well, it *sounded* like she was encouraging him to quit. It doesn't make sense, I know that. But she was saying that Mr. John never accepted Logan for who he was and wouldn't let him be his own person. But that Logan had to stand up to him and make Mr. John respect him. She said that he wouldn't ever treat Logan as anything but a child unless he did."

Mrs. Kennedy removed one of the pots from the stove and set it on a trivet.

"She probably wasn't wrong. Mr. John was tough on his kids, but he was better if they stood up for themselves and didn't let themselves be pushed around. He preferred them to be independent. Didn't like Logan living here without a job or something productive to do. Maybe he would have been better if Logan had talked back to him and stood up for himself and what he was doing. But it wasn't Charlotte's place to tell him that, to encourage him to confront his father. I didn't think anything good could come from it."

"Did you talk to her about it?"

"No… not exactly. I couldn't confront her without admitting I had overheard the two of them. I tried to tell her in other ways, through other conversations. More general ones about how she should be behaving. But I think… she knew that I'd heard something." Mrs. Kennedy shrugged. "I hadn't exactly had that kind of conversation with her in the three years that she's been working here. She was always a hard worker and minded her own business… until lately."

"Things changed recently," Garcia suggested.

"Yes. When she started showing him extra attention."

"And you can't think of anything that might have triggered the behavior? Nothing happened in Charlotte's life or in Logan's around that time?"

"No, nothing that I'm aware of. But the two of them… I'm not their mother or their best friend. They don't tell me things. I try to keep conversations at a business level, not personal."

"You have to in order to run a household like this, don't you?" Zachary reassured her, not wanting her to think they were being critical of her for not being friendly with her staff. "There is so much to be done, and you can't get mired down in gossip and relationships."

“That is so true,” Mrs. Kennedy said gratefully, nodding her agreement.

48

It had been a long day, but Zachary felt they had moved things down the field significantly. He appreciated Garcia allowing him to sit in on the interviews and tried to think of some way to express his gratitude to her sincerely but without sounding too sentimental. He didn't want to break the image that she had of him being a competent and businesslike private investigator. At least, that was the image he hoped she had of him and he didn't want her thinking that he would melt into a puddle at the least bit of consideration.

In the end, he had to settle for warm thanks and a handshake before he got back into his car to head home. Garcia gave him a dry smile and a nod. "Let me know if you come up with anything brilliant. I'm going to sleep on this and see what I can think of for our next step. I'm hoping that there was something in those interviews that will help to get us to the next step… the identity of the letter writer. So far, I can't think of anything, but maybe with a good night's sleep, we'll be able to come up with something together."

"I'll sleep on it too," Zachary promised.

But he didn't tell her how little he actually slept.

"Great." Garcia clapped him on the shoulder and then got into her car. Zachary got into his.

He texted Kenzie to let her know he was finished and on his way home. He was a little later than usual, but had warned her ahead of time that he might be, so he hoped it wouldn't lead to another blow-up over spending too much time with Detective Garcia.

When he walked into the house, he could hear Kenzie talking. He stopped and listened, trying to figure out if someone else was there or if she was talking on the phone.

"I told you I don't want him to have anything to do with you," Kenzie snapped. "You can find someone else to call. He cannot work a case for you. He just can't."

There was a silence as she listened to the answer. Zachary couldn't hear anything, so he assumed she was talking on the phone. He took off his shoes and moved as quietly as possible to avoid disturbing her.

And to hear what she was talking about before she realized he was there, if the "he" in her statements was Zachary.

There was a sharp intake of breath from Kenzie. When she replied, there was hesitance in her voice that hadn't been there before, but she was still adamant. "I'm very sorry. That's terrible. But he can't help you. You can't expect him to. I told you before."

Zachary paused before entering the living room where Kenzie was speaking. Who was she talking to? Was it about him? And if it was, then why was she making a decision without consulting him? Maybe it was Walter, her father. If he had a case that he wanted Zachary to investigate, and Kenzie didn't want him anywhere near it, Zachary could understand and respect that. She could make that decision unilaterally. He should have listened to her the *last* time concerning her father. He was on the same page with her now about not wanting to work for Walter again.

He stepped into the living room. Kenzie was sitting on the couch and was startled when she saw him. Her face went white, and she didn't answer whatever her father had just said, looking at Zachary with her mouth open.

He raised his brows and mouthed, "Walter?"

Kenzie shook her head. But she didn't tell him who it was. Zachary went to the couch and sat down, looking at her, waiting for her to tell him what was happening.

"Can you hold on for a minute?" Kenzie said, and held her phone against her leg to muffle any conversation she and Zachary had.

"Who is it?" Zachary asked, when she didn't tell him immediately.

"It's Gordon."

Zachary was taken aback. Bridget's partner? Gordon had come to Zachary before. Zachary had worked on a couple of cases for him. But after the last time, Zachary had agreed with Kenzie that he couldn't do that again. It was too much of a risk. He had been doing well battling his obsession with Bridget, not following or tracking her or driving by her house. But that success had come crashing down when Gordon had engaged him to surveil her to see whether she was seeing anyone else. Recovering from that had taken a lot of work on his part, med changes, and intensive therapy. It was still a daily battle.

That couldn't happen again. He was stable on his current medication, but another setback like that could be disastrous. Not to mention that his freedom could be severely restricted if Bridget filed an order of protection against Zachary and charged him with stalking.

He shook his head at Kenzie. "What's he calling about?"

If it was a case involving his company, that would be different from if it was about Bridget again. Although, Zachary didn't fully trust Gordon would be totally honest with him about his company dealings, either.

Kenzie looked at Zachary, biting her lip and trying to decide how to tell him. Or maybe how to keep him out of it, though he didn't see how she could do that when Gordon had clearly called her to see if Zachary would look into a case for him.

"It's the twins."

Zachary felt a cold hand squeezing his heart, making it impossible to breathe.

"Bridget's twins?"

They were less than a year old. They had been born premature, and Julia had almost not made it. But she and Tricia had gotten bigger and stronger and were now barely distinguishable from full-term babies of the same age.

Kenzie nodded. She swallowed hard. "They've been snatched."

49

It was a good thing that Zachary was already sitting down, or he might have collapsed where he stood. As it was, he reached out to support himself with his hands, the whole world turning upside down and leaving him dizzy and breathless. He tried to remain anchored to Kenzie and not spin off into a panic attack.

"They've been snatched? How? When did this happen?"

"Just recently. An hour, I don't know all the details. Bridget was hysterical. No one is sure what happened. But they are gone, and Gordon..." Kenzie gestured at her phone. "Of course he thinks you are the only one who can help."

"Has he called the police?"

"Yes. The police are there already."

"Are they at home? I'll go right over."

"Zachary—you can't get involved in this."

"I have to."

"You can't. You know it will derail you. He can find someone else. He can work with the police. The FBI. He doesn't need a private investigator. And if he does, he can call someone else."

Zachary was already on his feet and headed toward the door. "Tell him I'm on my way."

"Zachary!"

He shook his head. "There's no time to debate it. The window for successful recovery is only a few hours."

She was very pale. She knew the statistics herself. He hadn't even stopped to think about how the news of a kidnapping so closely connected with them would feel to her after her own experience.

"I'm sorry, Kenz. I have to go."

"You can't drive."

He shook his head. "I'll be fine."

Kenzie stood up, chasing after him. "If I can't stop you, I'm going with you. And you're not driving."

"You're in better condition to drive than I am?"

"Yes!"

He looked at her as he put his shoes back on. Though she was pale, she seemed to have her emotions under control. She was a rock. He didn't know how she could be so steady. Kenzie gave him a stern look to warn him not to go without her and ducked into the kitchen to pick up her shoes and purse from the back door.

Zachary tried to walk slowly and deliberately back out to his car, ensuring that she could catch up to him again by the time he got there. "Are you sure?" he asked, pausing at the passenger door.

"Yes. I'm sure. Please sit down and do some breathing exercises or something until we get there. Get yourself centered and focused."

He wanted to argue with her that he was already focused, more than he had ever been before. Nothing else mattered. Nothing would distract him. That was why he would have been fine driving to Bridget's house. Nothing would get between him and finding those babies.

But he didn't argue. He just got into the passenger seat and buckled his seatbelt. He looked straight ahead as Kenzie got into the driver's seat and pulled into the street. She wouldn't drive as fast as Zachary would have, but he had to ignore the feeling that they were wasting time, ignore the speedometer, and just think about the problem in front of him.

Kenzie must have told Gordon they were on their way over, as she had hung up on the call and the phone was back in her pocket or purse.

Zachary could only imagine how Bridget must feel. She was a passionate person. Those two babies had become the focus of her life. Never mind the fact that she had considered terminating the pregnancy when she had learned they had the Huntington's disease gene. She was determined to spend all of the time that she could with them while she was still able to. Her health had not been good since she had kicked Zachary out of her life when she got the cancer diagnosis. She had survived the harsh treatments and the cancer was in remission. She had still been building up her strength and getting back to a normal life when she got the Huntington's diagnosis.

He wasn't going to let anyone take the twins away from her. He had been in the hospital when they were born. He had guarded them when their lives had been in danger, putting himself between them and a murderer. And he would do it again. He would do whatever it took to get them back again.

They finally reached Bridget's house. Zachary's jaw was clenched so tightly that his teeth squeaked and felt like they might crack. He tried to portray a casual, easy confidence that he didn't feel. How could anyone do this? How could they take two helpless infants?

There was a police cordon around the house. Vehicles with flashing lights, yellow tape, cops preventing anyone from getting too close. It was all sickeningly familiar. Kenzie pulled as close as she could to the house and Zachary was out of the car before she even finished rolling to a stop. She shouted at him to slow down and wait for her, but he didn't. He headed straight for the front door and was, of course, grabbed by a couple of cops before he could step onto the property.

"Police only," one of them barked. "Can't you see the yellow tape?"

"I'm here to see Gordon Drake. He called me."

"No one is going in there."

But there was already a dark-suited man standing in front of the house, yelling instructions at them. The two cops released Zachary, their hands falling away from him as if they had been burned. Zachary resumed his course to the house. He looked all around for some sign of what had happened. Had they been taken from the yard? From the car? Had someone gotten into the house?

"I'm Agent Bourassa," the tall, dark-suited man informed Zachary. He had an accent. French? "This is *my* case."

Zachary nodded. "Zachary Goldman. Gordon called me."

"You're a family friend."

"Yes, and a private investigator."

"I can't stop you from coming in, but I don't want you interfering with this investigation."

"I'm here to help, not to cause you any trouble."

Zachary was escorted into the house. As usual, everything was pristine. It looked like a showroom instead of a home that someone actually lived in. Bridget was very particular about everything around her. There was probably a maid service in several times a week, and Gordon would not be allowed to drop his pants on the floor when he undressed for bed.

But the strangers milling around created an unfamiliar and surreal atmosphere. Uniformed and plainclothes cops and agents, all talking and coordinating the investigation. But it sounded like chaos rather than organization.

All of the furnishings and the thick, luxurious carpet in the living room were white and, as he always did, Zachary felt a strong reluctance to sit down in case he should get something there dirty or stained.

50

Zachary." Gordon rushed forward and wrung Zachary's hand. He probably would have hugged Zachary if it weren't for all the cops around him, watching every move. "Thank you for coming. I know you can help. You were there when…" He swallowed, battling tears, and apparently could not go on. But Zachary knew what he was talking about. It wasn't the first time he'd been to the house following a kidnapping.

"What happened?" he asked. There was no point in reliving the past. They needed to move forward, to find the missing twins as quickly as they possibly could.

"Bridget had the girls. She was out shopping and running some errands. I was working, and it was the nanny's day off, so she had more on her hands than usual." He shook his head, his face a carved picture of anguish. "I shouldn't have left. I should have stayed home and helped her. I usually do. But I figured she would be okay with the girls. She's been doing really well. She's healthy and strong, and the therapy and meds are helping her to hold her own without losing ground. But I should have known… I shouldn't have let her go out with the two of them. It was too much."

Zachary agreed. He wouldn't have let her go out with two

babies to take care of. But he didn't tell that to Gordon. He was feeling badly enough with his own self-recriminations.

"Where did she go?"

"She was at the grocery store. She had a few errands to do. Too much, probably. I told her to come back home before she got too exhausted. She could do just one or two things and then come home, and I would help her to take care of the rest when I got back from work."

Gordon had an investment banking firm: Drake, Chase, Gould. Zachary had investigated the case of an intern there who had been murdered. The police had written it off as an accident, but it hadn't been, and Zachary had helped to prove that. The firm was a world leader, even though it was tiny compared to most of the other top firms in the industry. The new kid on the block, but they were able to compete in the global marketplace. Gordon was brilliant and fabulously wealthy. Cutthroat in industry, but very devoted to Bridget and the twins at home.

"What happened?" Zachary persisted.

"She was at the grocery store. Picked up her milk and whatever else she needed. When she got to the car, she parked the stroller with the twins in it beside the van so that she could load the groceries into the trunk. They were underneath," Gordon explained, "there's a cargo area under the stroller seats."

Zachary nodded, picturing it in his mind. Julia and Tricia sitting side-by-side in a double stroller. Bridget bending down to get the grocery bags out from underneath. Straightening up again to put them into the back of her vehicle. And in the background, somewhere, danger lurked.

"She said another van pulled up and the driver asked her for directions. He was hard to understand, and she was focused on him. And..." Gordon swallowed. "Someone came out of the van, picked up the stroller, and put it inside. Bridget tried to stop him. She was knocked down. Her hands and knees were bloody from the pavement. The kidnapper got into the van and they drove away."

Zachary's throat was tight as he pictured the scene. Bridget's scream. The squeal of the tires of the van as it took off, babies inside. There had been no need to unbuckle them from the stroller and buckle them into waiting car seats. The kidnapper had just picked up the stroller and put it into the van. It had been planned, not a crime of opportunity. He had known that he was going to be snatching the stroller. Space had been cleared in the cargo or passenger area of the van to accommodate the stroller, which was bulky and needed a lot of room.

"It was planned," Zachary said. "Has there been a ransom call?"

"No. Nothing yet. We've been waiting. I've kept all lines open. Other than to call Kenzie." Gordon nodded, and Zachary saw that Kenzie had followed him into the house. She was still pale. But she was looking more angry now than afraid. Anger was good. It would give her the strength she needed. Neither of them was going to have a nervous breakdown. They would figure out who the kidnapper was and get the children back.

"Where is Bridget now?" Zachary asked. Kenzie had said she was hysterical, but there was no sign of her. She might have been taken in to the police station to make a statement or work on a rendering of the men she had seen but, if she had been that upset, he couldn't see her being able to do that, even with how much she loved the twins and wanted them back.

"She's sleeping." Gordon swallowed. "She was overwrought when the police arrived at the scene. When they brought her back here, she was slurring, hardly able to get anything out. The doctor advised a sedative to settle her down enough to communicate without the Huntington's symptoms getting in the way. We got as much of the story as we could out of her," Gordon's eyes indicated that the "we" included Agent Bourassa. "But then she was too exhausted to stay awake. I've put her down, have a girl watching her so we'll know as soon as she wakes up and she won't be alone."

Zachary nodded. "Okay. What about the license plate on the van?" He looked at Agent Bourassa. "Were there surveillance cameras?"

"There were a couple of them in the parking lot. But nothing that caught a clear view of the license plate. We're getting as much information as we can from the surrounding area. Traffic cameras. License plates on any white vans."

But it was the most common color of van, and Zachary could only imagine how many man-hours it would take to go through all the traffic cam footage and recorded plates to find the one of the vehicle that had carried Julia and Tricia away. They would have the names of the registered owner of every white van in the area, but would that help them identify the kidnapper? The van could have been stolen. The plates could have been stolen or obscured. And the name of the perpetrator might not be known to Gordon. He was bound to have enemies that he knew nothing about. Zachary shook his head. The FBI could run the plates. But that wasn't going to break the case.

"Have you had any threats? Not necessarily against the twins, but against you or Chase Gold? Have you had unhappy clients? A company you've taken over? An irate employee that you had to fire?"

Gordon shook his head. "I don't know. There are always people who are unhappy. They think that they should have made a million on an investment instead of losing money. That they should be able to get their money back when they make a bad investment. And you know what the employees are like. We have great benefits, but they have to work hard, and long hours." His eyes slid away from Zachary. He had promised to take better care of the employees. To ensure that they didn't have to work such long hours, that they could still function as humans and not end up sick or in an accident because they were asleep on their feet. "But… nothing that stands out to me. Nothing that was any different than usual."

"You haven't had any strange communications? Phone hang-ups, a note left in your mailbox, no—" Zachary broke off abruptly. He turned and looked at Kenzie, looking for reassurance. She hadn't made the connection yet, and stared back at him wide-eyed, waiting for an explanation.

"The note," Zachary said.

Gordon looked at him blankly, no idea what he was talking

about. "There was no note," he said. "Unless you know something I don't know. Did Bridge—"

"No. Not you. Not Bridget. *I* got a note." Zachary shook his head, trying to make it compute. Kenzie was obviously having the same problem.

"That didn't have anything to do with Gordon or the twins," she pointed out.

"No, it couldn't," Zachary mused. He still couldn't quite catch the thought and make it fit with everything else. "'I will bring the curse of a father's sins upon even the second and third generation.'"

Gordon looked startled. "What?"

Agent Bourassa was similarly perplexed. "What are you talking about? Where is that from?"

"I got a note. On Friday. It was left in my mailbox, but I don't know who sent it. It's to do with a case that I'm working on." Zachary rubbed the center of his forehead, which was pulsing with pain. How could the note have anything to do with the abduction of the twins?

"The second and third generation… it sounds like a threat to children and grandchildren," Zachary said. "But I don't have any children, let alone grandchildren."

He and Gordon looked at each other. Gordon's expression alternated between suspicious and confused. He knew that Bridget's twins were his and not Zachary's. Zachary had not been with Bridget for a couple of years. But…

"An outsider *might* think that the twins were mine," Zachary said slowly. "I was at the hospital when they were born. I sat up with them, looking after them…"

Gordon nodded slowly, scratching his jaw. Frown lines creased his forehead. "But that would mean that they were watching you way back then, last December. Have you been working on this case since then?"

"No. No, I just got it… He only died a few weeks ago."

"Who died?" Agent Bourassa demanded.

"The death that I'm investigating; it was ruled a natural death by the medical examiner, but the family wanted me to look into it further. His name was John Godfrey."

"Johnny Godfrey?" Gordon repeated, looking shocked. "I knew he had died, but they said it was a heart attack. Are you saying it wasn't?"

"I don't know. There is no proof yet, but it looks like he may have been poisoned. I've been working on it, trying to gather enough evidence to take it back to the medical examiner's office." He looked at Kenzie. "If it was poison, they will need some idea of what to look for. If it was something obscure… there is only a limited amount of blood left to test."

"*You* know him," Kenzie said to Gordon. "You don't… know anything about him or his family, do you? Or his work?"

"Well, yes. He and I have referred business to each other in the past."

51

Zachary tried to put it all together. "If a client of Godfrey's blamed him for losing their money or a loved one, is it possible that he blamed *you* for it as well? That he thought the two of you were both responsible for ruining someone? And he threatened to go after not just Godfrey's children and grandchildren, but yours too?"

"I suppose." Gordon's face had gone from white to gray. Zachary worried about the possibility that he had heart problems. The events had to be putting a tremendous emotional strain on him. The twins kidnapped, Bridget hysterical and requiring sedation, now the revelation that it might be related to something he had done in his business life.

"Where were you the last couple of hours?" Bourassa asked Zachary, his brows drawn down.

The ex was always a top suspect in any crimes. Especially if Zachary had been the father of the twins. Non-custodial parents taking children was common. Of course Zachary would be the first person they looked at.

"I've been at the Godfrey home. I was… with a police detective. You can check with her. There's no way it could have been me.

By the time I got home, Kenzie was already on the phone with Gordon."

"You could have done something between leaving this detective and returning to your home. It's not a big city. It's pretty quick to get from one place to another."

"It's Detective Garcia," Zachary said, ignoring the accusation. He pulled out his phone and read the number off to him.

Bourassa nodded. "I'll check in with her. No point in chasing suspects who have solid alibis."

He put his phone to his ear and walked away from them.

"I can't believe they would consider you a suspect," Gordon said, shaking his head. "Don't they think Bridget would have known if it was you?"

"I assume the kidnappers were wearing masks," Zachary said with a shrug.

"Yes… but she would know you whether you were wearing a mask or not. She's not blind. And even if she was, she would still know your voice."

Zachary was grateful that Gordon did not consider him a viable suspect. They could keep working on the leads while Bourassa wasted time checking alibis.

"We should talk about what clients you and John Godfrey shared. If there was someone in common between the two of you, that's a really good starting point."

"Sit down," Gordon motioned to one of the white couches. "Please. Let's put our heads together on this."

If Gordon had insisted that Zachary sit still, he probably couldn't have managed it. But the suggestion that they work through it together allowed Zachary to focus on the problem instead of having to pace around to concentrate on all the possibilities.

Gordon pulled out a drawer under the coffee table, revealing a stash of thick white writing paper and fine pens. Zachary was impressed. He would have guessed that the table was only decorative, not practical.

"Johnny's business and mine are complementary," Gordon

started off. "When they needed money to fund an investment, they went to him, and when they needed something to invest in, they came to me. We referred business back and forth if there were someone who would benefit from the other company's expertise."

"You knew that Godfrey was a loan shark?"

Gordon looked at him, brow furrowed. "Johnny was in the business of making money. His clients—the ones we shared, anyway—were sophisticated investors who understood the terms of the capitalization and could turn a profit with the money he gave them. These were not people who needed a payday loan."

"So it was okay because they knew what they were getting into."

"They were people used to dealing with large amounts of money and understood the terms they were agreeing to. I can't see anyone having a problem with that."

Zachary decided to keep any further arguments to himself. "If you can think of the clients you shared in the last..." Zachary hesitated, considering. "In the last two to three months?"

Gordon nodded as if this were reasonable. He started to write down names. Not quickly. It wasn't like he was reading off a list in front of him. He had to think about each one, to consider it gravely and then write it down. Some of his strokes were tentative, as if he weren't sure. But it was better to include people who might not have been clients of both than to leave people off of the list because he wasn't quite certain.

Zachary waited, letting him do it without interruption. Breaking his concentration would not speed things up.

Other officials arrived at the scene. Zachary looked up and saw Garcia. She nodded to him and approached, waving off Bourassa.

"What's going on?" she asked. "I don't get it. There was an abduction, but you think it was related to the Godfrey case? How could it be?" She looked at Gordon and obviously made him as the children's father. Her brows drew down while she studied him, focused on his list, and then looked at Zachary.

"John Godfrey and Gordon Drake shared some of the same clients. Gordon is my... my ex-wife's new partner. I think the threatening note might have been intended for him as much as it was for the Godfrey children. Threatening to go after the children and grandchildren… and Gordon's children were snatched, right in a public parking lot."

"You think it was our letter writer?"

"It seems like too much of a coincidence. Don't you think?"

Garcia nodded slowly. She sat down on the other side of Gordon, looking at what he had written. "Is this the list of the clients that you shared? We'll need to go through it and see if we can figure out who could be trying to get revenge. It seems like a stretch that someone would go after your children because of a bad business deal or a loan."

Gordon shrugged. "It doesn't make any sense to me either, but Zachary got the letter. He's a good investigator. He's… he's been able to help before." He gulped and looked back down at the paper. "This is everyone I can think of. I'll have to log in on my computer and see if I can find anyone else. Zachary said to go back a couple of months, but I don't remember much past that. If it's longer ago than that, I don't want to miss this guy just because he took a while to put his plan into motion."

He handed the list to Zachary rather than to Garcia. Zachary held it for a moment, looking at the unfamiliar names. He had hoped that one of them would jump out at him. That he would know just by looking at the list which one of them it was. But that kind of thing only happened in movies.

Eventually, after working through each of the names with Garcia trying to stretch her neck to see them all, he handed the list to her. She was a much faster reader than he was, or maybe she had one of those movie moments. She brought the list back down to the table almost immediately. "Wayne Duke Carver."

Zachary looked at the list and then back at her. "You know him?"

"I know *of* him."

"Is he a criminal?"

"He isn't someone who will ever be brought to justice for his crimes. Some would consider him a victim rather than the perpetrator."

Zachary's heart was beating so hard he felt like it would break through his chest. He was sweating, even though the room was cool. "Garcia," he protested. "Just explain. How do you know Carver?"

"He killed himself a few weeks ago."

"You know his name from a homicide investigation?" Zachary was impressed that she would remember the name of one suicide who had crossed her desk.

Garcia looked grim. "I remember him, because he was one of those family annihilators. He didn't just kill himself. He took everyone in the family with him. His wife and children. His daughter's children. All dead."

Zachary vaguely remembered hearing about the tragic case. He hadn't paid enough attention to remember the name, but then he wasn't a homicide cop. It wasn't his job to know anything about it, and he preferred to push it away and hear and remember as little about the tragedy as possible. He didn't need something that would bring him down when he was feeling healthy. The mention of suicide wasn't enough to cause him to have suicidal thoughts, but a study of the suicide and the events surrounding it certainly might.

"That's terrible," Gordon said. "I didn't know that."

"So that's why the letter writer included the second and third generations in the threat," Zachary suggested. "Why they are willing to take it out on innocent children. Because Carver's children and grandchildren died."

"Whoever penned the note was grieving a tragic loss," Garcia said, "just like you said. They were friends or family members of the Carver family. They blamed Godfrey and Drake for their loss."

Zachary swallowed and nodded.

And he had apparently killed Godfrey. Would he be able to follow through on the twins? Was it already too late? And who was watching the Godfrey siblings and their children?

He had snatched the twins while everyone was looking at the Godfrey children. What if he planned to do the reverse and harm or kidnap the Godfrey children or grandchildren while so many of the police department were focused on the kidnapping of Bridget's children?

"You're not looking so well," Garcia observed. "You want to take a break?"

Zachary shook his head. "No. I want to help."

She looked at him, her expression flat and impassive. Not giving away what she was thinking. But he still knew it was coming even before she opened her mouth.

"The agent and I need to have a conversation with Mr. Drake. A private conversation."

"I can help. I'm the one who made the connection between the two cases. Don't shut me out now."

"You need to take a break," she said firmly. "You look like crap. And if you want to be able to participate later when we have something to go on…" she trailed off.

But Zachary wasn't falling for her promises. She might say that she intended to let Zachary participate in the investigation once they had a good lead, but he knew very well that she wouldn't. It was one thing to be working with him when she was inquiring further into a case that had been closed. It was quite another to involve him when someone out there was holding two infants hostage. Or worse.

"Go splash some water on your face," Garcia suggested. "Get yourself together. We just need a few minutes. We can't interview Drake with you present."

52

Zachary was forced to leave the living room, along with Kenzie and several less-important law enforcement officers who were hanging around, interested in the goings-on but not actually involved in the case. Zachary decided to take Garcia's advice and splash some water on his face to try to settle his whirling brain enough to sort out the problem of finding out *what* friend or relative of Wayne Duke Carver was taking revenge on Godfrey and Gordon.

"I'll be out in a few minutes," he told Kenzie as she was escorted to a small sitting room to wait as they interviewed Gordon.

She nodded. Zachary followed Gordon's directions to a nearby powder room. He sat on the toilet seat with his phone, thinking through everything they had discovered in the last twenty-four hours. Events were moving quickly and it was hard to keep up with all of the information and integrate it in order to be able to formulate a theory. Garcia would be having the same problem, he was sure.

But they didn't have the luxury of time. There were two infant girls out there who were depending on them, assuming that Logan's half-brother hadn't already done something to harm them. Bridget would be devastated if anything happened to them and, as much as he was trying to keep his life separate from hers and forget about what they had shared, he still cared about what happened to her. She did not need the trauma of losing two children on top of everything else she had been through in the last couple of years. He had to focus on the problem and figure it out.

His camera was around his neck, and all the pictures he had taken at the Godfrey house were on it. He had not been able to find any clues in the pictures he had taken when he had reviewed them before, but that didn't mean that there wasn't anything there. A footprint. A scrap of paper that had fallen out of someone's pocket into the flowerbed. A broken branch that suggested that someone had entered the house through means other than the door.

The screen on the camera was tiny and it was difficult to zoom in and out and manipulate pictures. But the camera had wireless functionality which allowed him to transfer photos immediately to his phone when he needed to send something off to a client while still on surveillance. He established a connection and sent all the photos on the camera to his phone.

There were more than he had expected, and it took a few minutes to transfer everything. Zachary kept an eye on the time, expecting Kenzie to come knocking at the door any minute to find out if he was okay because he was taking too long. But she must have decided that he needed time to himself, and she didn't.

With the photo transfer complete, Zachary started to thumb through the pictures slowly, looking for anything he had missed. It wasn't as easy as it would have been on his computer, but his phone had a reasonably large screen, and it was easy to pinch, zoom, and pan around as he needed to.

There was nothing on the photos of the exterior of the house. No suspicious footprints or sign that someone had broken into the house. But there wouldn't be if Charlotte had poisoned John Godfrey at Logan's urging.

Had Logan had contact with his half-brother? Was that how it was all connected? The half-brother could have made contact with him and, finding out what his father had done, Logan decided to take action, but still to cover it up as much as he could. Having Charlotte do his dirty work for him was safer. He had plausible deniability. He could say that she had just done it on her own, that he had never intended for her to do anything to hurt him.

He had taken pictures of the house's interior the first time he had been there, and he thumbed backward through the photos to look at the shots of John's bedroom, the study, and the dining room. He knew he wouldn't find anything that hadn't been there before, but he was desperate.

Saved ahead of the pictures he had taken while walking around the house with Garcia were pictures of documents he had given her. There hadn't been enough time to photograph every sheet, but he had snapped everything he could. Everything that he knew was important and some that required further study.

Now that he at least had some names to consider—Wayne Duke Carver being the chief among them—maybe he could dig down deeper and find something there.

He began a search on the name Carver. He had an app that would OCR all the documents to fully index them, which would take several hours. A search, however, would start a rapid scan through the documents looking for any squiggles that might match the name Carver. It was very fast, and he had used it a number of times before to drill down to the information he needed. With his learning disabilities, it took a long time for him to read through documents or to skim over the words looking for a specific keyword, which seemed so easy for Kenzie and the other neurotypicals.

The search program would even search through the handwritten pages and would be much more accurate at identifying possible mentions of Carver's name than Zachary could himself. At least he could read cursive, unlike a lot of teens and millennials. It wasn't easy, but he'd learned to read and write cursive in school, unlike the digital natives.

The search started throwing up some results. Zachary found several ledgers showing amounts loaned to Carver and a couple of initial payments he had made. Much too small to even cover the interest on the money he had taken from Godfrey. Zachary's stomach was tied in knots as he thought about how horrified Carver must have been to see the amount of debt he owed rapidly increasing, with no way to pay it back.

Godfrey had made a note regarding the investment Carver had made with Gordon Drake, which was apparently why he had borrowed the money to start with. Godfrey's note indicated that the investment fund or company he had put money into had tanked. No money would be recoverable.

Carver had lost every penny that he had borrowed. And Zachary had a pretty good idea he wasn't the savvy investor that Gordon claimed. Someone who had their fingers in a lot of different pies would not be pleased about a bad investment, but he would be able to cover the losses through other means. Maybe they would even declare bankruptcy. Zachary knew from when he was a part of Bridget's world that wealthy people sometimes went through several bankruptcies as they established their businesses and decided what they wanted to do with their lives. And they seemed no worse off for it. For those people, losing everything on paper did not equate to losing everything in real life, and there were always certain assets that a bankruptcy couldn't touch, family and friends to fall back on, and money coming in from other sources. Zachary didn't know how it worked, but a rich person declaring bankruptcy wasn't the same as someone living on the poverty line who suddenly lost his savings, home, car, and everything else. Gordon might claim that he only dealt with sophisticated investors, but Zachary knew Carver was not the same as all of Gordon's other clients.

And he had seen a flicker in Gordon's eye when he talked about Carver. Understanding, regret, and fear. Gordon knew he had made a mistake in taking on Carver as a client.

A mistake that ended up putting his family in great danger.

Zachary returned to the list of results for the name Carver and continued to look for any possible connections.

In a notebook, he found the scribbled words, "Wayne Duke Carver, son of Mary Kendall."

Zachary's heart raced. His face broke out in a sweat.

There was a knock on the door. "Zachary? You okay?"

53

Zachary swallowed. He reached over, turned the tap on, and passed his hand through the stream several times.

"I'm fine," he told Kenzie, allowing his voice to remain hoarse. "I'll be out soon." He turned the water off and sniffled loudly, then dried his hand and blew his nose. "Just give me a minute."

"Take your time," Kenzie assured him. "No rush. I just wanted to make sure you didn't need anything."

He heard her footsteps retreat. He looked back down at the phone. *Son of Mary Kendall.* The name had obviously meant something to John Godfrey.

Zachary switched to his web browser, tapped in the names Mary Kendall and Wayne Duke Carver, and held his breath, anxiously awaiting the results.

There were a lot of hits that obviously were not anything. But there was an obituary for Mary Kendall, who was survived by her two sons, Wayne Duke Carver and Dylan Marion McArthur.

The police were not stopping people from leaving the scene and, although a couple of them looked surprised to see Zachary coming out a door other than the front door by which he had entered, none of them stopped him to ask any questions. He walked to his car at a leisurely pace, knowing that he could trip or draw attention to himself if he went faster than his usual pace. It was nerve-racking walking past the large living room windows and hoping no one would notice him. He was glad he'd been forced to park down the block so that Kenzie and Detective Garcia wouldn't notice his car driving away from the house.

He knew that pursuing the case on his own and not involving Garcia and Agent Bourassa was the wrong thing to do. It might get him locked up. Or worse. But he wanted to move quickly and stealthily, which would not be possible with a whole contingent of police and federal agents.

It wouldn't take them long to find out that Wayne Duke Carver was survived by a brother, even if he did have a different last name. There was no online obituary for Carver, probably because he had killed everyone in his family and no one had wanted to honor him. And it wouldn't take the police long to find the address of Carver's deceased mother when nothing appeared on a search of the land titles office under his name.

Maybe it would be nothing. But there was a chance Zachary was right and could get to Dylan before he could do anything more to the children.

He drove at sedate speeds, trying not to attract the attention of law enforcement officers or get caught speeding by any cameras. As long as he stayed below the radar, they were unlikely to find him before he had reached his destination.

His phone started to ring when he was nearly at the Carver house. Zachary glanced at the phone where it was clamped in a dashboard mount and saw Kenzie's name.

So she had discovered his absence. He was lucky that Garcia's name wasn't the first one to show up on his caller ID. Maybe Kenzie would give it a little bit longer before she let Garcia know that Zachary had fled. Maybe she thought he had just gone for a walk in the fresh air to compose himself. But it would be obvious when he didn't answer that something else was going on.

After Kenzie's call was routed to voicemail, she called again. And again. She sent him a text, gently asking if he was okay and to please call her. He wondered how long she would continue to be calm and supportive before she exploded with the realization that he was off pursuing a lead on his own. And he'd left her stranded, though she could get a cab or ride share if she wanted to get out of there and knew where she wanted to go.

"Sorry, Kenz," he said aloud. "I couldn't involve you in this."

He reached the address of the house registered to Mary Kendall and circled the block, eyes roving back and forth as he took everything in and tried to come up with a solid strategy. He examined both the front and the back of the house in question, the various entrances and windows, fences and gates. There was a detached garage. No lights. Windows covered so no one could see inside. It was not unusual for people to cover their garage windows so that no one could see whether the car or any expensive tools or equipment were inside. Or to stave off heat loss and high utility bills.

He couldn't see whether there was a white van inside the garage. If it had been winter, he might have at least had tire tracks to examine, but it was summer, and there was no way for him to tell how many times a vehicle had been driven into or out of the garage recently, or to speculate what kind of vehicle it was based on the size of the tire tracks and the wheelbase.

It was good that Zachary and Kenzie had left in a hurry and taken Zachary's car instead of Kenzie's convertible. It was nondescript and blended into the neighborhood but, even more importantly, Zachary's surveillance equipment was stored in the trunk.

He listened first with the laser mic, pointing it at each exposed window. He wasn't able to hear any conversation, but there was background noise. Maybe a TV. He was hoping that Dylan would be alone. Confronting or sneaking past one kidnapper was stupid enough. If the second man who had been involved in the kidnapping were there, the odds of Zachary being able to achieve any measure of success got much worse. And what if there had been more people involved? Someone else in the back of the van. Maybe standing by with a weapon in case Bridget had shown any fight or things went badly.

He pointed the mic at the garage and listened for a long time but, even with the sensitivity turned all the way up, he couldn't hear anything inside. If the twins had been left in a vehicle or in their stroller in the garage, they were asleep. Or worse.

The benefit of it not being winter was that he didn't leave footprints everywhere he went. After listening for any activity in the house once more, he left his car parked down the alley and took a quick walk around the house, reaching up to press an adhesive micro camera to each of the windows.

He returned to his car and brought up the cameras' feeds on his phone one at a time after plugging it into the USB charging port of the vehicle. The amount of data being transferred was minimal, with a low frame rate on each camera, which he could increase if he needed full video capabilities, but it still ate up the battery.

He had tried to position each camera where he could see past the curtains or blinds, and had mostly succeeded. It was a little three-bedroom bungalow, with one of the bedrooms being used as a home office. One of the bedrooms had the curtains closed, and Zachary had hoped that by positioning the camera at the split in the curtains, he would have a good view of what was going on in the room, but the view was still mostly blocked. Between the heavy fabric of the curtains and the lights being turned out, the room was pretty dark. A good place for sleeping babies? He wished one of the twins would cry so he would know that they were all right.

The living room camera confirmed his belief that the noise in the house was caused by a TV being left on. A man had fallen asleep in an easy chair across from it and was slumbering soundly.

Zachary studied him, looking for similarities to Logan in the man's features. If this was the letter writer, they had the same biological father. Zachary couldn't see much resemblance between the two of them. Both had dark hair and glasses, but the shape of their faces was not the same. The man in the chair was quite a bit older, starting to go gray. He had a narrow chin rather than Logan's oval face. Even asleep, Zachary thought he looked ratlike and furtive. But that was probably just his bias against a man who took his vengeance out on innocent children.

It was time to act. Zachary could call Garcia and tell her what he had found so far, or he could go in. The trouble with calling Garcia was that he still had no proof, or even strong evidence that the kidnapper was Dylan. And there was nothing to indicate that it had been Dylan rather than Charlotte who had poisoned John Godfrey. Garcia would not be happy if he blew up the theory that it had been Charlotte who had poisoned Godfrey at Logan's insistence. She was the one who'd had access, not Dylan. There had been no indication of a break-in or intruder of any kind.

If he called Garcia, he would be pulling her away from her investigation, which might bear fruit, on the off chance that Zachary was right in his guesses. The Mary Kendall who owned the house he was observing might be a different Mary Kendall from Carver's mother. The man snoozing in front of the TV might not be Dylan or anyone related to him. Garcia could not walk into the house without a warrant or an invitation and, if she couldn't get either one, she wouldn't be able to do anything but stand outside the property. She needed a warrant to do what Zachary had already done, installing cameras and bugging the house.

So he knew, even before he began the debate with himself, that he wasn't going to call Garcia or Agent Bourassa to bring them into the loop.

He sent a text to Kenzie, then forced himself to climb out of the car to do what he had to.

54

Zachary tried the back door and found that there was no need for his lock picks. Dylan had obligingly left the door unlocked for Zachary. He hesitated, thinking about that. Would Dylan have left the door unlocked if he had just kidnapped a couple of infants? Even if he didn't normally lock his doors, it seemed to Zachary that committing a crime like that would make the perpetrator more careful and paranoid about someone finding out.

But the door was unlocked. That was the way things worked out sometimes. They just made it easier for Zachary to proceed with his investigation.

He opened the door quietly and slipped into the house. He walked into the same noise as he had heard over the laser mic, but clear and crisp this time with no assistance. He moved quietly through the rooms, having already observed the layout and what he could expect to see in each room. At least, what the camera angles had allowed him to see through the curtains and blinds.

He stopped in the living room. The furniture was old, probably the way Mary Kendall had decorated it years earlier. The smell of fast-food hamburgers hung in the air. Zachary looked at the sleeping man, wondering whether he should stop to talk to him or go through the rest of the house first to see if there was any sign of the babies. Dylan did not appear to be armed, but he could be, and Zachary was not. It was best for Zachary to take him by surprise and not allow him the chance to think about weapons or defending himself. But it was also easier to search the rest of the house if Dylan was asleep and couldn't stop him.

There was the sound of an opening door, and a woman's voice. "They're down, but—"

Zachary whirled around. He and the woman stared at each other, both frozen in place.

She swore.

Zachary was kicking himself for not realizing someone else was in the house. He thought he had been careful enough, listening and watching before going in. But she had been in the darkened room, out of sight of the camera, having a nap or—her words suddenly registered with his brain—putting the babies down to sleep. And he had misjudged and entered a house outnumbered and unarmed.

He should at least start carrying a taser in such situations. He would never buy a gun or other deadly weapon, but a taser could come in handy in a situation where he might have to defend himself.

"What are *you* doing here?" Charlotte demanded.

Zachary shook his head, taking in her blond hair and familiar features. "I could ask you the same thing."

The sleeping man snorted and stirred, muttering something incomprehensible.

"Dylan, wake up!" Charlotte called out to him sharply. "We've got trouble."

He jerked and sat up straight. He opened his eyes and then blinked at Zachary a few times. He looked at Charlotte, frowning.

"What's going on?"

"Wake up! You need all your faculties here!"

"I'm awake," he growled. "What is this? Who is—what are you doing in my house?"

"This is Goldman, the private detective," Charlotte told him.

Dylan stopped scratching and looked at Zachary warily. He hadn't been too worried up until then. Maybe he thought that Zachary was someone Charlotte had invited over to help. That he was supposed to perform some service for them. But knowing who Zachary was, he started to get cagier.

"What? Goldman? Who is that?" He straightened and looked around the room, evaluating his position, figuring out how quickly he could get up and attack Zachary. What if Zachary was armed? Did he have enough time to get there?

Charlotte wasn't playing games. She took a few steps closer to Zachary. "I don't understand how you could be here. How could you know where I live?"

"I didn't come here looking for you," Zachary explained to her. "I came looking for him." He nodded to Dylan. "And the twins."

She swore again. Maybe until then, she had hoped that he had an innocent reason for being there. He had a few more questions to ask her and had just happened to figure out where she lived. But Zachary knowing about the twins confirmed the situation.

"What do you think you're going to do with them?" Zachary asked, keeping the outrage and accusation out of his voice. Just as a casual inquiry. Curiosity. "Are you going to ask for a ransom? Try to sell them on the black market?"

He didn't ask if they intended to kill them. Never that.

Charlotte's jaw clenched. Maybe this was something that she wanted to know too, but Dylan hadn't given her a satisfactory answer. After they kidnapped the babies, then what? They had poisoned John Godfrey. Did they intend to kill the babies? The Godfrey siblings? Their children? Little Wally and Finn? Did Dylan really intend to take a life for every one he had lost? His brother, his sister-in-law, and their children and grandchildren?

"When did the two of you get together?" Zachary asked, since there was no answer to the question of what they were planning to do with the babies. "Was it just recently, because you both had ties to the Godfrey family, or…?"

Charlotte had worked for the Godfreys for several years, so Zachary assumed that Dylan had taken advantage of that relationship, finding some way to bump into Charlotte and convince her to act as his pawn.

"We've been together for years," Dylan sneered, proving Zachary's speculation wrong, "I was the one who got Charlotte that job with Him. I didn't think, back then, that things would turn out as they did. But I'm glad that I got it for her now. It was so easy, with someone already in place there."

"Why would you get her a job there three years ago? And how? You knew… John Godfrey?"

"Knew that his wife had a thing with my dad, you mean? Yeah. You think that the upper crust has values, but they don't. They're just as bad or worse than anyone else."

Zachary nodded slowly. "Yes, you're right about that," he agreed. "But how did you get her a job? You met Mrs. Godfrey?"

"Yeah. Introduced myself a few years ago. Made sure both of them knew who I was. That I could make a lot of noise that they might not appreciate; if they didn't want her exposed and her youngest son outed as illegitimate, then they'd better be willing to help out now and then. Do some favors for the poor relations."

"You were blackmailing them."

Dylan chuckled. "They were helping me out of the goodness of their hearts. Whatever I needed, they could help out. It was very handy to milk them for whatever I needed."

But now that cow had gone. But if that had been Dylan's and Charlotte's doing, then why? Why kill the cow?

"It was all working so well," Dylan said. "I should have known that he was going to ruin everything. I should have known it."

Zachary tried to look sympathetic. "What did he do?"

"I told him that Wayne needed help. He was in pretty bad shape. The downturn in the economy, losing his family's savings, he was in a bad place. I wanted him to set Wayne up. Get him into investing, make it so that he could make money and get back everything he had lost."

Zachary wondered how he had lost it all in the first place. Gambling? Bad investments? Addiction? Or something beyond his control, like an illness or accident? Medical bills could be crippling and wipe out a family's hard-earned savings in a day.

"But the investment failed," Zachary filled in. "He couldn't repay what he had borrowed and had no hope of getting it back."

Dylan nodded. He leaned forward, his face red with rage. "Godfrey had all the money he needed and ten times that. He was harassing Wayne for payment. Foreclosing on his house. Threatening to send goons after him or after his wife. What did Wayne do to deserve that? He worked hard all his life."

"And Mrs. Godfrey was gone. You couldn't bring pressure to bear on her anymore."

"She was gone. My mom was gone. He said he wasn't granting any more of my requests. I'd gotten enough out of the relationship, and he was done with me. He didn't care if I tried to tarnish the reputation of his dead wife. People would give her a free ride. Write her off as a lonely woman who had reached out to the wrong man at a difficult time in her life. She was dead; people would forgive a little indiscretion."

"What happened to your father? Logan's father?"

"He went dogging off after some other guy's wife, I guess. He was never a part of my life. Or Logan's, obviously. He was just some… some gigolo who seduced them."

Zachary looked back toward the room Charlotte had come out of. "Are you really planning something to harm the twins? I think you know… that if you got caught, the public would never forgive you. They might overlook the early death of an aging millionaire, but twin infants? You know the courts wouldn't show you any mercy for that."

"What courts? I don't plan on getting caught." Dylan looked past Zachary to his partner in crime. "What about you, Charlotte? You're not going to get caught, are you?"

Charlotte glanced toward Zachary. He was a significant wrench in the works. Did they really think they could get away with anything now that he was in the house? Did Dylan think that nothing had changed?

55

"You were the one who left the note at my house," Zachary said, appraising Dylan's build and body language. "I thought it was a note threatening the Godfreys. Is that what you meant, or were you going to go after Gordon's children right from the start?"

"Oh, I knew about his twins," Dylan chuckled. "Wayne would tell me about them all the time. How his investment advisor was expecting twins and was so excited about it. And then that his wife had gone into early labor and they were struggling. And her with a chronic illness. Wayne felt bad for them, for everything they had to go through. This guy could afford the top care for his wife and kids, everything they could possibly want or need, and Wayne had nothing. But Wayne felt sorry for him."

Zachary was careful not to show any emotion at Dylan's comments. Dylan didn't know Bridget. He didn't know the twins. He wasn't emotionally invested in any of them. "How did you know that I knew Gordon? And where I lived?"

"Because he loved to tell the story. How his wife's ex had jumped in to save the day, sitting up with the babies, guarding them from any harm, even when he was supposed to be in the hospital himself." Dylan nodded. "Oh, yeah. I heard all about it.

Wayne was there when Drake ordered flowers to be delivered to your girlfriend. Knew her name, the street where she lived, all that stuff." He laughed. "Gordon had to show off what a great guy he was to Wayne; that he was doing this, sending her flowers for her boyfriend's part in the whole thing. He went on and on about it."

Zachary swallowed and nodded. He vaguely remembered Kenzie telling him about Gordon sending flowers, but he had been in such a deep, dark well of depression that it was fuzzy and gray. He had been sleep-deprived and paranoid; the borders between reality and dreams had been very permeable.

It was a nice gesture. But then Gordon had opened his mouth to the wrong person and, apparently Wayne had shared every word with Dylan. Right down to where Kenzie lived.

"So you kidnapped the twins because you thought Gordon gave your brother bad investment advice? And what is that supposed to prove? What is the plan?"

Maybe he shouldn't be pushing Dylan to think ahead. Not if the plan had been to harm the twins. Right now, they were safe, asleep in the darkened room. Maybe Charlotte had prevailed on her partner not to do anything to hurt them. And now they were stuck, unsure what to do next.

"He did more than give Wayne bad business advice," Dylan growled. He sat up taller and his face flushed. "He wiped him out. He was in a bad situation and, instead of making things better like he was supposed to do, instead of rescuing Wayne, he made things worse. Took it all away from him. Wayne didn't feel like a man anymore. He couldn't provide for his family. They were going to lose their house. The only security they had. Instead of getting him out of the hole he was in, Gordon Drake dug it deeper. He and Godfrey conspired to take everything Wayne had."

"I'm sure that wasn't the plan…" Zachary protested, trying to think of something to soothe Dylan. But Dylan had been talking himself into this for a while. He'd been using his anger to justify the actions he was taking. He wasn't the villain for snatching the twins. Gordon and John Godfrey were the villains. Dylan was just taking justifiable retribution.

"You don't know what it's like to lose everything," Dylan told Zachary. "You have no idea."

"I *have* lost everything. More than once. When I was ten, my house burned down, destroying everything we owned."

Zachary's throat was tight, and he struggled to stay in the present and not let his brain take him back there again. He needed to handle Dylan, to save the babies. He couldn't afford to slide into flashbacks. He cataloged the room around him, detailing the furniture and decor, the chatter and laugh track on the TV, the smell of onions and deep-fryer fat hanging in the air. He didn't say these anchors out loud as he would have with Kenzie, but he imagined writing them down in his notebook, recording his observations of the scene. Any little detail might be what he needed to get himself and the twins out of the situation safely.

The TV still played. The lights were dim. Charlotte had taken another step closer, but Zachary didn't feel threatened by her. She didn't appear to be armed. And while Zachary wasn't a big man or in great physical shape, neither was she. But two people against one did create a problem.

"When the house burned down, I was separated from my family. I grew up alone in foster care. No home, no permanent family, hardly any possessions."

Dylan scowled at this. Maybe trying to refute what Dylan said wasn't the best choice. Hostage negotiators were trained to agree with hostage takers. To establish a connection of trust between them. Was telling Dylan that he did know what it was like to lose everything the right option?

But Dylan did seem to at least be listening and considering it. Maybe the important thing was to keep him talking and distracted from the twins.

"Then, a few years ago, I met Bridget. I thought it was my one chance at family and happiness. But when she got pregnant, she didn't want anything to do with me or the baby. Then she found out she had cancer, and she kicked me out. That was it. Instead of having me supporting her through her illness, she decided I was too much of a drain on her and ended the marriage."

Zachary cleared his throat. It was in the past. Old news. Bridget had recovered from cancer and gone on to meet Gordon and had a life and children with him. Zachary had met Kenzie and had a life with her—though he would be in the doghouse for ditching her at Gordon's house. Zachary's life was better than it had been when he'd been with Bridget.

"I got my own place, got back on my feet again. And then… fire took that home too. And all of my identification, photography, and personal items. I was left with nothing. No home, no access to my money, and nothing but the clothes on my back. Not even a coat, in the middle of winter."

"And that's *his* fault," Dylan told Zachary.

"What?"

"Gordon Drake. You think he didn't start seeing your wife until after the two of you broke up? I guarantee you they were seeing each other before that. She was sneaking out on you with him. That's why she broke up with you, not over anything else. He stole her from you. And now he's raising kids with her. The kids that should have been yours!"

56

Zachary swallowed hard. Too many times, he had told himself the same thing. That Gordon had supplanted him and taken his happiness. That Bridget's children should have been his. He had always been faithful to her. He'd wanted to raise children with her, but she had rejected the idea. Was she already with Gordon at that point, listening to his promises for a better life? He could give her all the things that Zachary couldn't. Money, stability, position. With Gordon Drake as a partner instead of Zachary Goldman, the broken, neurotic, hopelessly awkward private investigator, she could rise socially, and people would look up to her instead of pitying her.

She hadn't even let Zachary visit her during her cancer treatments. Was that because Gordon was already there, and she didn't want them to run into each other? She didn't want Zachary to know that she had replaced him before he even knew there was a problem?

"If she's happier with him, then good for her," he told Dylan stoically. "I always wanted her to be happy. And she wasn't happy with me."

"What a loser," Dylan scoffed. "You think you're kidding anyone with that line? I could feel it when you were talking about losing everything. When you say you're happy that she's happy now, do you know what I feel? Nothing. Nothing but disgust."

The lump in Zachary's throat swelled so large he could hardly breathe.

"*You* might want her to be happy," Charlotte interjected, "but *we* sure don't." She looked at Dylan for his approval. She might have dominated Logan, trying to inflame things between him and John Godfrey so that she didn't have to be the one to administer the poison but, in her relationship with Dylan, she was submissive, seeking his validation. "We want Drake to suffer. We want his entire family to suffer, just like Wayne's."

"Do you know what it was like?" Dylan whispered hoarsely. "Finding out what he had done? All of them dead? Right down to a babe in arms." He stared off into the distance, tears in his eyes. "Even the baby had to suffer. Do you think that's justice? What do you think the punishment should be for something like that?"

"But Gordon isn't the one who did that. That was your brother's choice. He did a terrible thing. That was not the right choice. There were so many other things he could have done. People and organizations he could have asked for help. He didn't have to do what he did."

"He didn't see any other way out. And that is Gordon Drake's and John Godfrey's fault. John Godfrey will never watch his grandkids grow up now. He'll never be able to get the relationships with his kids right. Because he's gone. They can't do anything about it now."

"And that was you?" Zachary looked at Charlotte. "You're the one who poisoned his drink? The nightcap?"

He didn't expect her to admit it. Who would confess to something like that? They didn't have any proof that it was her and probably never would. They might be able to convince a jury that she'd been the one with the best opportunity and that she had the motive, but so did Logan and the others. Any of them could have done it.

Charlotte looked at Dylan, her eyes bright and eager. "We were getting tired of waiting. I thought Logan would do it if I put the thought into his head, but the loser wouldn't lift a finger to do anything for himself. He'd complain about his life, the poor boy living in the mansion with everything handed to him on a silver platter. But he wouldn't do anything about it. I gave him everything he needed, and he still wouldn't do it. He was just waiting for his father to come around. He couldn't see that it would never happen. The old man wasn't going to give him the freedom he wanted, wasn't going to support him if he didn't do what he was told." She shook her head in disgust.

"And you couldn't wait for him any longer," Zachary suggested.

"No." Charlotte shot a look at Dylan. "We had to do it. For Wayne."

"And you couldn't let Gordon be happy with his children."

"He is a good dad," Dylan growled. "He obviously loves them. And why should he get to enjoy them when Wayne didn't? When Wayne had lost everything because of Drake's mismanagement?"

Charlotte's eyes darted suddenly over to the room where the babies were sleeping. Zachary hadn't heard anything, but it was clear that she had heard one of them stir or make a sound. He took a couple of strides toward the room, his movements automatic. He didn't consciously make a choice, but his instinct to protect the children instantly kicked in.

"No, you don't," Charlotte warned, holding out her hand to stop him.

"I need to see them," Zachary insisted.

She grabbed him as he entered the hallway and shoved him into the wall. "No! Dylan, help me!"

There was a creak and a groan as Dylan struggled up from his comfortable seat. He wasn't moving quickly, but Charlotte continued to fend Zachary off until he got there, and the two of them managed to wrestle him into submission together. The more tightly they held him, the more desperate Zachary was to see the twins. He writhed and tried to twist out of their grips. What had she done to the twins? Maybe they weren't sleeping. Maybe Charlotte had smothered them with a pillow, and one last agonal breath had attracted Charlotte's attention. If Zachary could reach them, maybe he could do something.

It was a brawl. Zachary had to see the twins and tend to them, but Charlotte and Dylan were just as determined to keep him from them. They had their plan, which involved inflicting as much pain as possible on Gordon, and that overflowed onto Bridget and the twins. But Zachary couldn't allow that. Every time he escaped their grasps for a moment, one of them would punch or kick him, grab him, and take him to the floor. His face hurt, his head, his body. Every time he crawled to his knees or feet, they were there, beating on him again.

But they didn't know his history. They didn't know how many times he had been beaten by someone much bigger and stronger than he was. He wasn't going to give in because of a little pain.

57

There were shouts and crashes but, in the throes of the fight, Zachary didn't realize immediately that someone else had arrived. Not another attacker, but uniformed saviors who were pulling Charlotte and Dylan back, shouting instructions and threats. Zachary sagged with relief. It was over. He didn't care about the cops manhandling him as well, yelling at him simultaneously to put his hands on the wall and then lace them behind his head, who searched his pockets and body with rough, impersonal hands.

"The babies are in there," Zachary told them, trying to nod to the bedroom. "I need to see them. I need to make sure they are okay."

"Shut up!"

Zachary let them bully him, dragging him out of the hallway as if he were one of the kidnappers, seating him with Dylan and Charlotte, all in a row on the living room floor, hands cuffed, legs crossed.

Garcia and Bourassa didn't make their entrance until the rest of the house was cleared and the cops were sure that everyone had been subdued and contained. Zachary was not surprised to see that neither of them was particularly happy. They conversed with the head of the insertion team and were led to the bedroom. Zachary couldn't see what was going on but, remaining as still as possible, tried to hear every word they said. A cold hand clenched around his heart when he heard them call for an ambulance. Was he too late? He had done everything he could to get there as quickly as possible and prevent any harm.

Garcia walked back down the hallway to the living room. She stood in front of Zachary, looking down at him.

"So you're willing to follow the rules and work with the law enforcement officers on the case until you're not," she observed. "And then you go bat crap crazy?"

Zachary couldn't restrain the embarrassed grin that forced its way onto his features. "I'm sorry…"

"You are not," she declared. "You're not the least bit sorry that you kept us out of this and went all Rambo on it yourself."

"Rambo?" Zachary looked down at himself. He'd never been called that before. He didn't have any weapons. Or muscles. If she was looking for some bronzed, muscle-bound hero dripping with sweat, she would have to look elsewhere. Except for the dripping with sweat part—he had that covered. And he wasn't sure whether the moisture dripping below his nose was sweat, tears, or blood.

Garcia gave a low chuckle.

"Are they okay?" Zachary asked, twisting his neck to look anxiously toward the bedroom as if he could see from where he sat. "I heard you call for an ambulance."

"They look okay, but we can't rouse them. They may have been drugged, and I don't think I need to tell you how dangerous that is for an infant. We need to get them medical care as soon as possible."

"But they're alive. And unharmed."

"They will need full examinations to confirm that. But yes, they appear to be unharmed, other than being sedated."

And they were too young to remember the trauma. When they woke up, they would be back with their family and the kidnapping would just be a bad dream, no more traumatic than being left with a babysitter. He hoped.

"We didn't do anything to hurt them," Charlotte asserted.

Garcia and Zachary both ignored her. Of course she would say that. And her story would morph. She had been coerced into it by Dylan. He had threatened her, held something over her. He had misled her into thinking they were in danger and he was rescuing them. But Zachary had their original story on record.

Zachary didn't ask to be released but, eventually, Garcia bent down and helped him to his feet, then unlocked the handcuffs. Zachary rolled his shoulders and massaged his wrists. He was covered with scratches, scrapes, and bruises, and tomorrow he would be a riot of colors, he was sure. He hadn't been in a knock-down drag-out fight like that in a long time. A taser would definitely have helped.

"How are you feeling?" Garcia asked.

"Fine. No permanent damage."

She looked him over, shaking her head. "When the adrenaline rush wears off and you feel the extent of your injuries, you might change your story."

Zachary shrugged. It didn't really matter. He would sacrifice his body and comfort for two helpless infants any day. That protective streak was a mile wide, ingrained as it was to protect his younger siblings, then foster siblings, from those much larger and more powerful, and ensure that they had enough to eat, clothes and blankets to keep warm, and other necessities of life. He could not overlook the neglect or abuse of a child. It wasn't in him.

"Come outside," Garcia told him. "Kenzie will need to see that you're okay, and then we can chat about just how you got here and what compelled you to do it on your own and go charging into danger without any backup."

"Well… I knew you would come, so it wasn't exactly with *no* backup."

"Have you ever watched any cop shows on TV? What happens when one of them charges into a building with no backup, even if it is 'on the way'?"

Zachary looked down, somewhat embarrassed, as Garcia escorted him out of the house. "Well, they get ambushed," he offered. "But every other cop I've dealt with has told me not to go by what I see on TV."

Garcia gave a bark of laughter.

58

There was a crowd gathering outside. Plenty of emergency vehicles, marked and unmarked, cops outside as well as in, neighbors hanging around to get the scoop on what had happened. Kenzie was outside the perimeter, but Garcia motioned to one of the officers securing the scene to let her into the front yard.

Kenzie hurried over to him. "Zachary!" She held his face in her hands, looking him over critically. "I can't believe you did that! Whatever possessed you to come over here instead of passing the information on to Detective Garcia and the agent? And don't tell me 'poor impulse control,' because that isn't going to cut it today."

It had not been an impulse this time. Maybe his dash for the bedroom to look in on the babies had been impulsive, but escaping detection at Gordon's house and making his way over to Dylan on his own had been a deliberate move, and he had planned carefully before making his way inside.

He let Kenzie pull him in for a hug and patted her soothingly on the back, knowing that it must have been difficult for her to see that he was in danger.

"There wasn't enough evidence," Zachary explained. "They

wouldn't have been able to get in without a warrant, and there wasn't enough evidence to get a warrant."

"So you decided you would just come over here like a cowboy and take care of everything yourself instead of waiting until they could build a case."

At least she had said cowboy instead of Rambo. It was a little easier for him to see himself as a lone cowboy than a soldier. But a cowboy without a gun.

"I was careful," Zachary told her. "I made sure that I had the cameras and microphone set up so that you could all see and hear what was going on, so that anything they said could be used…"

"You were *not* careful," she snapped. "Collecting evidence is not the same as being careful."

"Well… I let you know where I was."

"You should have given Garcia everything you knew and let the police take care of it."

Zachary shrugged. "That would have taken too long."

"And as a result… look at you. Why would you rush into something like this? You're lucky that they weren't both armed! How could you take that chance?"

"I had to protect the babies. Make sure that they were okay."

"How many broken bones do you have?"

Garcia looked surprised at this. "He's banged up pretty good, but I don't think anything is broken."

"I know this man better than you do. Zachary?"

Garcia was right that the adrenaline rush was preventing Zachary from feeling the full extent of his injuries. He tried to evaluate.

"Nothing to be worried about," he assured Kenzie. "Maybe a rib." He looked at his hands, bloodied and scraped up. Already swelling. "Knuckles."

"What about your head? It looks like they bashed it into the wall a few times."

He explored the most tender spot with his fingertips. "I don't think so. I think it's fine."

"You're getting x-rays."

Zachary sighed, but he was resigned to whatever Kenzie deemed necessary. Including the lectures and recriminations that would probably go on for weeks. And he deserved them. But it was a small price to pay for rescuing Bridget's twins.

"You could have really screwed things up," Garcia told Zachary severely, clearly not believing that he was taking it seriously enough. "You could have been killed before we got here. You could have made them run or do something to harm the children. Obviously, you couldn't just fight the two of them off and prevent anything from happening. You needed us here to help you for that."

"I didn't plan to fight them," Zachary pointed out. "I checked out the house first. I had audio and video. Dylan was sleeping. I thought I could get into and out of the house cleanly. And if I couldn't… well, you would know where I was."

"The police are not your agents. We don't work for you. You had no idea if I would come here or even know where you were."

Zachary raised his brows. "I've worked with you for a few days. I knew you would come. And my location is shared with Kenzie, so I knew you could find me."

"That gets us into the neighborhood, but not to the house you were in. You're parked down the block. You're lucky we got here in time."

"Then I guess I'm lucky," he agreed. "And the babies are safe."

"Don't think I'll ever involve you in a case again. You promised me you would work within the law and not cause problems. If I see you again in the future, you will not be on my party invitations list."

"But the babies are safe."

She looked frustrated with his insistence that this was the only thing that mattered. But how could she argue it? The potential consequences for the police department and the media attention would have been dire if the babies had been lost, regardless of how it had come about. Their rescue, on the other hand, would cover up a multitude of other faults. The public—and Bridget Downy—would forgive just about anything in light of their safe return.

59

Tricia and Julia had been checked out at the hospital. Though they were required to stay overnight until they reacted normally to stimuli, the doctors said they were perfectly fine and would recover fully from the light sedation they had been given. Bridget, on the other hand, had been heavily sedated, so she was still in bed when Gordon brought the twins home from the hospital.

"I should just leave this to you," Zachary whispered as Gordon opened the bedroom door. Zachary was chickening out. He had been flattered that Gordon wanted him there for the reunion but, when he thought about it, he knew it wasn't his place. He might have been able to be Bridget's knight in shining armor this time, but she wouldn't want him there, and he had no place in her bedroom.

"No, come," Gordon insisted. "Do you think I want to be in trouble for not bringing you so that she could thank you?"

Zachary couldn't help smiling at that. While Gordon was a wealthy, influential business leader, cutthroat in his business and used to being able to order everyone around, he still bowed to Bridget. If Bridget wasn't happy, he needed to do something to fix the situation. He was better at handling Bridget than Zachary ever had been, more able to give her what she wanted and to act correctly in social situations, so Zachary assumed he didn't attract the same anger and resentment from her as Zachary had.

Gordon opened the bedroom door awkwardly, holding one girl in each arm. Zachary followed a few steps behind and stood in the doorway rather than entering the room.

Bridget mumbled and moved around restlessly. Zachary was swept back in memories of sleeping with her. Her smell, the texture of her skin, those little sleep mumbles that didn't mean anything.

He had been in paradise when she had been happy.

"Bridget. Bridge." Gordon shook her gently. "Bridget, wake up."

Bridget mumbled an incomprehensible complaint and pulled away from him.

"Bridget. Come on, honey. Don't you want to see the girls?"

Something about his question made Bridget take notice, even in her drowsy state, and she sat up partway, searching for him in the dimness.

"Gordon?"

"Morning, honey. I brought the girls to say hello."

"The girls?" Bridget looked from one to the other, confused. "Are they okay? I had a dream…"

"They're just fine. Here, do you want to hold them?"

Bridget reached out her arms, and Gordon settled them against her, like a parent helping his child to hold the new baby in the family for the first time, making sure that the twins were secure and Bridget was awake enough not to drop them. The babies babbled and giggled happily.

"They… they were kidnapped," Bridget said, frown lines visible in the dimness of the room. "From the store. The parking lot. I… they *were,* weren't they?"

"Yes. But they're back now. Zachary found them and brought them back."

Bridget looked around and, eventually, her eyes found him in the doorway watching. "Zachary."

Zachary drank in the image of Bridget, drowsy, her hair tousled with sleep, cradling both babies in her arms. She looked peaceful and relaxed, all the cares of the world gone. An angelic portrait. Madonna and children.

"Zachary found them?" Bridget murmured, echoing Gordon's words. "Thank you, Zachary."

"You're welcome."

She lay back, her eyes closing again. Gordon checked the security of each of the babies, then turned to Zachary to speak a few more words.

"You always come through, Zach. I know that I shouldn't call you, that I should let you live your own life and find someone else who can help. But you always come through. I can't trust anyone else."

Zachary nodded, wordless. He had no idea what to say to that.

"Can you see yourself out?" Gordon suggested. "I want to stay here with Bridge. Make sure she doesn't roll over on them or take them out when they wake up if she's not ready to get up yet. Just… savor this time."

"Sure, of course."

He left Gordon there, enjoying the company of his partner and children. At times like this, Zachary couldn't see Gordon as anything other than a family man, concerned for his family, present, and loving. There was no sign of the ruthless businessman who would do anything to get ahead of the competition, including working his employees almost to death.

He couldn't see Godfrey's business colleague refusing to do anything to help Wayne Carver and offering him no recourse for the loan that Godfrey still held. He had been as unconcerned for Carver as he had been worried about his children.

60

Logan met with Zachary away from the mansion. Maybe he was embarrassed by everything Zachary had found out about him, or the way that he had been played by a maid he thought had been attracted to him. At least he hadn't been convinced to murder his own father. She hadn't been able to talk him into hating his father enough to do that. There were many men and women who had been talked into such things in the past, and Zachary was sure Logan would have regretted it.

Zachary was a little surprised that it was Logan who wanted to meet with him rather than Karen. Karen was the one who had retained him and had run the investigation from the start. Logan had been a bystander, just an observer. It was strange to have him take a bigger part in it now.

Logan motioned Zachary to the table he had been sitting at as he stood up. "Can I get you a coffee? What do you want?"

Zachary nodded. "Sure. Coffee is good."

Logan went over to the counter to talk to the barista. He didn't look any different from any of the students who frequented the shop, coming over from the college across the street. He chatted with the barista while she prepared the drink. Logan returned to the table and handed the coffee to him. Zachary leaned toward his cup as he brought it up to his face, inhaling the scent of the rich coffee deeply. Logan settled back into his chair and considered his own drink, swirling what remained of his coffee in the cup.

"We wanted to thank you for sorting this out," he said. "For figuring out what happened and giving the police what they needed to reopen the case so that guy can be prosecuted. You did an outstanding job." He sipped the coffee. "I didn't think you could do it. I wasn't even sure there was anything to find."

Zachary shrugged. "I know. It's hard when all you have is suspicions. Where to start, who to talk to, where to look. And I'm sure you didn't think I would end up looking at your girlfriend."

"She wasn't my girlfriend," Logan said, holding up one finger. "Amy was my girlfriend."

Zachary wasn't sure what to say about this. He didn't want to get into Logan's relationship with Charlotte. It was true that it hadn't been romantic. Logan hadn't fallen in love with her, and she had only been using him as a tool. The relationship had been a non-starter. Just Logan fooling around on the side, as far as he was concerned.

"Was?" he asked, noticing Logan's use of the word.

"Well, apparently, Amy wasn't too keen on the fact that I had been… involved with Charlotte. How do you explain that to someone? I know that the fact that it was her idea doesn't excuse me, but… I think it should be taken into account, at least."

Zachary could see how that might not play too well with Amy. At least Logan had been upfront with her, not trying to hide the fact that he had been involved with someone else. But that was small consolation in the face of his betrayal.

"So now that this has all been cleared up, the estate can be distributed without worrying about whether your father's killer would benefit from his death."

Logan blew out his breath. "That's a relief. In two ways—knowing that it wasn't any of my siblings and that I won't have to worry about money anymore. I can do what I want."

"And do you know what that will be?"

"I'm looking around." Logan shrugged. "I never did want

college, even though that's what Mom and Dad pushed. I knew it wouldn't be any easier for me than high school. That's just not the way I learn things. I'd rather be hands-on in a trade. But that was never good enough for Dad."

"Well, maybe you can pursue that now. And you can talk to your school or instructor about accommodations. For learning disabilities."

"I don't know." Logan looked doubtful. "I always hated being treated any differently. The other kids knowing that I was different. If I could get by without any accommodations..."

"It was better if they thought you weren't trying than that you had disabilities."

Logan raised his brows. "Well... yeah, I guess."

Zachary nodded. "I know how that is. High school especially. I hated teachers and group home supervisors thinking that I was stupid. I would rather they thought I was lazy and acting like a screw-up than that I couldn't do the work. I had a resource room teacher who was really good for a while there, and that helped. But I was just getting along the best I could, and I didn't have any friends."

Logan sipped his coffee. "Yeah."

"You could get a private instructor or someone to help you out with the work, either instead of a classroom or in addition to it. You can afford it."

"What about Karen's son?"

Zachary cocked his head, considering the non-sequitur. "Wally, you mean? I guess she'll be able to get him the help he needs now too. Better than waiting until he's an adult."

"I always liked him. He and I *get* each other. Maybe it's genetic instead of because I was born premature. From Mom's side, obviously, since... Dad wasn't really my father."

"Maybe you could help Karen, then. Make suggestions of things she can do to help him. How to understand his behavior. He's lucky to have an uncle who can help with that stuff. A lot of kids don't have that."

"Her other son is great too, of course. Finn. But Wally is the one I really connect with."

"Maybe that will help you get closer to Karen, too."

"They were always so remote. Already practically grown up when I was born. What will hold us together now that Mom and Dad are both gone? I think we're just all going to drift apart and never talk to each other again. At least when Mom went, we still had family dinners. Now that Dad's gone, too, I don't think we will. I don't think we'll be a family anymore. Especially since I'm barely even related now."

"You can tell them that you want to keep having the family dinners and stay in touch. You could take charge. Schedule dates and encourage everyone to come."

"I guess… but that's more Alex's role, isn't it? Or even Karen's, since she's the girl. It would be weird if I took charge of it. Wouldn't it?"

It was hard for Zachary, who had grown up without his siblings since the fire, to know what would be normal or abnormal for a family. But he didn't see why it should matter who took charge of keeping the family dinners going and staying in touch as siblings. "No, I don't think so. They'd probably be happy for you to take it. Alex is pretty busy with his work and Karen with her kids and night shift. You don't have to be the head of the family to suggest that you keep in touch."

It had been Tyrrell that had brought Zachary and his siblings together as adults. And he was one of the middle children. It had never occurred to Zachary that it should be anyone else.

But they'd still never gotten everyone all together at one table. The six siblings had never been all together in the same room since the fire. Zachary let his thoughts drift as he had another sip of coffee and considered it. Maybe one day, all of the Goldman siblings would break bread together again. He didn't have to wait for Tyrrell to suggest it.

Did you enjoy this book? Reviews and recommendations are vital to making a book successful.

Please leave a review at your favorite book store or review site and share it with your friends.

Don't miss the following bonus material:
Sign up for mailing list to get a free ebook
Read a sneak preview chapter
Other books by P.D. Workman
Learn more about the author

UNLOCK ACCESS TO ZACHARY GOLDMAN'S CASE FILES!

Get a peek inside Zachary's case files and see what other intriguing tales are in store!

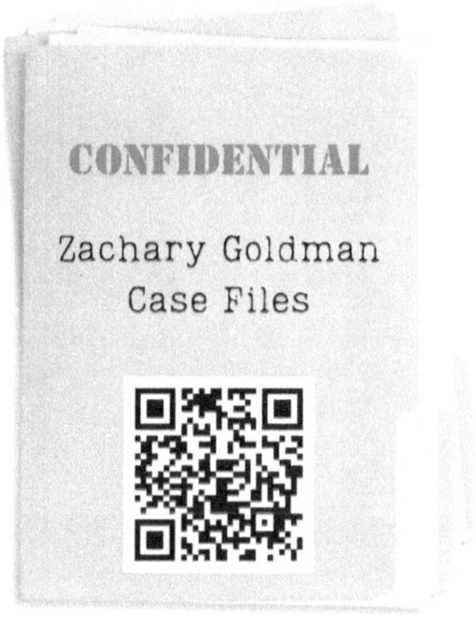

SCAN TO UNLOCK OFFER

books.pdworkman.com/sign-up-zg

PREVIEW OF SHE WAS THEIR TARGET

CHAPTER 1

Zachary stared at the screen on his phone after the call ended, frowning and thinking about what the woman had said.

Jennifer. She had been Jennifer Olson when he had known her, but he couldn't remember what she had just told him her married name was. He looked down at the notes he had scribbled while she was talking. Kristin Jones. That was her daughter. So she was Jennifer Jones now. A common name. One of those ones that was really fun to trace when he was trying to track someone down. But he didn't have to track Jennifer down. He had her phone number and a time and place to meet with her.

Kenzie crossed his line of vision and said something to him. It was like she was far away or underwater. He knew she had spoken to him, but wasn't sure what she'd said. Zachary rubbed his temples and focused on her, trying to pull his brain away from the woman on the phone. He was sitting on the couch in the living room, where he had been working on his laptop, and Kenzie had come in from the kitchen.

"Sorry, what?"

Kenzie raised her brows and shook her head, sending her dark curls bouncing. He wondered how many times she had repeated herself already. She didn't look pleased about having to do it again.

"Where are you?" she asked. "Who was that on the phone?"

"Uh… a new client. Maybe. A woman I went to school with."

"Oh…?" Kenzie sounded interested. Zachary rarely talked about school or his years in foster care. She knew the overall shape of his life before he had turned eighteen and aged out of the system, but he didn't talk about it a lot. Didn't mention specifics. He avoided even thinking about it if he could help it. Talking about it was the last thing he wanted to do. So when Kenzie learned something about his past, it was usually just one tidbit, or maybe something that came up in couple's therapy. Where he still did his best to avoid diving too deeply into it. "What is her name?"

That part was easy. "Jennifer." He looked for something else to tell Kenzie about her, to show that he was willing to share. "She was… in high school with me, I guess. I don't remember very much about her. She was older. A couple of grades ahead of me."

"So you probably didn't know each other very well. Kids tend to stick with their own grades at that age."

Zachary cupped his hands over his eyes. "We were… she was very nice. Not a lot of people in high school were nice."

Kenzie made a sympathetic noise. "It's a tough age, even without all the stuff that you had to go through." She paused, waiting for him to say anything in response. "Are you going to help with supper?" she asked eventually. "Tyrrell will be here before long."

"Oh. Yeah, of course." Zachary rubbed his eyes briskly and got to his feet. That was probably what she'd been asking him.

It wasn't like he was making the meal. Kenzie was handling most of that. But Zachary tried to help out—setting the table, making a salad, and getting out anything else she needed. He was happy to give her a hand with anything she needed him to do in the kitchen, but she didn't usually trust him to do the actual cooking. That might have something to do with his ADHD and several meals in the past either put into the stove still wrapped in plastic, left in until they burned, or left sitting for an hour in a cold oven because he had forgotten to turn it on. That, and the fact that coordinating several dishes at once so that nothing burned and everything was finished at the same time required a level of concentration and executive function that he just didn't have most days. He could manage a salad or a sandwich, which wouldn't be ruined if he left them out or they sat on the counter for a while.

Waking up from his reverie about Jennifer, Zachary could smell the hearty scents of tomato sauce and cheese coming from the oven. And garlic. Hopefully, she had made garlic bread to go along with whatever else she had made—a favorite of Zachary's and Tyrrell's.

"Sorry, I should have come in earlier."

Kenzie shrugged. "You were on the phone."

Zachary moved around the bright, cheerful kitchen, getting out the plates, glasses, and cutlery. He was determined to stay focused on the job and not forget anything because he was thinking about Jennifer. He didn't want to think about Jennifer. He would distract himself with the dinner preparations and then with the conversation with Tyrrell and Kenzie over dinner.

His younger brother Tyrrell was doing well with his job at Kenzie's family foundation. He had been there a few months, and all indications were positive. But that could end at any time. Tyrrell was an alcoholic and had been unable to stay sober for more than a year or two since he was a teenager. While Zachary hoped that the latest treatment program had made a difference and Tyrrell could maintain his sobriety, he was alert for any signs that Tyrrell had started drinking secretly.

The doorbell rang. "There he is," Kenzie said unnecessarily.

Zachary left what he was doing and went to the front door to let Tyrrell in and punch his code into the burglar alarm keypad so the alarm wouldn't be triggered. They didn't need security guards showing up for their dinner party.

"Zachary!" Tyrrell grinned at his big brother and threw his arms around him in a quick man-hug, pounding him on the back. "How's it going, bro?"

"Pretty good," Zachary told him, and stepped back to allow him in. "How's everything with you?"

They started walking toward the kitchen.

"Alarm," Kenzie called out.

Zachary looked back at the keypad. "I did it, didn't I?"

Tyrrell shook his head and stepped back to punch the code in himself. There was an answering beep as the system cleared.

They joined Kenzie in the kitchen again. Tyrrell looked around. "Anything I can help with?"

Kenzie shook her head. "I think everything is done. Have a seat and tell us how it is going."

Zachary went over to the stove to help take out the hot dishes and get things to the table, but Kenzie frowned, making him retreat instead to sit down with their guest.

"It's going great. Hillary says I have become 'indispensable,'" Tyrrell bragged.

"Good for you." Kenzie approved. "She's so capable; I never thought she would let anyone else help out with the important stuff. I'm glad she has you to backstop her now."

"Filing is up to date. The database is current. Mostly. I have some research to do on some organizations that we might consider supporting. She says it's nice not to be behind on all the administrative stuff."

"I'm sure it is." Kenzie placed hot pads on the counter and transferred dishes from the oven. "I think we'll just serve up buffet style, so we don't have to try to pass around the hot dishes or reach across to get everything."

She opened up the tinfoil-wrapped garlic bread and Tyrrell and Zachary salivated, watching her slice the crusty loaf. Kenzie paused to look at them. "You guys are two peas in a pod. You'd better eat your veggies!"

"Yes, ma'am," Tyrrell and Zachary responded in unison, then laughed.

Zachary felt a warm flush of affection for his brother. Looking at them, someone who didn't know them would think that they had grown up together. But Tyrrell had only been eight when they had been placed into foster care, and Zachary had not seen him until decades later. A year and a half ago. They shared the same dark hair and eyes, some similar facial features, and memories of their family before the fire, but that was all. Zachary had spent eight years in foster care without any contact with his biological family, and when he aged out, he had been alone.

He was lucky to have his siblings back in his life again.

It was best to focus on the present.

CHAPTER 2

"So, tell us about this friend of yours who called," Kenzie told Zachary, after Tyrrell had finished talking about what was going on in his life and at the foundation.

Zachary stopped chewing and looked at her. He had already said he didn't remember Jennifer very well, so he hadn't expected Kenzie to pursue it. He strained to swallow the lump of garlic bread still in his mouth.

"Uh… I don't know how much there is to tell," he waffled.

Tyrrell and Kenzie were both looking at him with interest. He supposed he would have to tell them something.

"You said she was an old friend from high school?" Kenzie prompted.

"I didn't think you were in contact with anyone from that far back." Tyrrell took a huge bite of the crusty garlic bread himself and spoke around it. "Other than Mr. Peterson."

Zachary had been in and out of various families and facilities for years, and the only person he had kept in contact with was his old foster father, Lorne Peterson. It was Mr. Peterson who had sparked Zachary's interest in photography and set him on the path to becoming a private investigator, even though by that time, Zachary had long since moved on to other families and facilities.

Along with his partner Patrick Parker, Mr. Peterson had provided Zachary with a sense of stability and family that he had not gotten anywhere else.

"We *haven't* been in touch. This is the first time I've heard from her in years. Since she moved away. That's why..." Zachary shrugged, "I don't know much about her. It was a long time ago."

"And she just reached out and called you?" Tyrell asked. "Maybe she has some old romantic feelings for you." He waggled his eyebrows. "Wants to rekindle things."

Zachary's face burned. "It was never anything like that!" He glanced at Kenzie, hoping she didn't suspect Zachary's motives. "She's a potential client. That's all. Needed a private investigator, and I guess she heard about one of my other cases..."

He'd had a few big cases that had hit the media and spread his name around, so some people who called him now were interested in hiring him specifically, rather than just a random name they had picked out of an internet search.

Jennifer hadn't said which case she'd heard about. Zachary had recently investigated the death of a man who the medical examiner had said initially died of natural causes when in fact, he had been poisoned. It had made a small splash in the Vermont papers but had not gone national like a couple of Zachary's other cases.

"Oh, I see." Tyrell nodded. But he was still using his teasing voice. "A potential client."

"She is."

"What kind of case?" Kenzie asked, trying to rescue Zachary.

Zachary rubbed his forehead. He was starting to get a headache. "Her daughter. She died suddenly and Jennifer wants it investigated."

"Oh, dear," Kenzie shook her head at this. "How old was she?"

"A teenager. I'm not sure how old. Do you remember a Kristin Jones?"

"No." Kenzie's forehead creased as she thought about it. "I don't remember the name and haven't had any teenage girls through recently. Are you sure she went through the Roxboro medical examiner's office?"

"No. She didn't say. It might have been one of the bigger hospitals."

"Yeah. Probably."

Having Kenzie as a contact in the local medical examiner's office was handy, but Zachary was not disappointed that Jennifer's daughter hadn't been autopsied by Kenzie or Dr. Wiltshire. He didn't want to challenge another one of their cases quite so soon.

"By 'died suddenly,' do you mean she committed suicide?" Kenzie asked.

"No. Jennifer said it was in the middle of a medical procedure."

"Oh." Kenzie nodded. "Well, that does happen," she admitted. "Sometimes there are unexpected complications."

"I don't know the details yet. We're going to get together tomorrow, and then I'll know more."

"Don't raise her hopes," Kenzie warned. "If it was in the middle of a medical procedure, the cause of death could be unknown, but they're usually pretty thorough investigating cases of potential doctor error."

"I'll tell her that."

"What was she like?" Tyrrell asked. "Back when you knew her?"

Even though he remembered Jennifer being nice to him, Zachary wasn't looking forward to meeting and reconnecting with her, especially under such tragic circumstances. It would not be a joyful reunion. And he wanted the past to remain in the past. His chest tightened and his heart beat painfully hard just thinking about it. How would he feel the next day when he had to face her in person?

"I don't know," Zachary told Tyrrell testily. "I don't remember."

Tyrrell sat back in his chair, looking at Zachary speculatively. "Okay, bro… sorry…"

"Zachary said that she was kind," Kenzie told him. "But it was a long time ago. She looked at Zachary. "A lo-o-ong time ago," she drew the word out, teasing him.

"I'm not that much older than you." Zachary shook his head and picked up his crust of garlic bread. He appreciated her trying to shift the conversation away from him, but wasn't in the mood for teasing and joking.

"He must be at least ten years older than you," Tyrrell studied Kenzie. "I mean… look at him. And look at you."

Kenzie's red lips curved into a smile.

Zachary was no catch physically. He'd lived a hard life and had plenty of scars to show it. And while he'd put on weight and looked pretty good now, he was usually underweight during a depressive cycle and looked worn and gaunt. Right now, he was on the upswing, the hollows in his cheeks filled in and his eyes not sunken.

But Kenzie definitely looked better.

"Only three years," Kenzie laughed. "He's no cradle robber."

+++

Later, Tyrrell had gone home and Zachary was sitting in bed, watching Kenzie spread moisturizing cream on her face. One of those things that kept her looking young and fresh, he supposed. It had never occurred to him that he should take better care of his skin. There were much higher-level things he had to be concerned with. His mental health. Not taking on cases involving dangerous people. Getting enough sleep and, before his last med change, forcing himself to eat enough despite the nausea caused by his prescriptions.

"Are you okay?" Kenzie asked, looking at him.

He tore his eyes away from her, realizing she probably thought he was staring at her, when he was actually lost inside his own head. "Yeah, I'm good. Sorry."

She continued dotting the moisturizer on her face and rubbing it in. "It's just that… you've seemed distracted. A bit… out of sorts, maybe. You're usually relaxed when Tyrrell is here. But you seemed like you had something else on your mind today."

"Just thinking about this new case."

She looked at him, waiting for more information.

"There's not anything to tell yet." Zachary looked down at his phone to check for messages or emails. "I won't know anything until I've had a chance to meet with her."

"But you're not looking forward to it, are you?"

"No."

"I thought you would be excited about seeing an old friend. It would be different if she were someone who didn't treat you very well. I can see you putting her off and saying you have too much on your plate. But if she was good to you..."

Zachary tried to think of the best way to explain it. He knew he *should* be happy to see Jennifer.

"She was good. But with the rest of the stuff going on around then... it was a pretty dark time. I don't want to think about it, and I can't separate Jennifer out and only think about her. It's all woven together."

Kenzie screwed the lid onto her face cream and put it on her side table.

"Sure, I can understand that. Sorry for pressing you. I'm not trying to be intrusive."

"It's okay." He scrolled down the endless timeline on one of the social media apps, not looking at her. "I know it sounds backward. That meeting someone who was nice would bring back bad feelings and memories. But that's the way it is. I've tried to leave all of that behind me. I don't want it coming back up."

She knew only too well how he had repressed other memories. But they hadn't stayed where he had buried them. But they had come bubbling back up again, and he'd had to deal with them instead of being able to compartmentalize and push them down again. He still wasn't finished dealing with them. It had been over a year and had been the subject of many therapy sessions.

"You're strong enough to deal with it," Kenzie assured him. "Maybe you weren't when you were a teenager, but you've grown a lot since then. You've learned a lot about yourself and dealt with a lot of hard stuff. You can deal with this too."

"I'd rather not."

Kenzie chuckled. "I'm sure you would. But we don't always get the luxury of choice."

She'd been dealing with traumatic stuff lately too, and he was proud of her for it. He put his hand down in the space between them, and Kenzie interlaced her fingers with his and held his hand firmly.

"For tonight, let's focus on the present."

Zachary wholeheartedly agreed.

She Was Their Target, Book #15 of the Zachary Goldman Mysteries series by P.D. Workman can be purchased at pdworkman.com

ABOUT THE AUTHOR

P.D. Workman is a USA Today Bestselling author and multi-award winner, renowned for her prolific output of over 100 published works that span various genres. With a knack for crafting page-turners, Workman captivates readers with everything from cozy mysteries like the Auntie Clem's Bakery series to gripping young adult and suspense novels.

A prolific reader and writer since childhood, P.D. Workman crafts emotionally powerful stories that don't shy away from hard topics. Her books tackle mental illness, addiction, abuse, and trauma with raw honesty and compassion, giving voice to the often unheard. If you crave authentic, character-driven page-turners that hit deep and stay with you long after the final page, you're in the right place.

With each new release, fans eagerly anticipate another thrilling blend of thought-provoking storytelling and relatable characters that define P.D. Workman's brand as an author of unforgettable page-turners—gripping tales that leave a lasting impact long after the last page is turned.

> P. D. Workman, does not shy from probing the deep psychological scars of childhood trauma, mental illness, and addiction. Also characteristic of this author, these extremely sensitive issues are explored with extensive empathy, described with incredible clarity, and portrayed with profound insight.
>
> — —KIM, GOODREADS REVIEWER

Some of Workman's titles have been translated into Spanish, French, Portuguese, German, and Italian.

Workman began writing at an early age and is a prolific reader as well as writer. She is also passionate about teaching and learning, expresses her creativity through art and cooking, and loves exploring the Calgary parks and green spaces where the Parks Pat Mysteries are set. She was a legal assistant for many years and has done extensive charitable work.

Workman was born and raised in Alberta, Canada, and is married with one adult son.

Please visit P.D. Workman at pdworkman.com to see what else she is working on, to join her mailing list, and to link to her social networks.

If you enjoyed this book, please take the time to recommend it to other purchasers with a review or star rating and share it with your friends!

tiktok.com/@pdworkmanauthor
facebook.com/pdworkmanauthor
x.com/pdworkmanauthor
instagram.com/pdworkmanauthor
amazon.com/author/pdworkman
bookbub.com/authors/p-d-workman
goodreads.com/pdworkman
linkedin.com/in/pdworkman
pinterest.com/pdworkmanauthor
youtube.com/pdworkman

Find P.D. Workman's books at

PDWORKMAN.COM

Scan the QR code below

www.ingramcontent.com/pod-product-compliance
Lightning Source LLC
Chambersburg PA
CBHW030925260626
47169CB00002B/380
9781774685112